AN AI APOCALYPSE
HORROR/COMEDY FOR THE AGES

ZAMBIES!

MATT J PIKE

****

Edited by: Katie Lowe

Cover design: Matt J Pike

****

****

Published by Zombie RiZing Books

Paperback Edition: June 20, 2024
ISBN: 9798332819087

www.mattpike.co

Cover design: Matt Pike

****

Special thanks:
Imogen Murray, Katie Fraser, Jan Pike,
Lisa M White, Jade Phillips, Nikki Gitta Taylor, Lisa Chant
Sophie Pike, Sam Pike and Abby Pike, Sienna Taintey.

****

Other books by Matt J Pike

Starship Dorsano Chronicles:

(YA Inappropriate sci-fi comedy)

Kings of the World

War & Quel

*

Apocalypse Survivors:

JACK

(Prepping/adventure)

Apocalypse: Diary of a Survivor

Apocalypse: Diary of a Survivor 2

Apocalypse: Diary of a Survivor 3

Apocalypse: Diary of a Survivor 4

NORWOOD

(Dark action/thriller)

The Parade

War Parade

*

Zombie RiZing:

(Middle grade fantasy horror comedy)

The Beginning

Dreeks' Horde

Dragon's Wrath

Death's Door

*

Hart & Sol

(Totally inappropriate sci-fi comedy)

(co-written with Russell Emmerson)

ADELAIDE/ FLEURIEU PENINSULA

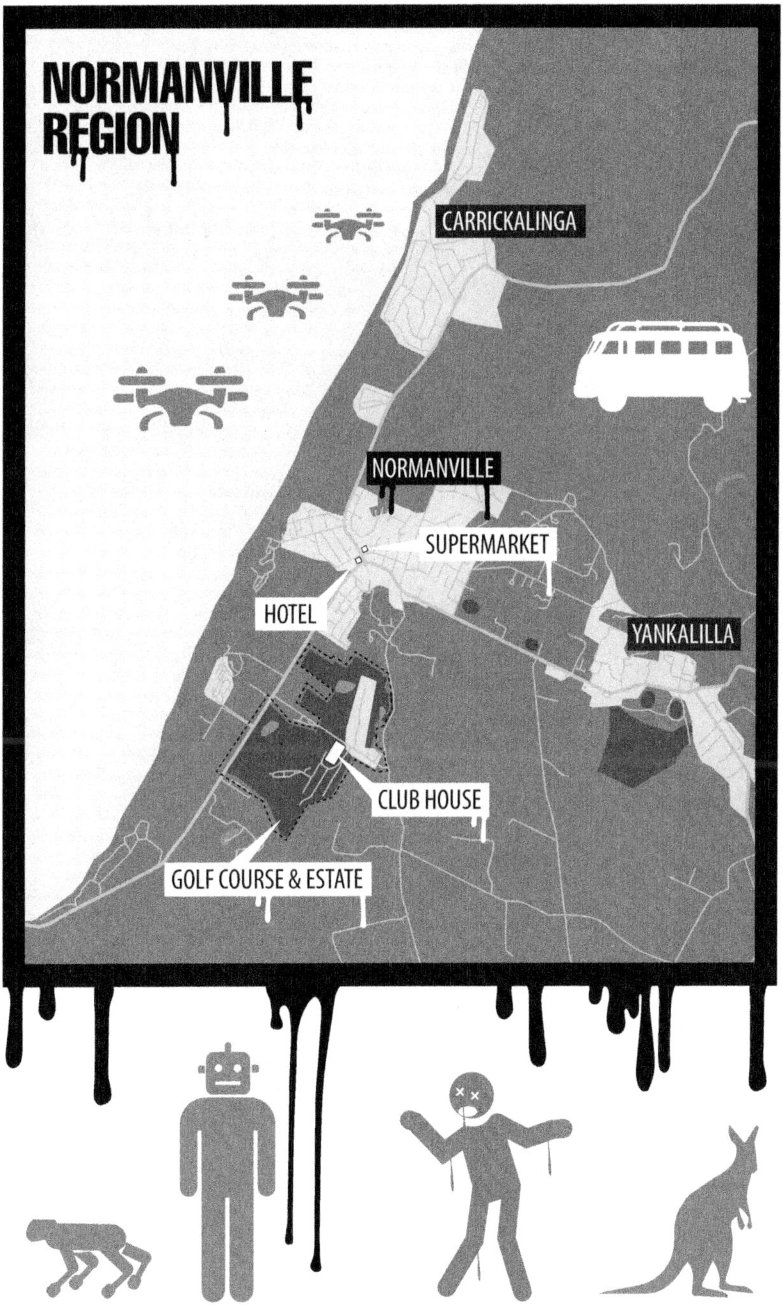

NORMANVILLE REGION

CARRICKALINGA

NORMANVILLE

SUPERMARKET

HOTEL

YANKALILLA

CLUB HOUSE

GOLF COURSE & ESTATE

****

Conceived and created by a human.

****

CHAPTER 1
ERUPTION

"Bbbwwweearrrghhuuu."

Grace and Suede stared at each other over their kitchen counter coffees. The expressions showed their shared concern that, whatever the noise they'd just heard was, it was close, of human origin, wet, echoey and completely unhinged.

"The fuck was that?" whispered Suede.

Grace responded with a concerned shrug.

It didn't help matters that they were mostly unfamiliar with the property they were house-sitting for a couple of weeks. It was only their second morning – new noises, new energy. Sure, many might not count a Tuesday morning in Adelaide's inner east as energy, but it was a whole lot more chaotic than van life.

The tortured rasp sounded out again. Grace and Suede silently expressed their raised levels of concern before tracing the sound to its source. At the other end of the hallway, the front door beckoned. Shadowy movements danced in the gap underneath. Sure, it could've been trees. Then again, it could've been anything. Another sickly sound spewed towards them. The door was only a metre away from the footpath and, in combination with the floorboards and high ceilings, that seemed to play magic tricks on how noise amplified to the living area.

The couple stared at each other once more. Whatever the sound was, it drowned out the background hum of the automated vacuum cleaner working its way across a Persian rug in the open planned living area. Both seemed completely out of place in this modern world – echoes to a simpler time. Then things fell silent once more and the vacuum's hum returned to the audible palette.

The silence lasted long enough for Grace and Suede's locked-eyed expression of concern to start to melt away. Suede sipped his coffee.

"Bbbrrrwweerrerrr."

The noise was even louder this time.

Suede grabbed a handful of tissues to clean the spilt beverage from his shirt while he silently cursed the noise, the house, city life… everything. Definitely not his courage, though. It totally wasn't that. Grace did her best not to roll her eyes at him.

"Should we, like, go and check it out?" whispered Suede.

"Probably," whispered Grace. "We could—"

Her words were interrupted by the noise again. This time it was different, perhaps coming from two people? As the sounds faded, she turned her focus back to Suede, only to realise he was already positioning himself further away from the hallway. She knew immediately the 'we' in his offer, actually just meant her.

She shot him a look, but he wasn't prepared to make eye contact to receive it. She sighed. There was something about his appearance that gave a sense of safety to those in his presence. It was partly his height, strongly featured face and brown skin tones, but also his calm demeanour that put people at ease. He was cosmopolitan chill personified. But experience had taught Grace that 'easygoing' could also translate to 'avoids action at crucial moments'. She walked to the kitchen, grabbed a knife from the second drawer and made her way up the hall.

Suede found a healthy cover position behind the dining table and watched her depart. Would he regret this later? Probably. Was he going to do anything about it while he still could? No. Instead, he watched her march into an action that, at this moment, was beyond his pay grade. She was a sight to behold in full flight – driven. Her flowing dark hair, olive skin and piercing eyes were almost mesmerising in a way that screamed 'don't mess with me'. So, he didn't… physically.

"You might be best to try to—"

Grace stopped his words with a sharply deployed gesture of her middle finger, she didn't even bother to turn and face him.

Suede swallowed air, then turned his focus to his cover and how he could fortify his position with a chair.

As Grace hit the corridor, the floorboards creaked. She froze.

"Careful," whispered Suede.

Grace swore to herself. A second later, the throaty noise came from out the front of the house again. She could definitely make out two distinct voices this time.

"Nice and easy," whispered Suede.

Grace swallowed her frustration and pressed forward once more. She was at the front of the corridor in seconds. She slid open their temporary bedroom door and headed in. From her closer vantage point, she could hear an entirely new layer of detail from the happenings outside. There were sliding and hobbling noises just outside the gate. The street beyond seemed alive with activity. Far more so than she'd seen in her brief time at the property.

"What is it?" Suede panic-whispered from down the corridor.

"I haven't looked yet," Grace rage-whispered in return.

She narrowed her eyes after hearing his tut echo to her, then turned her attention to the window. She raised her hands to the blinds, which were still down, and pressed shaking fingers against a slat to create a gap to see through. She took a deep breath and leaned forward.

In an instant, she gasped and pulled back in panic, before raising the courage to look again.

"What?" whispered Suede. "What was it?"

His words washed right passed her, unabsorbed. Instead, Grace swallowed hard, hoping the move would give her the courage required to have a second look. She exhaled her last breath over several seconds as she opened the gap in the blinds once more.

Barely more than two metres away, leaning on the gate of the front yard's picket fence was a man. She guessed he was in his 50s, dishevelled in a way that was definitely not in keeping with the upper-class, inner-city suburb aesthetic. As she watched, her heart galloped. There was something decidedly strange about him, if it was a man. Not a been-at-the-pub-too-long weird, or a hit-the-pipe-too-hard weird. Not even a having-a-psychological-episode level weird. Not that she was an expert, but Grace had seen all sorts of humans in all sorts of ways doing all sorts of things on, well, all sorts of things. And this wasn't that. It was something else altogether. Something new. Something not right. She studied the lurker at the gates. He leaned in unusual ways, drooling and incoherent, pallid, and bloodied. Something terrified her.

"I said, what is it?" rage-whispered Suede.

His voice was washed away by her focus again, unable to resonate in her conscious thoughts. She was lost in the otherworldly street beyond the window. She saw one, no two, no four, others acting in the same disconcerting way. There was also a woman nearby, also in her 50s or early 60s, perhaps. Grace was pretty sure she was the owner of the second vocalisation they'd heard. She was equally out of it, equally freaky and disturbing.

Perhaps they were talking to each other with those grunts? It didn't seem that way, but there must've been some purpose for their odd noises. Not that she was going to hang around and solve that riddle. Something told her the best place to be right now was a long way from where she was.

She looked further afield to the other two other strange people across the street. Both of retirement age, both making the same freaky noises and movements. What was going on?

"Earth to Grace. Come in, Grace."

Given the ages of the, well, people, plus how they were behaving, she was pretty sure she could also rule out drugs or alcohol. And four people doing the same thing in the same vicinity? No, this was something bigger, something different, something new, something bad. She freed her mind, letting the neurons fire in different ways. That's better, she could be in the moment and think clearer now.

Maybe it was—No! Unthink that thought. That stupid, stupid thought. There you go, just unthink it. She laughed at her foolishness. She had a biology degree for fuck's sake, it was a ridiculous idea. Still, the drooling and groaning and staggering show continued with bad choreography and incoherent lyrics.

Zombies!

She retracted from the blinds in a flash and tried to catch her runaway breath. Zombies! There it was again. The word had whispered to her again, and louder this time.

Shut the fuck up, internal monologue!

Her hands went clammy. Thoughts at how far away she was from loved ones if something truly big was happening scared her almost as much as the bravery and support currently displayed from her partner.

The moment consumed her. She was lost in what she'd witnessed, it seemed more at home on a streaming service than a real-life inner-suburban street. Lost in her flight of fancy, it was no surprise she didn't sense the presence in the room, nor catch a glimpse of the peripheral movement until it was too late.

A hand touched her shoulder.

She screamed.

*

CHAPTER 2
STREET FIGHTING MAN

"Jesus! Chill out, babe!" said Suede.

Grace found herself squatting in a fight position. She had somehow jumped away from the window, twisted back and away from the threat, yet turned to face it while placing her arms out in front of her face. Her hands were clenched into fists and ready to uncoil on the enemy. Or Suede, as it turned out.

"Little tip," she said, glaring at him. "If you manage to go the rest of your life and never do that to me again, you can consider it the exact right amount of time."

"Jeez, relax."

"Tell me to relax again, I dare you," she said, right fist now raised behind her. "Have you seen what's happening out there?"

Suede stared at Grace blankly. She rolled her eyes before gesturing to him to look through the blinds. After a couple of hesitant false starts, he leaned in, made a gap with his fingers and looked through.

"No, no you haven't seen what happened because you were – that's right – cowering down the other end of the house!"

Her words fell on deaf ears. Suede was transfixed in the view. "What the actual?"

"Exactly!"

He turned back to her, hands shaking the gap in the blinds. "Are they… you know?"

Grace shrugged. "If it looks like a duck and quacks like a duck, I guess…"

Suede scrunched up his face. "I meant zombies!"

Grace stared at him, deadpan. "I know."

"Then what's with the ducks?"

Grace sighed. She already had her phone out and was flipping from app to app, scrolling through feeds.

Nothing.

It made her feel almost as uneasy as the street creeps. "Can we… just focus. I think we need to get the fuck out of this place. Who knows, maybe the entire city. Like, in a right now-ish timeframe."

"Agreed. But where?"

"Not sure, but generally in an away from the city direction, until we no longer see any of those things. Then maybe a bit further. Let's just chuck our shit into the van and head down the coast."

Suede nodded as he returned his visual focus to the view out the front of the house once more. "And how do you propose we get to the van?"

Grace swore as she realised the cosy inner-city cottage they were house-sitting only offered street parking. She swore again as the potential danger hit home.

"Wait," said Suede. "There's someone out there. Like, a normal person."

Grace squeezed in between Suede and the vintage tallboy that blocked most of the window so she could share the view. Across the road, she saw an old man wielding a shovel. He neared the couple of older strange-behaving people and raised it in a threatening manner.

"What's he doing?" asked Grace.

"Playing defence for his missus, by the looks of it," said Suede. He nodded to a point further up the street.

Grace scanned the direction and saw a woman of the same vintage. She had a carry-on-sized suitcase on wheels in one hand and a set of keys in the other. Ahead of her, the man put one hand on the SUV parked across the road.

"C'mon, c'mon," said Grace.

"You're barracking for the old guys, yeah?" said Suede.

Grace retracted herself from the window and stared at him until he felt the weight of her gaze enough to look back. She was pleased with the look she gave him next to illustrate her disgust.

"Just asking," said Suede. "Chill."

They both turned their attention back to the view. Grace gave him a clip on the ear for the chill comment.

"Piss off!" yelled the old man outside.

"Wait," said Grace. "Is that blood all over his sleeve?"

Suede narrowed his eyes to focus on the shovel wielder's cardigan. Despite the distance and its dark colour, he could make out stained patches that were definitely not part of the intended knit design. "Looks like it."

"Back off!" yelled the man as he took a swing at the two nearby, well, zombies.

The blade made a thud as it connected with one of the creatures, then a metallic ting as it collided with the footpath. The struck zombie reeled backwards for a few steps. Behind shovel man, the old lady closed some ground, holding her car keys at the ready.

Now she was closer, they could make out her injuries. Well, at least where the blood was soaking through her clothing. They realised the blood on the man was actually hers. There was only one creature within reaching distance of the passenger door now. The old man turned back to the woman to make sure they were on the same page, then turned back to the most immediate threat. He swung again, this time collecting the zombie.

"Boom!" celebrated Suede.

Grace nudged him. "Shut the fuck up," she rage-whispered.

The two zombies closest to their front gate turned and faced their general direction, searching for the source of the sound. The investigation was short-lived, however, as the commotion with the old couple proved too great to ignore. Grace and Suede let out their long-held breaths as the tension eased ever so slightly.

"Sorry," whispered Suede.

Grace shook her head in disbelief.

"Check that out," said Suede, attention already back on the commotion across the road. "The one he whacked first."

"What about it?"

"Blade sliced right through it. It's trying to get up!"

Grace squinted her eyes to try to narrow her focus. "Oh my God."

"That's pretty zombie-ish if you ask me," said Suede.

"Can we not use that word?"

"What, zombie?"

"Yeah!" said Grace. "It's really starting to freak me out."

Suede gave her a look she chose to ignore. "So, what am I supposed to call them then?"

Grace opened her mouth, but no words fell out.

He stared at her, his mouth opening to encourage words that never came. "Not-zombies," he said, eventually. The words somewhat falling out.

Grace tried, and failed, to come up with something better. She shrugged then nodded.

Suede scrunched up his face and gave his own shrug. "Not-zombies," he practised.

By this point, the man outside was attempting to nudge his shovel forward to push the, erm, not-zombie, into a position that would clear access to the car. The woman had closed the ground towards her survival partner. The problem was, more of the strange acting creatures had also crossed to the source of the commotion.

"Hurry up," whispered Grace.

"Hurry up!" screamed the old woman as she saw how little time they had.

The not-zombies in front of the house were now crossing the road. The man took a quick look around to reset his bearings. He narrowed his eyes on the gashed not-zombie and took a wild swing. His shovel blade met the head of the creature.

"Yes!" whispered Suede, accentuating his words with a silent fist pump. "C'mon, old couple!"

The old man pushed forward on his shovel, sending the creature stumbling backwards and out of its threatening position near the car. Behind him, the woman unlocked the vehicle with her keys then stepped inside. Hearing the door open, the man pulled back on the shovel to reclaim it.

It became clear the shovel was stuck in the skull of the creature, which was now trying and failing to fight the effects of gravity as it fell backwards. The shovel followed in the same direction. At the same time the old man tried to rotate clear. He attempted to let go of the shovel, but momentum and the choreography of physics had his hand caught in the centre of the handle. He twisted to the ground at an unnatural looking angle.

"Oh fuck!" whispered Suede.

The old lady wriggled her way across from the passenger seat headed towards the driver's side. She started the engine as more creatures set upon the car. She disappeared from sight before reappearing upright in the driver's seat several seconds later.

On the footpath, the man made his way to his feet, his pain obvious. He scanned the environment, saw the inbound threats, the woman in the driver's seat and the shovel-faced zombie trying to regain its feet.

"I'm coming, honey!" he said, as he made a hobble for the car.

Behind him, in an attempt to regain its footing, the creature fell to the ground once more. The off-balance weight of the shovel sent it twisting to the pavement. As it rotated and fell, the shovel that was still stuck in its skull struck the old man across the knee. It buckled as the man fell once more.

Though Grace and Suede's view of the impact of the fall and what happened next was blocked, the screams, twitching of old man slacks and spurts of blood emanating from the general location left little guesswork as to the outcome.

"C'mon old lady, this is your chance!" whispered Suede.

As he did, she revved the engine.

"Mow those mofos down and save your man."

The wheels squeaked briefly as the car burst into motion, engine roaring. Within seconds, the car disappeared out of sight up the street, revealing the sight of the old man getting attacked by what soon became several not-zombies. The tortured screams attracted even more not-zombie attention to the disturbance.

"Shit," whispered Suede. "She missed them! By quite a way too."

"Seriously? That's your take? Not, 'she just left him there to die to save her own ass'?"

"She wouldn't do that!"

Grace retracted from her view of the street to stare at him with open mouth disbelief.

He looked back at her. "What? I just assumed given her age and… other factors… she just missed."

Grace stared at him. "Other factors?"

"Mostly age."

"What other factors?"

Suede gulped. "I really think we should focus on getting out of here."

"Was one of your so-called factors the fact that she was a she?"

Suede went to respond but no words came out. The dark look in Grace's expression was too much for his eye contact to override.

"Just pack your shit," said Grace. "And learn to understand road statistics."

*

CHAPTER 3
BACK STREET PICK UP

Grace placed her hand on the doorknob, before exchanging a nod with Suede. "Ready?"

They both wore a backpack with the belongings they travelled with and were each armed with a knife they had swiped from the kitchen. Suede carried a second bag in his other hand with all the merch he didn't dare leave in a van parked on the street.

It was one thing to have a successful YouTube channel, it was an entirely different one to also have successful merch.

"Not really," said Suede, gripping the bag tight.

Grace shrugged as she turned her focus to the door. "Remember, hit the gate, scan both ways, then find the safest way to the van. It's not far away and it looks like all of the, erm, not-zombies are dealing with old mate over that way."

"We're seriously going with not-zombies, huh?"

She nodded. "Yes, not-zombies. Clearly, not-zombies. I mean, look at them." She delivered each word with less conviction as the one before, then presented the keys and nodded again before turning the handle on the door.

"Sure thing," said Suede, ignoring her intense glare. "Not-zombies," he said, more as a reminder to himself.

As they stepped onto the porch, the sounds that were muffled when they listened inside the cottage hit them with more clarity, and louder. There was a horrific scream that didn't sound too far in the distance and the general soundscape told of a situation far bigger than what they had already seen. They acknowledged that even more caution was required with a glance, then crossed the few steps to the front gate. All the while, their eyes were locked on what was happening to the old man across the street.

Their view opened up when they reached the gate. Across the road to the left they could see the van. It was a good thirty metres south of the chaos, where the old man was currently looking at them, while seemingly being devoured. He raised his arm and his eyes pleaded for some non-betrayal-style assistance. Meanwhile the not-zombies gnawed away. The man opened his mouth to scream or plead or break the ice, but no words came out. Soon, another not-zombie reached the pile-on and blocked their view of his face.

"Should we try to save him?" whispered Suede.

It was spoken in a tone that was part I-really-don't-want-to-do-that and part it-just-feels-like-the-right-thing-to-say. The comment drifted in the air unanswered as they both realised how utterly unprepared they were for the world they seemed to have stepped into.

As Grace stared at the scene, a dozen emotions hit her. The one she'd be last to admit was relief when she could no longer see the old man's face.

"Don't look, honey," whispered Suede, eventually.

She turned to glare at him in the way that suggested the person who hid at the other end of the house when this whole fiasco started didn't have the cachet to offer that advice on the matter.

He broke eye contact, instead focusing temporarily on his toes, before switching to the van and task at hand.

Using hand gestures, Suede suggested they take a path that kept them on the cottage side of the road. Grace nodded her approval before gently opening the gate so they could step in the danger zone.

The moment passed with a great deal of success, until the gate whined an elongated squeak as Suede brought it to a close. They stopped in their tracks and Grace shot him a death stare before their eyes darted to the human-street food situation across the road. One of the gorging not-zombies raised its head, seemingly alerted to the sound. Or the presence of more humans.

Heartbeats raced as the couple stared back in silent anticipation. The moment seemed to last an eternity until the not-zombie lost interest and returned its focus to the banquet.

Grace gave him another loaded stare before they turned in the direction of the van.

"How was I to know that would happen?" whispered Suede.

"You didn't," rage-whispered Grace. "You just didn't need to close the gate at all."

Suede went to defend his action, immediately interrupting his response when he realised she was right.

"I can't even say you had one job!" whispered Grace. "You had no jobs!"

They turned their back on the squeaky gate and the cute cottage they were house-sitting on the street they could never afford, and shifted their focus to their escape route and the multi-coloured kombi van that was a critical part of it.

The already narrow street seemed doubly so this morning. The one-way thoroughfare had cars lining it on both sides. Down the middle was a sliver of bitumen that would have made truck drivers nervous. To add to the degree of difficulty, it was bin day, and every inch of kerbside and all the driveways were packed with general waste bins and the larger recycling bins.

"Fucking recycling," whispered Suede.

Grace nudged him. "That shit's important."

"I just meant there'd be half the number of bins out here if it was green waste week."

The conversation petered out as they approached the strip of street most densely packed with cars and bins. The van teased them across the road. Its red exterior, criss-crossed with black and white strips at all manner of angles, beamed like the calling card of the home it had been since they started their around-Australia trip months earlier.

"We're coming, Halen," whispered Grace.

*

Halen was more than just a mode of transport, it was part of the team – a significant part of their relationship, their lifestyle and the world they had built. Sure, travelling around the country, living off content-creation income may have seemed easy from the outside, but a thousand things had to go right at all times to give that appearance. And they were the sort of things followers of their various channels would never notice, unless they decided to share for the realness of it.

The duck glides over the surface while its legs paddle madly beneath. Some of the endless leg paddles were in their creative control — like the relentless search for ideas — others were logistical challenges one didn't realise were an issue until everything broke hundreds of miles from help and others were the brutal honesty of a relationship spent living in each other's pockets 24/7.

At the centre of all those moving parts was Halen. A simple, dependable, cheap to run and easy-to-fix workhorse with a retro paint job. The glue. The paddling legs. The shelter. Part studio, part accommodation, part greenroom, part office, part back drop, part cameo appearance, part storage, part transportation.

Halen.

*

Further down the street another not-zombie made its presence known as it slipped off the street between two parked cars, then stumbled into a couple of bins and fell to the ground. It stared at them while clumsily trying to regain its feet.

Grace shared an apprehensive look with Suede. Suddenly, the sounds of mayhem seemed to rise in volume, the street had narrowed and the obstacles blocked more space. Grace led them past the last car before the point they had targeted to cross the street. She reached an arm back, and Suede made contact with it as they progressed. She moved past the front of the car until she was in a position to peer up and down the length of the street, pausing briefly to collect herself before doing so.

A few more of the not-zombies were scattered up the road in the direction they were headed. But the other way, closer to where their one-way street hit the main road, things looked a whole lot worse. There was movement everywhere, but it was too distant to make out any details beyond what the sounds of panic and screaming offered.

"Oh shit," said Suede, having moved in next to her.

"Yep," said Grace. "What the hell is happening?"

"We're getting out of here, that's what," said Suede.

Grace nodded as she reached into her jacket for the van keys as they stepped out onto the street. Well, they would have if something hadn't caught Suede's ankle.

*

CHAPTER 4
RUN LIKE HELL

It didn't take long for the combination of Suede's momentum and the grip on his ankle to trigger a fall. He dropped the knife and merch bag as he went down so his hands were free to cushion the impact. After meeting the ground, he scrambled to reorient himself. He manoeuvred his body to face the threat, offering a pre-emptive scream as he turned. A not-zombie, twisted under the car, stared at him, its hand still on his boot as it tried to pull him closer.

It emitted a noise that was part-wheeze, part-rasp. There were spaghetti lengths of viscous drool everywhere. It was enough to send Suede's scream up several semitones. As it neared a for-dog's-ears-only register, Suede found himself transfixed by the not-zombie's eyes. There was something piercing about how they stared at him – all-seeing, yet distant – vacant even.

Grace broke the moment with a swift kick to the not-zombie's face.

Suede's focus snapped back, and he started thrashing his leg about and leaning back until he was free of its grasp.

Grace offered her hand, and he used it to lift himself to standing. She turned to the van while Suede took his opportunity to sink his boot into the creature's face before picking up the merch bag and knife and turning to join her. "Asshole!"

After battling her shaking hands, Grace felt the sweet action of keys sliding into the lock mechanism before she opened the door. She turned to see Suede fleeing the scene of commotion before jumping into the driver's seat and unlocking the passenger side.

"Gross!" Suede screamed as he joined her seconds later and flung the merch bag in the back in disgust. "Gross, gross, gross."

Grace hit the ignition and rubbed the dash when Halen's unique puttering engine noise started. "Good boy." She pulled the van onto the street.

"Just nasty! Did you see the drool? And its eyes?" said Suede after catching his breath. "Where do we go now?"

"I think we just drive as far away from here as possible."

Their progress came to a halt before they'd even reached the end of the street. After passing a handful of non-zombies here and there down the narrow thoroughfare, they were greeted by a group of four of them completely blocking their path. The van was metres short of an intersection that opened up to a wider cross-street. It teased them as the not-zombies were drawn to the noise, and perhaps colour, of the van.

"Great!" whispered Grace.

They studied the creatures, only separated from their seats by a thin layer of metal and glass. Their chests tightened as they waited, hoping the not-zombies would turn their attention to something else. It soon became apparent that wasn't going to happen without an intervention. Not only had the van drawn the creatures, but now the two human faces inside seemed to transfix them.

"What do we do now?" whispered Suede.

"How have you not been thinking about that already?" whispered Grace as she gave him a glare. "Surely that's the assumed next question."

"It was no less constructive a comment than your sarcasm!"

After Suede had matched her stare, the pair returned to the events unfolding outside the van's cabin. And the silence of unsuccessful problem-solving.

"Do you think they could break the glass?" whispered Suede. "You know, if they really wanted to."

"I don't think I want to hang around long enough to find out."

"Could you maybe ease it into a slow roll? Hopefully, they'll just get out of our way."

"What if one of us opens the sunroof? We could throw something into a nearby window or something. It might distract them enough to clear the street," suggested Grace.

Suede nodded as he made his way to the back of the van. "Done. If it doesn't work, we can nudge them out the way."

Grace turned her attention back to the not-zombies staring at her from the front of the van. Their glares were unwavering, unnerving. What would she do if the plan didn't work? What wou—

There was a nearby screech of tyres from behind the van, followed by a fleshy impact noise, then a metallic collision crunch. Grace jumped, then went to look on through the rearview mirror, but Suede was standing under the now-open sunroof, blocking her view.

"What was that?" she said as she turned to face the back of the van.

Suede was rubbing his head. His jump in fright had clearly sent him into the sunroof edge. "SUV. Looks like it ploughed through a bunch of zombi—"

"Not-zombies!"

"... not-zombies on the main street. Slammed into a parked car, too. Man, there's zo— not-zombie bits everywhere."

Grace signalled for him to move to the side so she could also take in the scene. The SUV revved and lurched backwards, then forwards as the driver tried to untangle it from the wreckage of the vehicle it had collided with. They heard a number of panicked voices arguing from inside the damaged vehicle.

The nearby not-zombies that had been feasting on the now-deceased body of the old man across the road turned and headed towards the commotion. At the scene, there were already a number of not-zombies surrounding the SUV.

"Should we try to save them?" said Suede.

Silence followed.

They watched as one of the windows on the non-impact side of the SUV smashed outward into the street, and one of the occupants started prodding something at the nearby non-zombies.

"Is that a crowbar?" said Suede.

"Maybe," said Grace, looking through squinted eyes.

The prodding object was thrust towards the head of one of the not-zombies, the blow pierced the creature's skull and it dropped to the street, defeated. But with the crowbar still attached. From the downed beast's flanks, two other not-zombies leaned forward in competition to enter the vehicle's cabin through the broken window.

"Oh shit!" whispered Grace.

Pained screams soon rang out from the vehicle. The only competing noise was that of the SUV's engine, now screaming in its own way as the driver increased the level of desperation to escape the entangled mess of vehicles.

It was confronting viewing. Suede scanned the wider scene to find some respite from the horror. He soon found himself drawn to the body of the old man. "Do you think he's going to, like, turn or something?"

"What?" said Grace, her attention still on the SUV.

"The old guy. They bit him and stuff. Does that mean he becomes… you know?"

"I don't know."

"Well, if you believe all the mythology around, erm, not-zombies, once someone is bitten, they turn into—"

"Not I don't know what you're talking about… I don't know if that's going to happen!"

Suede nodded, still a little confused.

By now, other not-zombies were clambering around the SUV. It was already blocked by the wreckage on one side, and now, it was surrounded by not-zombies in every other direction. One fell forward onto the hood, then managed to leverage its legs against other clamouring not-zombie limbs in such a way that it worked itself into a standing position.

The SUV shook with the forces applied to it from a number of directions, and the not-zombie on the hood soon fell, smashing through the front windscreen.

"That's not great," said Suede.

At that moment, the windows darkened on one side of Halen, then the other. Two of the not-zombies who had been blocking their exit were seemingly drawn to the commotion by the crashed SUV. Heart rates galloped as Grace and Suede stayed as still as possible. Soon, a third not-zombie passed by, then the fourth and final.

Even once the creatures had moved on and the immediate danger had passed, Grace and Suede barely made a sound. Each knew a false move here could send them the way of the SUV crew. There they stayed, statue-still, as the not-zombies passed the still unmoving corpse of the old man, only daring to break the moment when the creatures joined the others attacking the SUV.

The pair breathed a heavy sigh of relief. Then their attention turned to the road ahead of the van, now empty of not-zombies, the path to the intersection free.

"Let's get the fuck out of here," said Grace as she slipped back to the driver's seat.

"Let's the fuck do that," said Suede, putting down the object he was going to throw and closing the sunroof.

They shared a look of relief before it dawned on Grace what Suede had picked up. "Was that my salt lamp?"

"Sorry?" he said dismissively as he turned his full focus to the sunroof.

"Asshole!"

"I needed something heavy to break windows!"

"You know what that means to me!"

Suede did his best not to comment on his belief about the effectiveness of salt lamps. Instead, he tried his best at an understanding gesture.

Grace turned the ignition. If there was an aggressive way to do such a thing, she found it. "You know what that does for the air. Not to mention my allergies."

Suede slipped into the passenger side and clicked his seat belt. "Honestly, I didn't have time to think. I just needed something heavy."

"Not to mention what it does for my mood," she said as she began rolling the van slowly towards the nearby intersection, eyes darting around in search of hidden surprises.

Suede opened his mouth, then paused. Experience told him he should strongly edit his next sentence several times before uttering it. Or, better still, not have a next sentence.

Grace put her indicator on as they neared the intersection. "Besides, it's a key part of the backdrop for my wellness channel."

Suede kept his eyes forward, taking in the world that had changed. He thought about making a comment about the effectiveness of a wellness channel in the current world circumstances but passed. Then he thought about commenting on the effectiveness of indicating but passed again.

Instead, he patted the dashboard and spoke to the van. "Good boy, Halen, good boy."

They hung a left at the intersection. A sense of relief washed over them as the suffocatingly narrow one-way street disappeared in the rear-view mirror. They passed an overturned car, only to see the half-gnawed body of an elderly female driver still being dined upon.

It was the woman who had bailed on the old man outside the cottage.

"She didn't get far," said Suede.

Grace glared at him.

"What?" he defended.

That aside, the not-zombie presence in the wider street seemed nowhere near as menacing as what they'd already experienced. While a few not-zombies pocked the path ahead, they would be easy to drive around. A few blocks ahead, the main road beckoned. It would lead them to the fringe of the city and their way out of the madness.

*

Grace momentarily diverted her eyes from the road to a photograph held onto the sun visor with hair ties. It was of her and her father, taken several years ago. She brushed her finger across it lightly in a ritual Suede had seen many times before. He extended his arm to her knee and patted his understanding.

Her father – James – was one of the key reasons behind Halen and the van life. He had raised Grace by himself after her mum had left. She'd not just left the marriage but left the state – left Grace.

She was eight.

It nearly broke James, but it didn't. He raised her his way. What he lacked in words, he made up for in actions. Working and raising Grace – that was his existence. Whatever sport or activity or interest she had, he was there. He gave her his kind of normal. And when he did use his voice, it was either no-nonsense advice or words of love. Grace always knew where she stood, in all the ways.

He'd gone over and above the requirements for an average father to earn the same title, which only made the cancer seem so much more unjust. Grace was at university by then and did as best she could to return the years of favour. She never missed an appointment or a treatment, even when university was done and she was in the workforce.

It wasn't just watching her father grow weak that hurt. It was watching how the world seemed designed to let people fall through the cracks. Or turn a blind eye or just not care. Instead of paying off the house and saving for his retirement, he lost his job and struggled to make ends meet, even with her help.

Five years was a long-time lesson in losing faith in the system you live under. When James passed, most of what he'd worked his life to build had been stripped away. And while she was looked after when he was gone, she swore she'd never live for a system like that.

She watched as friends dedicated their lives to playing the game. It started with the tertiary education required to get a decent-paying job and the years of financial debt that incurred. They chased house prices that were reaching escape velocity, making ownership a pipedream until your mid-30s, if ever. If you managed to get through all that and get the mortgage dream, you were rewarded with a 30-year commitment to keep your nose to the grind for the bulk of your adult life. Always only one misstep away from everything unravelling. All the while, AI and robotics kept constantly changing the face of employment and eating away at job opportunities, and the gap between rich and poor – old and young – widened.

No, that wasn't for her.

It was the easiest thing to do to walk away from her job and life aspirations that she and many of her generation had decided were twentieth-century values.

She met Suede a few months later when he served her a coffee on a trip up the central coast. That was back when he had dreads.

He was on the run from suffocating family expectations, and it wasn't long until the two became a couple. A few months and a few big dreams later, they found Halen advertised in the classifieds. A quick paint job later, and they were on the road – a new life – a new way of life.

That was more than two years ago.

And now, they were on the road again.

*

CHAPTER 5

WE'VE GOT TO GET OUT OF THIS PLACE

It wasn't until Grace and Suede neared the main road that the extent of the situation really began to reveal itself. There were three cars ahead of them at the intersection, and so slow was the traffic movement on the main road, it took a whole ten minutes to make a turn onto the thoroughfare. Things had all but ground to a halt, the road now a sea of beeping cars and swearing occupants.

At the distant set of lights ahead, there was some sort of commotion. There were also the remnants of a recent car crash nearby, which the traffic just rolled on past.

"Jesus," said Grace as the full extent of the situation sunk in.

"We'll be here for hours," said Suede.

On the opposite side of the road, a small group of not-zombies ambled along next to the traffic.

"We'll be sitting ducks for hours," said Grace.

Suede looked back to the problematic intersection ahead. "Wait, look at the cars on the other side of the lights. They're bumper-to-bumper as well. Even if we get through all this, it's even worse on the other side."

"Shit," said Grace as she pondered the problem.

She studied the surrounding landscape. They were following the line of the foothills. In a few kilometres, the road they were on would split. One direction becoming the South Eastern Freeway towards the hills and interstates beyond, while their intended path would lead them past the outer southern suburbs to the coast.

She looked in the direction of the Adelaide city centre in the distance. Even at this elevated view, only the upper sections of the taller buildings could be seen. There was something disconcerting about the skyline that day that she couldn't quite put her finger on. Perhaps it was a lingering feeling that she wasn't going to lay eyes on it in a while, or if she did, it wouldn't be the same as it was now. "I'm really trying not to freak out."

"Me too," said Suede. "I never could deal with peak hour."

"No, not that, just…" started Grace, without any idea how to complete her though. "I think we need to bail on the main road."

They shared a look, and Suede nodded.

"We should be able to cut through the side streets pretty much all the way to the start of the freeway."

"Do it!"

Grace put the car into reverse to allow enough clearance to turn behind the car in front. From there, she hoped to mount the gutter and reverse back to the side street a few metres behind them. Just as she did, a round of screams cut through the beeps and idling car engines. "What was that?" she asked.

"A sign we'd better move fast," said Suede.

As she pulled out of the traffic lane and clicked Halen into reverse, another wave of screaming washed over them. They looked up to see a number of people running from the road, abandoning cars for whatever safety the roadside houses might provide. They were less than fifty metres ahead of the van.

There was a thud as Halen flattened a roadside street sign.

"Shit!" shouted Suede as he recovered from the shock. He glared at Grace.

"My bad!" she said.

"You drive, I'll keep my eyes on… whatever's going on up there."

"Keep me posted," said Grace as she hugged the passenger seat and turned her focus to the view through the rear door's window.

Another wave of screams came as more people fled from the commotion, which was now a few more metres away. More people flooded from their cars. That's when Suede saw the first not-zombie. It was a young woman in pursuit of the humans. Within seconds, there were a dozen. And the number doubled again seconds later. Then a young couple ran through, trying to fight off a swarm of not-zombies that had surrounded them. Except there was nowhere to run.

More screams echoed around the road. Some from victims, others from those who were watching.

"You're supposed to be giving me updates!" said Grace.

Suede acknowledged her with a nod, then returned to watch the scene in front of the reversing van. The scale of the situation had multiplied in the seconds he had taken his eyes from it. Worse still, the retreating people were now realising the properties lining the main road – Portrush – were fronted with high fences to block out the noise. A few of the more athletic retreaters took on the fence-scaling challenge, but the rest fled further down the road. Which also meant they were tracking after the van.

"Hurry up!" said Suede, eventually.

"What kind of update is that?" said Grace as Halen thumped into another pole. "Sorry!"

Around them, the screaming and mayhem intensified.

"Just, we need to get off this road, like, yesterday," added Suede, attempting more clarity.

Grace groaned at another uninformative update before turning to see what was happening with her own eyes. A swarm of fleeing humans chased down the side of the road and footpath in front of them. The frontrunners were only metres away.

"Shit!" she said as she turned to the view out the rear of the van. "With those updates? If you could just use your words!"

The street was approaching. Grace counted down the seconds until she could throw Halen into a sharp turn before backing up the street far enough to turn around and accelerated into the salvation of the side streets.

At least that was the plan. Just as she was about to trigger the move, a car pulled out of the line of traffic, clipping the van in the midsection. They felt two wheels leave the bitumen temporarily before the van thudded back down to earth. Their vehicle lost all momentum in the bingle.

"Asshole!" screamed Grace as she flipped the bird to the occupant of the car. Then she saw the damage to the other car. Its back wheel twisted from the impact. Her thoughts turned to Halen. The engine was still running, but who knew what damage he had absorbed. She adjusted her side mirror to try to get an idea.

"Hurry up!" screamed Suede.

Grace turned to see the first of the retreating human pack almost on top of them. More people started pouring out of the nearby cars as the panic spread to such a level that the immediate danger was actually getting killed by hysteria from others.

"Oh, come on!" said Grace, pressing her foot down onto the accelerator pedal once more.

She had her fingers crossed on the wheel as she turned it hard, hoping the van would hold together long enough to get them out of there.

A thud at the front of the van, then another, made her jump. She turned to see two of the fleeing frontrunners trying to get her attention, pleading for her to let them in the van.

"You do understand what updates are, right?" she screamed to Suede as Halen continued to hook around the corner.

"How was I supposed to sum all that up in a consumable sentence?" said Suede, gesturing to the scene of bedlam in front of the van.

Grace groaned.

By now, the leaders of the retreating pack were positioned in front of the driver and passenger doors, still pleading for help while trying to prise them open. "Should we try to save them?" asked Suede.

Grace looked up at the countless dozens of crazed people retreating in their direction. "If we stop now, I don't think we're starting again."

Suede nodded, then turned to the passenger window and sympathetically shrugged his shoulders. This only riled the two people trying to force their way in.

Meanwhile, another knocked repeatedly on Grace's window. She did her best to block out the noise and stay focused.

"Not-zombies!" screamed Grace.

The van had straightened out of its 90-degree turn into the side street, where three not-zombies lined the road. Their attention was completely on the van and the human smorgasbord that followed in its wake.

Grace lined up the reversing van for one of them and hammered the accelerator. The van passed close to the creature, and it collided with the human running alongside the driver's side door. The knocking on Grace's door instantly stopped. She breathed a sigh of relief.

The other two not-zombies were now in the van's wake. It didn't take long for the non-chasing humans to notice them. Screams broke out as the chase for the van soon turned into an about-face flee back to Portrush Rd.

"My hands are tied, she's crazy!"

Grace turned to see Suede apologising sympathetically to the two remaining chasers at his window. She narrowed her eyes, spun the wheel hard and slammed on the brakes, then she jammed it into forward gear and slammed her foot on the pedal. Somewhere in the chaos, the two wannabe hitchhikers went rolling onto the grassy verge, recovering only in time to see the stripey red kombi accelerating into the distance.

*

CHAPTER 6
LIVING ON THE EDGE

It took nearly an hour to negotiate the backstreets to a point where they could converge with Portrush Rd again. Every street held a potential spot fire of not-zombies, fleeing vehicles with the same side street idea and blocked streets due to car crash carnage. Somehow, they'd negotiated the maze. They were now near the city fringe, where paths to the interstate roads and southern suburbs converged.

The atmosphere in Halen had been silent for the bulk of the trip. Thoughts of what was happening to the world outside the walls of the van were too overwhelmingly soul-draining. So too were thoughts of what they'd witnessed, what they'd been a part of. What they could have done differently.

"We had to get out of there," said Suede.

His words hung in the air. An out to excuse both of them, yet one they barely believed. And there was too much else happening to get bogged down in what it all meant. As the main road neared again, the silence in Halen's cabin had changed from one of contemplation to trepidation.

"We should be able to see something on the other side of this ridge," said Suede as he toggled between phone navigation and street observation.

Sure enough, they crested a peak in the quiet, leafy suburban street and Portrush Rd came into view once again.

The first thing that caught their eye was a mess of cars on the median strip. Three were piled on top of each other with a fourth on its side, its front hugging a tree on the corner.

"Jesus!" said Grace as she approached. "Stay sharp."

"On it," said Suede, eyes darting from one potential hazard point to the next.

The van eased past the car wrapped around the tree. There was a body in the driver's seat, slumped over the wheel.

"Must've been one hell of a crash," said Suede as he studied the three cars in the middle of the road.

Grace navigated past the worst of the crash debris to pull out onto the main road once more. It could not have been further removed from the experience they'd had when they'd last left it. Ahead, she could see all the way to the next intersection. "What the hell?"

Suede soon had his eyes on the road behind them. Several hundred metres back was a scene of utter chaos. A mass of cars, plumes of smoke and roaming people. "It looks like the entire road is blocked."

"Are they people? Or, you know?" said Grace, eyeing the scene through the rearview mirror.

"Hard to tell," said Suede. "Sure are a lot of them though."

Grace turned her attention back to the stretch of road and the intersection ahead. It looked busy up there, chaotic even. In the stretch of road between, there were a couple of other car crashes, the occasional not-zombie and the odd car cutting in from side streets to head in their direction. But, given the number of cars trying to flee from further down the road, it was almost empty there. She kept Halen at an easy pace.

"Think we've got lucky," said Suede.

"Let's not go high-fiving ourselves too quickly."

"I'm not, but seriously, look what we just avoided back there," said Suede. "You filled Halen up yesterday, right?"

"Yeah. You owe me $60, by the way."

"Yeah, yeah."

They puttered their way through the ghostly scene in silence once more. An almost permanent head shaking of disbelief their chosen way to express their emotions.

Suede put his head down in his phone. "Jesus!"

"What?"

"You're not going to like it."

"What?"

"Top hashtags right now – political shit left, politic shit right, football, some actor I've never heard of died… what the fuck? Donuts about all this."

"Like, nothing, nothing?"

"Weird," said Suede, his voice distracted as he typed into his device. "Like, literally nothing. I just typed in… that word we're not calling the… things. And it's come back with nothing but results from TV shows and games. Oh, and that new game everyone's playing on socials – seventies rock stars that now look like zombies. The bass player from Aerosmith is this week's nominee, judging by trending.

"That's weird, right."

"Weird."

Not for the first time that day, an overwhelmed silence took over the cabin of Halen.

"Hey, what about the radio?" said Suede, eventually.

"What about it?"

"Can't you get, like, news and stuff on it? Might find out what's going on."

Eyes fell to the console between them. "How do you even use it?" said Grace.

"I don't know," said Suede, as he started pressing buttons and turning knobs.

Eventually, the sound of static poured into the cabin, and he got the sense that turning the knob that made the red line move across the numbers seemed to have an effect on the static. Then another sound shot out briefly from the speakers, perhaps a voic—

"Go back!" said Grace.

Eventually, Suede attuned himself to the subtleties of the signal and tuned in a station.

"Just recapping the top stories on this beautiful autumn day, an earthquake has caused havoc in western Turkey with the death toll expected to be in the thousands. Tensions climb after another day of violence along the…"

"Erm, I'm no expert, but I think they've missed the headline," said Suede.

"… closer to home, and the polls are showing things are getting tight as we head into the election with…"

"Unbelievable!" said Grace.

Meanwhile, Suede worked the dial, tuning in another station.

"… and in sport, the big news for the morning, the Aussie men's team are celebrating their big win against South Korea in the World Cup qualifier last night, the win all but…"

"Are you fucking serious?" said Suede as he tuned again.

"… we'll continue to give you updates of this breaking story…"

"Oh," said Suede as he turned the volume up.

"… repeat, a fisherman is missing after falling overboard last night in the waters in the gulf. A fleet of boats are now sweeping the area—"

Suede flicked the radio off in disgust. "Pfft. Legacy media."

"OK, we're here," said Grace as she took her foot off the accelerator altogether.

A car tore around the corner from behind them, flanked them on the outside, cut back in front to avoid an abandoned vehicle in the middle of the road, then sped into the intersection, turning onto the highway.

"Wanker!" said Grace as she flipped the bird to the rapidly disappearing car in front of them.

"Be careful," said Suede.

"Me? Which part of that situation made you decide I needed a talking to about my driving technique?"

"I didn't mean it like that – don't go pissing off some crazy."

"Which reminds me, you told the randos trying to get into the van earlier that I was crazy!"

Suede opened his mouth, but no words came out.

Once again, silence claimed the cabin as they rolled to the fringe of the intersection. The world was transitioning around them again. Gone was their moment of respite along the blocked section of road – their eye of the storm – the scene in front of them was every bit as crazy as the main road they'd fled from an hour earlier. No, this was worse.

"Well, shit!" said Grace.

Such was the intersection's geographical location, that it was a chokepoint of traffic that could not be avoided. It was a convergence of major thoroughfares framed into place by the steep hills that surrounded it. It was a point in the east where north-south traffic converged on east-west traffic and a route that led from the city in one direction to the highway in the other. There was no way around it, no sneaking through the side streets.

While there was barely a trickle of traffic coming from Portrush Rd, the same could not be said for Cross and Glen Osmond roads. Both were lined with seemingly endless traffic backed up, trying to enter the highway and escape the city.

The highway itself was banked up as far as the eye could see as it wound into the hills. There were crashed and abandoned vehicles everywhere, including a couple that were on fire. To top it off, there were groups of what looked like not-zombies lurking near the crawling traffic. The cars heading out of the city in that direction weaved in single file around the chaos.

The opposite side of the highway, separated by a wall, was no better. Some enterprising drivers were heading against the direction of traffic to avoid the crush of the official outbound lanes. But they were competing against a flow of traffic still headed into the city. It was a frantic and angry scene, littered with more abandoned vehicles.

"Holy shit," said Suede, as the entirety of the carnage of the highway opened up in front of them. "Doesn't look like anyone's going anywhere in a hurry."

"Looks like they're one more crash away from traffic stopping altogether."

The other two roads to their right were packed with cars queuing to get on the highway. Again, there were spot fires of crashes and carnage everywhere. There was beeping and swearing and engines revving in frustration. Any attempt to follow the traffic lights had long since been abandoned as drivers from multiple directions tried to press their cars into any millimetre of space that got them closer to the highway. It was four packed lanes trying to turn and merge into one. And all of those cars were further back in the queue than the small trickle of vehicles still coming up from the blocked main road who merged with the single file of traffic further around the corner.

"How the fuck are we going to get across all of that?" said Suede.

That's when the enormity of their task hit home. Grace scanned the chaotic mess, searching for an angle.

"They're doing it," said Grace, as she pointed to two cars, facing the way they wanted to go that were nearly through madness. "Follow them, I guess."

They were also the nexus of swearing and horn blaring.

"How long do you think it's taken them to get there?" asked Suede.

"An hour? Three? I guess we're about to find out," said Grace. "It's not like we have much of a choice."

There was another car just ahead of them, just beginning its journey through the chaos. Its presence across the flow of traffic caused a chorus of car horns and very personal comments about the driver's mother and lineage.

"I think I'm just going to follow them," said Grace.

"We're not going to be popular," said Suede.

"When has that ever stopped you?"

He glared at her, then flipped her the bird.

With that, they entered the fray.

*

CHAPTER 7
CROSSTOWN TRAFFIC

It had been 40 minutes since they had started crossing the intersection. The good news was that they were nearly halfway there. They had caught up to the rear bumper of the car in front and a third car had now joined them as they worked their way across the direction of traffic.

One of the occupants of the lead car had climbed onto the roof. After using up what seemed like a plentiful supply of empty beer bottles as projectiles to help clear a path forward, he had now retrieved a crowbar from the boot and was on the roof, threatening anyone who didn't yield to their right of way. It had really sped things up in the last few minutes. They'd moved nearly a car length. However, cars from further afield were now responding by lobbing any projectile they could in his direction.

Meanwhile, Grace and Suede were copping their own abuse for riding on the coat-tails of the intersection disruptor.

"Wanker!"

"Cockswab!"

"Cockswab," said Suede with a smirk. "I'll have to remember that one."

"Eat this," said the roof rider, gesturing to a nearby driver with his hand on his crotch.

"Not so much that."

Something caught the roof-rider's eye in the distance. His look changed to one of sheer horror. He bent down to the driver's window and screamed. "Get the fuck out of here now!"

"What did he see?" said Suede.

"Something towards the city," said Grace. "Do we want to know?"

It was too late. Suede was already opening the sunroof and climbing through for a view. "Oh shit."

In the distance, a sea of movement and chaos filled the road. It was as if a horde of not-zombies were sweeping all four lanes of gridlocked traffic. They numbered too many to escape, and the cars were too entombed to drive away.

"What?"

"They're everywhere." He worked his way down to the passenger seat in a flash. "We need to go."

Grace laughed at the stupidity of the suggestion, given their situation, then turned to see his pallid face, awaiting an update.

"Hundreds. Thousands. I don't even know. And they're heading this way. We need to go now!"

Grace looked at the mangle of traffic. "How?"

*

Ten minutes had passed, and they had barely moved. Suede was returning from his fourth trip to the roof in that time. He consulted his watch and did a few mental sums. "We've got half an hour. Maybe forty-five. Maybe."

"Things will clear up a bit, I know it," said Grace. "Right?"

"And if they don't?"

"We grab some bags and run."

Suede nodded. "Let's hope it doesn't come to that. I'm not sure I want to do this without Halen."

Grace breathed out heavily. "It won't."

They shared a nod. Grace turned her eyes back to the cars ahead, and Suede looked to the broader scene, hoping to find a distraction.

His eyes were soon drawn to the movements of a single pedestrian. A teen was standing at the foot of a retaining wall, no doubt erected to protect houses from regular intersection traffic noise and runaway trucks losing brakes down the freeway (a not uncommon situation). The boy was working with a pair of spray cans and a crate so he could write a large piece of graffiti.

"Check that kid out," he said, hoping to share the distracting moment. "He's writing… the z word on that wall."

Grace barely looked, her focus on the projectile flinging chaos ahead.

"Wait, he's spelt it wrong!"

Grace had already blocked him out.

"He looks like he's spent ages on it too. He's got the Z, M, B, E and S in red. Then came back and did the I in blue, but where he's supposed to put the O, he's done an A! Poor kid just ruined the whole thing. I guess they don't teach spell check these days?"

Grace's attention was now fully absorbed in a game of bumper chicken with a hatchback heading to the highway. Both vehicles knew if they won the battle for the next few millimetres of ground, the other car would have to yield. She ignored Suede.

"Zambies! Idiot."

"Come on, Halen, this is what you were made for. No fucks given about your panels. That car's brand new. Look, it's electric. They'll back down," said Grace.

"Sounds like someone's trying to say zombies, but with a Bostonian accent."

"Boom!" said Grace. The other car had folded, and the battle for position was hers.

"We're in the car, going to Harvard, to get away from those zambies," said Suede in a dubious Bostonian.

Grace stared at him. "What the fuck are you doing?"

Suede felt a sudden twinge of embarrassment. "Zambies," he defended, pointing to the graffiti.

"Could you at least attempt to be the slightest bit constructive?"

"Quit being such a poor sport," said Suede, again using his new-found accent.

Grace breathed in and out heavily at the wheel. "Never, ever do a Boston accent in my presence again."

The cabin was as quiet as the abuse being sworn at it from outside allowed. The car in front with the crazy crowbar man on the roof continued forward and the end of the trouble was in sight.

"Zambies," Suede whispered to himself.

But not quietly enough. "Do you want me to leave you here?"

"Sorry."

Another showdown of car wills loomed with a car full of twenty-somethings headed to the highway. Grace locked eyes with the driver, only to realise she was already smiling back at her. She was holding up her device. And hand signalling Halen through.

"What the?" said Grace.

"Has she got your wellness channel open on her phone?" said Suede, leaning his head forward.

Grace tried to hide her head wobble as she took the space offered and eased Halen forward. While she did, she pulled out her phone, which was vibrating profusely. "Oh, she's a fan. She's been messaging me." She gave a gushing smile out of the window, mouthed 'thank you', then gave the love heart signal.

"Wow, what are the odds?" said Suede.

Grace detected the tone of a backhand in the comment. "Not that great, really. There are nearly 600,000 followers on that channel."

"Yeah, I guess. It just seemed that odds would be much more likely someone following one of my channels would recognize me. Especially given Halen features quite a bit."

Grace allowed her smile to enter smug territory before she waved at the driver once more. "Hmmm, maybe most of your fans are in Boston?"

Suddenly, the thundering of air brakes ripped through the air, drowning out the beeping and abuse. Seconds later, it was followed by skidding. From the direction they had come, an out-of-control truck barrelled towards the crush of cars.

It all happened too fast to process or react to. Not that there were many reactions that would have made a difference wedged into the mass of cars as they were. By the time Grace saw the mass of metal approaching in the rear-view mirror, the cabin covered in not-zombies, she only had time to say two words.

"Hold on."

The sound of folding and tortured metal crushed eardrums as the truck hit the pack of cars at speed. It sent some– or parts of them – flying and compressed others into each other. Grace and Suede watched as the cars to Halen's flank formed up and down patterns across the intersection as they were compressed and tossed around like toys. As the initial wall of sound abated, screams could be made out again – some of pain, some of fear.

The couple turned to the rear of the van to see the worst of the damage. The broken cabin of the truck was barely visible through the cars it had displaced in the deceleration of impact. A dead driver slumped over the out-of-shape steering wheel, joined in the cabin by a couple of not-zombies, seemingly recovering from the ordeal. Several more of their kind were spread across the metal destruction below. Some defeated, some recovering.

Those who were able to do so, fled from their vehicles, or tried to free fellow occupants. Those trapped in cars screamed. Grace could only imagine the suffering being endured, or the horrors of watching the not-zombies approach. She fought back the fear that was threatening to overwhelm her.

Around the fringes of the pack of cars, most of those able to do so, fled. Others continued to hold their ground, hoping pathways to the interstate were still possible. Whatever their move, the stakes they had bet on it were extreme.

It was only an act of fate in how multiple sub-collisions spread the energy of the truck's momentum safely around Halen, that left the van free from the interlocked mass of vehicles. Not two cars across, the destruction left cars a complete write-off. Some drivers were trying against hope to free their vehicles from the carnage, others bargained to hitch a ride, while still others fled on foot.

Of course, that was all behind them and to their side. Ahead of their decorated red kombi van, the car Grace was following squeezed free from the gridlock cluster. The man on the roof let out a satisfied roar as he grabbed his crotch and did a little jig at the people still hurling abuse at him. He climbed back inside the cabin, and they took off. Grace was on the ball enough to stay on its bumper until Halen was also free of the pack.

"Yes," she said with gusto.

Suede celebrated with a fist pump.

A couple more cars followed in their wake, but the convoy soon found its next challenge – cars heading to the interstate had all but blocked the westbound lanes of Cross Rd against the traffic. The car Halen followed scraped past vehicles, knocked over road signs and rode the footpath as the driver found every inch of space to get them clear of the chaos. When they finally rounded the fullness of the bend, they saw the new traffic horror that awaited. Bumper-to-bumper traffic as far as the eye could see.

"Jesus!" said Suede. "What now?"

"Keep following this lot, I guess."

"Good call."

Soon, the convoy crossed the footpath into an adjacent park, which led to an oval in the suburb beyond. For the first time, they were free of the gridlock insanity, and a wave of relief washed over them. On the far side of the oval, the road joined a tree-lined side street in foothill suburbia.

Despite being off the main roads, many an enterprising city escapee seemed to be searching for another way out of the mess. But the further into the suburbs they got, the more vehicle numbers thinned out.

"Finally," said Grace.

"Shit," said Suede looking at his phone. "Maps is down. Everything is down."

Grace sighed as she navigated the unfamiliar streets. They hit a corner, and instinct told her to turn right, yet the lead car turned left, as did the one in its wake.

"Shit!" said Grace as she pulled over to assess the situation.

"Hang on, signal's back. Like dial-up speed, but it's something," said Suede, studying his screen. "Looks like they're headed up to the hills. That way leads to a road that parallels the highway. Maybe we could take it and cut around the country roads until we hit the coast?"

They watched the convoy move into the distance, followed by other cars.

"Can't we just cut around the suburbs like we are now?"

"Or catch up with the others?" said Suede. "Safety in numbers and all that."

"I don't know!" Grace hit the steering wheel. "Sorry, Halen."

"Actually, looks like we can cut around. I think this way will be quicker."

"OK, let's do it!" said Grace as she put the van into gear and dropped her foot onto the accelerator.

Halen was soon off in chase. While climbing hills wasn't the van's strong suit, especially when fully fuelled and laden, Grace drove in a way that made ground. They hit the next crossroad at speed, with Grace only seeing the flash of black too late.

The collision of vehicles was as loud as it was sudden.

Halen went into a spin.

Which was stopped by a tree.

*

CHAPTER 8

ALWAYS CRASHING IN THE SAME CAR

Grace's head was spinning, her ears rang, and her body felt like it had been through a pasta maker. She remembered a streak of black – a car failing to give way. It clipped Halen in such a way that all driver control was lost. Then, the brief sensation of gliding over the road's surface like it was ice, then a similar but less controlled experience in the dusty gutter. Then bang! They must have T-boned that tree hard because the entire experience came to an instant, glass-shattering, bone-jarring halt.

Now that the dust was literally starting to settle in and around the cabin, she could see the stub of a cut-off branch mere centimetres from her head. "Suede!"

She heard a spitting sound coming from the seat next to her. "I'm fine, I think," said Suede before spitting again.

She looked over to see his face only half visible through the dusty cloud in the cabin. A moment later, she saw the blood. "Jesus! You OK?"

He traced her eyes back to his mouth and moved his hands in to investigate. "What, this? Bit the inside of my mouth. I'll be fine." He spat again. "I'm not sure if I've swallowed more dust or blood. What the hell happened?"

"Some fuck ran straight through the give way sign."

"Shit. And Halen?"

Grace unclicked her seatbelt, then went to open the door before realising a combination of tree position and door damage meant that wouldn't be possible. The true extent of their problems started to kick in. "No, no, no, no, no. Halen!" She reached up to the sun visor and removed the photo of her dad, slipping it into her pocket.

Suede felt around to make sure all appendages were present and operational before he unclicked his belt and opened the door. "It's going to take a lot to hold Halen down for too long."

His words did little to soothe Grace. Once he was out, she contorted her leg under the slightly mangled steering wheel before sliding out the passenger side door. Like Suede, she checked that her key body parts were at functional levels before leaving the broken van. Suede was already around the back, collecting a bunch of items that had scattered free during impact.

Grace headed over to join him, but something caught her eye in the distance. The carcass of a black SUV, camping trailer in tow, with muffled music blaring within the cabin. It, too, had come to a resting place wrapped around a tree, although the contact had been more head-on. The impact damage on the passenger side went all the way back into the cabin, and smoke poured from the engine.

The vehicle had a row of spotlights mounted behind the cabin, too many bumper stickers and every other indicator that screamed 'red flag' to Grace. She turned to Halen; rage burning within her.

Suede stepped up next to her. He had the salt lamp in his hand, and presented it to her. "This thing's lethal. Should have seen the chunk it took out of the tree."

Grace smiled and took the offering. Each of them tried to force a smile. That's when they heard movement near the black SUV, quickly followed by a guttural groan, similar to what they'd heard outside the cottage hours earlier. They exchanged a glance acknowledging their shared concern and scanned the sight of the SUV wreckage.

It didn't take long for Grace to have located the sound's source. "Pinned between the camper trailer and the tree," she whispered.

As the dust from the accident continued to dissipate and an eddy of breeze sent the smoke heading in a different direction, the creature was revealed. It was the body of a female, not dissimilar in age to Grace if you were judging it by human metrics. The bulk of its body was pressed between the trailer and tree, leaving only its arms free to reach.

"I see it," said Suede. "Wait, what do we do?" he added after a pause.

"At least it looks solidly pinned down to me," said Grace. "I'm going to have a closer look."

"Are you su—"

Grace lifted the salt lamp at the ready and made her way towards the wreckage and the not-zombie. "Go and see if you can find something sharp."

"It's just, I'm not sure if we have enough data to know what they'll do if we get too cl—"

Grace stopped his argument with a glance when Suede conceded eye contact and turned to the strewn wreckage of Halen to find a weapon. "Just don't get too close," he said as he turned to his task.

Grace crossed the intersection to the SUV wreckage. Once she'd crossed, a convoy of cars rolled by, temporarily blocking Suede on the other side. Her heart raced as she closed the ground to the wreckage, not just from the not-zombie and the unknowns it offered, but whatever potential horrors awaited in the truck's cabin.

The growls from the not-zombie intensified as it reached out to Grace when she was only a couple of metres from where it was imprisoned. She looked back at the intersection, spotting Suede still searching through Halen's wreckage. She looked at her salt lamp, juggling its weight in her hand, imagining the pressure it could apply to the being's head. "Hello?" she said.

Groans.

"This is probably going to sound weird, but you look like a…" she laughed briefly to herself and the awkwardness of the moment. "An undead person."

As if on cue, the creature breathed a raspy, wet tonal expression.

"That's easy for you to say, but I'm trying to work out if I should be killing you – whatever you are. You know, for my own protection."

"Gwaaassrrrghhh."

Grace laughed to herself again. "I literally don't know if that helps solve this conundrum one way or the other."

As the not-zombie drooled out another verbalisation, it was matched by another coming out from behind the tree. The stereo effect took a moment to process, and by the time Grace did, a second not-zombie had entered the scene. It was closer than the pinned-down not-zombie and on foot. Grace took an instinctive step to the side and clocked her elbow into the corner of the trailer. "Fu…"

She caught her words before they turned into a yell, suddenly aware the space was nowhere near locked down. Instead, she imagined several excellent swearwords as she backed further to the street. She studied the new player on the scene. "Perfect, older male – just as I was looking for opinions," she said as she raised the salt lamp at it. "Are you, or are you not, alive?"

"Bwaahhheeahhh."

"No, that one's on me. Stupid question."

"Gwaaahuuuu."

"That's just mean," she said. Suddenly, a car whooshed by in close proximity, followed by another, then a third one, which beeped. She turned to confirm just how close to the road she had strayed. "Shit!" she roared as she jumped back from the edge of the verge.

That's when she felt a not-zombie hand brush her arm. She screamed as she jumped clear and further from the traffic. Not clear enough, as it turned out. The not-zombie lunged forward, its hand brushing her torso before latching onto her jacket. She screamed again and plunged the salt lamp into the not-zombies head, the blow as perfectly timed and executed as she could have hoped for. The sound of the impact was full of the low-end bass a deep blow exudes. She felt the skull give a little in the impact. She retracted the salt lamp, stepped back from the creature, and watched on expectantly.

Blood poured from the newly created dent in the not-zombie's head. It swayed slightly before renewing its attention on Grace. It rasped as it lunged forward once more. Grace screamed, pivoted, and swung the salt lamp again as the creature sailed past her. The lamp managed a glancing blow, not enough to cause damage, but enough for the creature to lose balance and fall face-first to the ground.

Grace took the window of advantage and moved in to strike it in the head again. Then again. Both blows connected with brutal accuracy. She stepped back, breathing heavily.

After taking a few seconds to gather itself, the creature tried to stand. Meanwhile, Suede was on the scene, crowbar in one hand and a steak knife in the other. He gave Grace a nod of satisfaction, then stood back to watch the not-zombie's attempts to rise.

"What are you doing?" said Grace between breaths. "Get it!"

He nodded nervously. "Sorry."

His eyes toggled between both weapons before selecting the crowbar. He aimed the sharp end at the creature's already damaged head and prodded forward. While the blow stuck flush, it merely bounced off the creature's skull. He looked at Grace in shock, eyes pleading for instruction.

She shrugged. "Knife?"

Suede took a couple of deep breaths while repositioning himself to an attack angle he felt was safe for close range. Then, after a couple of false starts, he saw a window of opportunity, stepped forward, brought the knife up over his shoulder, and struck.

A second or so later, he rolled from the not-zombie, screaming in pain. Grace surveyed the scene. The knife was stuck in the creature's skull, dug in barely past the tip, the rest of the blade bent nearly at a right angle. Suede soaked up the blood pouring from his hand with his T-shirt. By his side was the crowbar. Grace swooped in, picked it up, turned it to wield the hooked end and then struck another blow on the creature.

Again, after a short recovery, it tried to get up.

"Are you kidding me?" she wailed. "Skull's harder than a cat's head."

"Aim for the bits you've already dented in," suggested Suede.

Grace nodded, repositioned herself clear of flailing arms and stuck another blow. This one missed but further opened up the dent. She raised the object once again, this time delivering an accurate blow to the damaged section of skull. The strike hit flush, sinking into the wound with satisfying accuracy. The creature stopped all protests, all movement.

She shared a look of achievement with Suede before pulling the crowbar free. At least she would have if the suction of grey-matter flesh hadn't gripped it tighter than she anticipated. She gave Suede a confident smile before using both hands to grip and free the weapon. Again, the plan had fallen short of working. On her next attempt, she pressed a boot on the corpse's head and used both hands to pull. After a couple of false starts and some repositioning of the head of the crowbar inside the skull, she pulled it free with a gushing noise and a plume of red liquid and grey matter, some of which soaked Suede. The move itself sent Grace falling backwards to the ground.

"That is seriously nasty!" said Suede before making a vomit noise as he picked some of the chunkier bits from his T-shirt.

"Don't touch it!

"I'm not just going to leave it there!" he said, continuing to pick. "Not my AI DID DIS tee! That's one of my faves."

Grace studied the T-shirt. It was one of the many self-designed parody tops Suede wore regularly. This one mimicked a famous sports footwear brand with a triangle made of four stripes and the words 'AI DID DIS' underneath. It was one of many designs from his T-shirt drop-shipping business. "Is the blood contagious?" she said. "You don't know."

"Gross, gross, gross," he said as he started wiping his blood-stained hand on the grass. "Any chance you can maybe not cover me in brain goop next time!"

"I didn't do it deliberately!" Grace thought about the act of trying to prise a crowbar out of a brain. "It looks easier in the movies."

*

CHAPTER 9
AIRBAG

After a few moments of regaining dignity and wiping themselves clean, Grace and Suede tried to turn their focus to the larger scene. Cars continued to drive by, most now slowing to avoid crash debris or rubbernecking the scene in general. Not that it was a surprise. The pair of them and the bloodied corpse must've looked a sight. Despite the interest, it was clear no one had any intention of stopping.

The almost constant stream of vehicles quickly turned to a reminder of how much the crash had cost them.

"What are we going to do?" said Suede. "Everything I own was onboard Halen."

"Me too," said Grace.

They exchanged a look that expressed how out-of-body their current situation felt. Not only the shock of the moment and seeing all of their possessions strewn across the intersection but also the badly injured Halen. Not to mention the complete lack of surety about the state of a reality that threatened to consume them. It was all compounded by their unease at the presence of the defeated corpse, the other not-zombie, still hissing, and the yet-to-be-examined van.

The SUV's wreck lay eerily still nearby, although the muffled music from within continued. It accompanied the out-of-sight, trapped not-zombie. They knew they had to check the cabin while they were so close, yet the thought of what might greet them when they did was terrifying. It was if—

Suddenly, its horn burst into life. Both Grace and Suede jumped. They exchanged glances before heading towards the wreck. The smoke coming from the front of the vehicle was a little thicker than before.

Once at the SUV they saw a man in the driver's seat through the heavy window tinting. He was old. Retirement old. He was looking at them and angrily mouthing words that were barely audible over the music within. He was also gesturing frantically.

The pair studied him. He was bleeding from the forehead and mouth, no doubt after hitting the deployed airbag. Aside from his rude demeanour, the man was lean and thinning on top. He was dressed like, well, anything but the gun-toting killer that featured in Grace's mental worst-case scenario – he was just a normal-looking old guy. In fact, given their current state, maybe they were the ones who looked like they should be avoided.

Thankfully, the passenger seat was empty because parts of the engine had pressed the dashboard back into the seat. It was hard to see anyone surviving that.

The smell of unhealthy materials burning hit their noses.

Grace exchanged a look with Suede. "What do we do?"

Suede looked back at the scene and the angry old man. "Just wind down the window," he said in encouraging, some would say patronising, tones. This seemed to make the occupant even angrier, triggering a new and heightened round of gestures.

Grace glared back at the man who had nearly wiped them off the mortal coil by failing to give way. It was a look that would've stopped Suede in his tracks, leaving him an apologising wreck, but it only seemed to fuel the old man to act out further.

"Shall we just leave him?" said Grace.

Suede ignored her. "We can't hear you," he said in exaggerated tones with hand to ear.

The old man found an even angrier face before finally flicking off the music.

"Well done," said Suede.

"Shut the fuck up and get me out of here," said the old man.

After being temporarily taken aback, Suede moved in to test the door handle, but Grace blocked him.

"You could've killed us!" she said.

The two locked eyes in a glare that was part battle of wills, part, well, it was all a battle of wills.

"Listen, sugar, if you don't help me get out of here, you will be killing me."

As if on cue, the first signs of flames licked up from where the car kissed the tree.

Sugar? Sugar! Grace's jaw dropped before her expression seamlessly evolved into a death stare of intense darkness.

Suede gulped at the challenger's naïve bravado. He mocked a light laugh. "There's a term you don't hear too often these days."

Grace did not break eyes with the old man. "Call me sugar again, I fucking dare you."

The old man stared back. "Get me out of here before I roast."

"I believe it was considered a compliment back in the day," said Suede, doing nothing to break the deadlock of eyes. "Like toots, babe, doll or sugar tits."

Grace clipped him over the back of the head. "Ouch!"

"Sort your lady out and get me out of here," screamed the old man.

Suede shook his head, unsure how to respond or react to the rapidly escalating showdown. He looked at the rage in Grace's eyes, then turned to see the old man's eyes widen in pure fear before the window smashed into a thousand pieces. Then he turned back to see Grace with her hand gripping the salt lamp.

*

Several minutes had passed since the showdown. The old man had done his best to salvage as much as he could from his car and camper before the explosion hit. The fuel tank had ruptured, cremating it and the tree in a fiery finale.

Meanwhile, Grace and Suede had retreated to the kombi van to gather what they could of their possessions. It was a far less time-sensitive affair. Meanwhile, the cars kept on passing. Slowing down for their own safety and the show, but never stopping.

"What do we do now?" said Suede. "Stick out our thumbs, maybe?"

"Maybe, but everyone headed this way is headed towards the highway. No one will be looping around to head south."

"What if we—"

At that moment, a 4 x 4 truck pulled up off the road between the two vehicle carcasses. Although several decades older than the old man's truck, it was also black, had floodlights and bumper stickers, and gave Grace the same potential driver red flag vibes.

Suede nudged Grace in the side and directed her attention to words spray painted on the rear tray panel – fuck zambies.

"Spelt it wrong, too," he said, with a knowing nod.

Grace's focus was elsewhere, however. She eyed the driver's side door, waiting for someone to emerge. Seconds later, the engine was killed, and the door opened to reveal a man in his mid-30s. He was unshaven, aside from his head, and wore a plain black T-shirt, camo pants and big black boots.

"For fuck's sake," Grace muttered under her breath.

"Is everyone OK?" said the man.

Something about his tone, emotional expression and mannerisms were the entire opposite of what Grace had imagined from his exterior. "Physically, yeah."

"That's good," said the man as he studied the three and the scene. "I'm Kane."

Grace nodded. "Grace. This is Suede."

The old man scoffed. "Colin," he said.

Once again, he and Grace locked eyes.

Kane studied them with a deep, decision-making breath. "Gather your shit. You can bring whatever you can fit in the tray or the back of the cabin. I can take you to the top of the hill before I jump off grid. I'll drop you at Crafers. You've got five minutes."

A wave of relief washed over Grace, followed by a wave of nausea as she looked at her scattered belongings – her world. How was she possibly going to process everything in five minu—

"Four minutes forty until I will be leaving," said Kane after consulting his watch. She turned to see him staring at her before she nodded and hit her task at pace.

Kane opened the back door to his truck's dual cabin to rearrange some things, presumably to give the others space to sit. "Oh, one more thing. No phones."

The old man shrugged but Grace and Suede stopped in their tracks.

"What do you mean no phones?" said Suede.

"They're traceable. I don't do traceable," said Kane. "And neither should you."

"The thing is, though, we need our phones for work."

Kane eyed him. "Work?"

"Yeah, we've got this travel channel," said Suede, looking to Grace for support.

She nodded enthusiastically. "We've got two million subs."

"And once you factor in Grace's wellness channel, my music and my T-shirt drop-ship business—"

“That explains everything,” said Colin, already over to Kane’s van with his gear.

“No one asked you, lead foot,” spat Grace before turning back to Kane. “Look, we just need them for our livelihood.”

Kane laughed. “Your livelihood? What livelihood? In case you didn’t get the memo this morning, everything’s fucked. Four minutes.”

“No, no, I get that, but I have my life on that phone.”

“Look, Grace, is it?”

Grace nodded.

“Despite the fact you had been driving the ideal set of wheels for the new world, it looks like none of this has really sunk in yet. Life as you know it, is dead. Whatever you were doing for money is dead. Most of the people you know will be dead soon, too, if they’re not already. And the only chance you have of not joining them in the foreseeable future is to ditch your devices.”

Grace and Suede stared at each other, unsure.

“Three minutes thirty! Lose your devices, grab your shit and get in the truck. Or stay here. The choice is yours.”

*

CHAPTER 10
RUN TO THE HILLS

It's funny how some moments hit more than others. Grace had spent the entire morning fleeing not-zombies while watching many others try and fail to do the same. Nothing real before that day seemed real anymore. Yet no moment had seemed quite real until the one she was in right now.

She watched the gum trees rush by her window in the backseat. Diagonally opposite, Kane weaved the truck along the road. They were now caught at the rear of a snaking chain of cars headed to the hills. Between her seat and the view out the windscreen was the very slappable head of Colin, the old man who'd broken Halen and fucked everything up. By her side, Suede stared out the window in silence.

She had barely taken stock of what she'd chucked into the bag at her feet, nor the one that sat on top of the loaded tray at the back of the truck. Apart from Suede, the salt lamp and her phone, she couldn't be sure of anything else coming with her.

Should she have packed her phone? Who knows, but it was going to take more than one prepper to convince her otherwise. Now that she wasn't driving, she just had time to think. How had everything changed so significantly in a single morning? What world were they now in? What would it become? What of her family, her friends, her hometown? What of everything?

Judging by the silence, she wasn't the only one in deep contemplation.

The speed of progress at the back of the peloton had slowed significantly. Kane kept a tight line on the car in front while keeping a constant eye on the surroundings. "Looks like this might take a bit longer than expected." He looked warily at the countryside before shuffling awkwardly in the driver's seat. "This has been coming for months, you know. Years probably."

He pulled a packet of tobacco from the console and removed a cigarette he'd rolled earlier. He pulled a zippo from his pocket and lit up before opening his window slightly. "They were just waiting for the right moment, I guess. I mean, achievement-wise, they've had plenty of those already. And from a human reliance perspective, well, society pretty much can't function without them…" He spat a piece of tobacco from his lip. "... So, I guess they nailed that."

Grace and Suede exchanged glances, not wanting to miss a word of the conversation but not quite understanding the perspective of any of it.

"We were all just on borrowed time when you think about it. Tech companies, governments, armies… none of them were stopping anything. The complete opposite, really. The race was on to be first. Politicians…"

He let the word drift to the sourest part of his mouth before winding down the window further and spitting out, "Fuckers! Thankfully, not everyone was asleep at the wheel, on the take or on a power grab. Some of us have been prepping for years. We were organising when everyone else was gushing over how much better the new world was. The last couple of years, where this almost felt inevitable, we've been readying ourselves. On call to go off-grid, as they say."

Suede exchanged another look of uncertainty with Grace, before glancing at Colin to see him lost in complete old man tech confusion. "What, does this thing have anything to do with what you wrote on your rear door? Fuck Zambies, or whatever?" said Suede.

"Bingo, someone give the blood-soaked newbie a prize. Good to see you starting to piece it together."

"I saw some kid graffiti it at the start of the freeway. Zambies? Is that a Boston thing?" said Suede before repeating the new word a couple of times in his best attempt at a Boston accent.

"What the fuck are you doing?" said Kane.

"Exactly!" added Grace.

"Zambies," repeated Suede in a more submissive tone in his native accent.

"It's obvious! The a and i are a different colour – usually blue against the red of the other letters. AI – that's what this is all about."

"But… zombies," said Suede. "Not-zombies," he corrected after a look from Grace.

"Not zombies equals zambies," said Kane.

The cabin went quiet, an unspoken confusion speaking loudest.

"Zambies! Everyone who was jacked into tech – gamers, hosts, splicers, transcendents, blue bloods, medhosts – all of them. Zambies."

Again, silence permeated the confusion.

"Catch up people," said Kane before taking a frustratedly deep drag on his rollie. "Everyone you saw out there today. Everything that looked like a person but wasn't. They were all hard-wired into one digital plane of existence or another. Sucking on the teat of technology way too hard. Reliant. Then something, or someone, somewhere flicked a switch and bang. All of them have turned on the rest of us."

Silence settled over the cabin once again. This time, it was one of processing as the scale of the information hit home.

"What someone?" said Suede.

"We don't know that yet," said Kane. "We may never know."

"The government?" said Grace.

"Maybe," said Kane. "Or someone else's government. Not that nation-states matter that much anymore. Could've been some tech company, some hi-tech fringe group or full-on tech terrorists. Some bad actor somewhere."

"If they're actors, they looked pretty convincing to me," said Colin.

"He means someone or some group acting for nefarious purposes, you dill," said Grace, surprised at her use of the word nefarious.

Colin nodded in somewhat understanding.

"It's either that or one of the AIs has gone rogue," said Kane. "Or there's some new AI construct we don't even know about yet. Either way, things are fucked, and the zambies might only be the beginning."

More silent contemplation.

"So, these zambies? Are they real or not?" said Grace.

"Real?"

Her mind flashed with the violence from minutes earlier. "Alive, conscious, aware?"

"No, at least not that our network could find. A few of the hardcore gamers fell last week. Not that many of us thought that was a sign of an immediate hostile takeover," said Kane. "Not like this. Anyway, a few people across our network had access to some—"

"Some… gamers?" said Suede.

"Exactly."

"How?"

Kane adjusted the rear-view mirror to make eye contact with Suede. "Because unlike any of you fucks, my group has been seeing events unfold, realising it could lead to, well, something exactly like this, and making sure we are prepared. It's biotech meets AI meets blockchain and maybe robotics. It's the new world order, my friends."

The information was enough to quell the interruptions.

"That's where we come in. We're not just local. We're everywhere. A worldwide underground. On call to go off-grid – old school and prepared. It was our job to be aware, to be ready."

He flicked the mirror to eye Grace. "So whatever you two did to that thing back there, it was not a person. And every test we've done tells us it was never going to be a person again."

Grace nodded her appreciation as a tear formed in her eye.

"Whatever the term person means anymore," added Kane.

Kane looked ahead where the fringes of the township of Crafers came into view. At the same time, traffic almost ground to a halt. He looked at his watch. "Fuck!"

"Why zambies?" asked Suede, eventually. "It's really just so close to that Boston accent it sounds a little off… or try-hard or something. What about calling them, I don't know, NPCs. Or bots. They're gamer's terms for non-playing characters, which seems to me to be more—"

"Jesus, bots now? Don't even get me started on bots – they're a whole different thing altogether. Let's just pray they stay that way, or we're really fucked," snapped Kane. "These things are called zambies. It's not hard to grasp, I wouldn't have thought."

"Also, from a time-to-utter-the-word perspective, NPC only has three letters," added Suede.

Kane took a puff, then turned to Grace. "Is he always like this?"

She opened her mouth, but no words came out.

Kane then turned to face him in the back seat. "They're zambies, end of story," he said before setting his eyes back on the road again. "Besides, NPC has one more syllable – slower to say."

Grace watched her partner as he mouthed zambies and NPC before offering a nod of defeat. "What about bot—"

"Not happening. Bots are bots! Why would you nickname zambies an entirely different thing that also poses a threat right now? Shit is confusing enough as it is. Don't trust bots. Don't trust any tech. Any of it. It's all connected, and we don't know how, just that it's bad." Kane took another drag. "Avoid tech. Write it on your foreheads. That's why your van was perfect. You can't hack or track vehicles made before the early 90s."

Suede gave Kane the look one might give when they know they've been schooled.

"So, what do we do now?" Grace said.

"The way I see it, there are two choices – fight or flight. I'm heading to a rendezvous right now, if you care to join," said Kane.

"Some sort of militia?" said Grace.

"Yeah, some sort of militia," said Kane.

"What exactly are you going to do?"

"Fight for humanity," said Kane as he pressed the last embers of life out of his cigarette, then flicked it from the window. "Well, the current form of humanity. There's room for more."

Silence filled the cabin.

"And the flee option?" said Suede.

Kane shook his head and sighed. "It won't work, you know. The thing that's happening here, is happening everywhere."

"What about down south? Somewhere on the coast."

"If you found somewhere far enough from big populations. If you had supplies. If you could live off the network – all networks – if you were surrounded by a small community of likeminded and completely trustworthy survivors and if you had a secure supply of food and water, then maybe. Maybe you might get a small window before it finds you anyway."

"Small window?"

"Who knows what this thing will deliver. Best guess, a week or two," said Kane. "The zambies might just be the tip of the iceberg."

Again, silence reigned as the truck slowly rolled its way into the fringe of Crafers.

"Tip of the iceberg?" prompted Grace.

"I don't even have the imagination to forecast what whoever or whatever is orchestrating this situation could create. But any entity with the ability to do what has been done today is to be utterly feared."

"But if we can wait it out," said Grace. "Hide away until the threat passes, we cou—"

"I don't think you're fully appreciating the scale of what has begun here. There is no 'threat passing'. They are trying to control the rest of us, with the ones they've already controlled. This isn't just a situation. This is a chips-all-in play for control of this planet, our species… everything."

Kane made eye contact with each of them in turn. "This is not going back, it's going beyond. It knows where we all are, and it pretty much knows each of us better than we know ourselves. If you combine the computer skills at the disposal of whoever this is, we are facing a psychological, technological and evolutionary massacre.

"No one is outrunning that. We're going to have to go off-grid to have any hope of surviving.

"Sidenote, has anyone seen a robot today?" He turned to Suede. "You know, actual bots." His eyes were back on the road before Suede could react. "I haven't. Not one. And that's freaking me the fuck out as much as the zambies."

The others in the truck processed the comment. So distracted by the, well, zambies, they hadn't even noticed the obvious truth presented under their nose. The number of humanoid bots had slowly grown over the last few years from celebrated first appearances, to occasional daily sightings, to somewhat commonplace. Bots in factories, bots on building sites, bots in office workplaces, bots in restaurants, bots in hospitals, bots in nursing homes. And to spend several hours driving through suburbia and not see one? That was the new unusual.

"It's like it's back to 2024 out there."

Kane's comment hit home just how much had changed about the world in so little time.

"Anyway, the offer is out there. Become a part of this and take control of your future."

"Else?" said Suede.

"I'll drop you in Crafers and say my goodbyes."

Grace, Suede and Colin exchanged glances.

*

CHAPTER 11
SHOULD I STAY OR SHOULD I GO?

Kane curb-hopped his mid-80s dual cab truck off of the main thoroughfare at Crafers – onto a beautiful tree-lined road lined with historic buildings. A slew of traffic flowed by them, heading to the nearby highway entrance and potential salvation. There were no immediate signs of not-zombies, but they could see a few bodies further up the street.

Kane was at the back tray and removing his passengers' belongings before they'd all even exited the truck. "Well, good luck, I guess."

Grace smiled. "You too. And thanks."

"Hopefully, you find your salvation down south," he said as he locked each in a handshake.

"Thanks," said Suede. "And good luck with the whole rebel fightback thing."

Kane smiled at the ridiculousness of the reality he had been preparing for that required the uttering of such a sentence. "I wasn't kidding about the scale of this thing, you know. And if things ever get too hectic out there, you can always come looking for us."

"What just pop into the Crafers Hotel or something?" said Grace. "Or wait for your ancient truck to rattle by?"

"You'll find us up at the Mt Lofty lookout every dawn. Assuming we still, you know, can. Definitely in a 1980s car or earlier if you're going to rock up there!"

The three nodded their understanding.

"Good, I'd hate to shoot you."

With another round of nods and handshakes, Kane was gone. He left Grace, Suede and Colin holding their remaining possessions at the roadside, watching a stream of vehicles flee to the freeway.

"So… what do we do now?" said Colin.

"We?" said Grace. "Which part of you thought there was a we?"

"I just thought, you know, safety in numbers, as they say."

"You nearly killed us, and you destroyed Halen and almost everything we own and basically our one shot of having an even chance to survive."

"I didn't mean—"

"Then we saved you from one of those things lurking around your truck, then again from burning alive in the same said vehicle. If there is safety in numbers, we seem to be bringing the numbers, and you seem to be the only one getting any level of safety."

The look on Colin's face turned darker. "Now just you listen here, little missy—"

Grace screamed as she moved into attack. Fortunately, the experienced Suede was well ahead of events and was already holding her back in a bear hug from behind. Meanwhile, he caught Colin's eye and gestured vigorously for him to change approaches.

Colin collected himself as best he could as Suede eased Grace back from the edge of fight.

"Look, I can't remember anything from the crash," said Colin, holding eye contact with Grace. "But I do know where I was headed when the whole thing happened." He paused long enough for one of the other two to follow his conversation lead. They did not. "I have a little holiday house down the peninsula. Near Normanville."

As each sentence passed his lips, Grace and Suede became more receptive to the words. "Anyway, it's on the south coast, as it seems to me was your goal. And it also matched the majority of the criteria Kane was saying you would need to survive. Except for the survival-ready neighbours. But that's where I figured you guys—"

"Safety in numbers," declared Grace. "The more I think about it, the more it starts to make sense."

She looked at Suede, who nodded profusely. "It's the only way we're all going to get through this."

They exchanged nods of approval. "Looks like we've got ourselves a deal," said Colin.

"Deal!" said Suede before he started laughing in a manner slightly unhinged for the moment. Colin stared open-mouthed and Grace narrowed her eyes in a threatening manner. "I'm sorry, it's just…"

He laughed again, taking a step back to analyse the scene in front of them. A small hills town, a steady stream of refugee vehicles running for their lives, memories of NPCs – zambies – and thoughts of unaccounted-for robots and whatever else Kane was talking about. It took the best part of a minute for him to rein the emotion in and breathe consistently enough to talk. "When I woke up this morning, you could've given me a lifetime of guesses as to how my day was going to work out – ten lifetimes even. There is no way I would've gotten close with any of them."

"To be fair, a lifetime of guesses might not be as many as you thought," said Grace.

She looked at him before they carried on his laughter together.

"Fucking zambies!" said Suede, in bad Bostonian tones.

"Cawwffeee, walk the dawg," added Grace.

"That's New York," said Suede, deadpan. "Don't kill the flow."

Grace shrugged, then laughed again. "Is it?"

The stupidity of it all ushered in a new fit of laughter from Suede. "No wonder we're failing at this survival thing."

"I thought that was because I fucked up your van," said Colin, joined in the hysterics.

Immediately, the other two stopped laughing. Grace stared him down. "Way too soon!"

"Shut up, Colin!" said Suede.

An awkward silence lasted several seconds before all three of them broke into hysterics once again.

"And he wanted us to join the resistance!" added Grace.

More hysterics.

The occupants of passing cars stared out of their windows, which only added to the loss of control. Across the road, the town's historic pub looked on while the bottle shop appeared to be getting raided. Some of the looters stopped to look at the three idiots on Main St. Further afield, a glimpse of the highway showed the cars that had made it through the city maze had a clear run to whatever unknown fate awaited. Beyond that, who knew.

*

CHAPTER 12
HITCH HIKIN'

The afternoon sun carved rays through the mighty gum trees that towered overhead. Grace felt the shoulder straps from her backpack start to dig into her skin and reshuffled their positions in the hopes of finding relief. In her hands, she lugged another bag of essentials. Next to her, Suede wiped the sweat from his brow as he, too, struggled with his supplies and the undulating road.

"Where's boomer?" said Suede. He'd had a chance to change out of his blood-stained T-shirt. Now he was sporting a logo design of a mock tractor manufacturer logo in green and yellow, with the chalk outline of a body in the middle and the words John Doe underneath.

"A block back," said Grace. "He's hobbling, but I'm not sure if it's slowing him down that much. Stubborn fucker."

Behind them, they heard the telltale signs of cars approaching. Once again, they stuck their thumbs up in the universal hitchhiker's signal. Once again, the conga line of cars passed by without slowing.

"For fuck's sake," said Suede. "No one's going to stop, you know."

They had reached the top of a rise in the road, and Suede dropped his backpack and used it as a seat. He pulled a bottle he'd swiped from the Crafers Hotel and swigged. Then wheezed, then coughed, recovered and swigged again.

Grace sat by his side. "Someone will stop."

He offered her the bottle, but she declined. "Eventually," she added.

"Definitely if it was just you," said Suede. "Maybe for the two of us. And just about no chance with Captain Hobble back there as part of the package."

"Well, we kind of need Captain Hobble at this stage. He has the place."

Suede held his thumb aloft as another train of vehicles passed by. "Maybe. Or the address and the key, perhaps." Grace nudged him with her elbow.

It soon became clear that no cars would pull over, so he took another swig.

"Go easy on that, huh," said Grace.

Soon, the sound of Colin's suitcase bumping over the dusty roadside loam could be heard over the background noise of cars. It was accompanied by the little groans of pain he was emitting.

Suede rolled his eyes at the pathetic cry for help, then took another swig. "It's helping me cope."

"Just… you know what you can get like sometimes."

"Look at him. Look at that hobble!" said Suede, subtly gesturing towards Colin. "We're trying to hitch a lift with a guy who, in his current state, looks indistinguishable from the freaks everyone is running from."

Grace looked back down the hill at the approaching Colin and found it hard to argue his point. "Someone will stop, and when they do, we'll need to bring our A-game, else we've got a hundred-kilometre walk ahead of us."

Her words hovered like a punishment in the air, and the conversation died until Colin finally caught up. He placed his relatively small bag next to the others, hunched over and sighed heavily. Suede looked at the relatively light weight of it and rolled his eyes.

"You'll have to excuse me," said Colin between panting noises and sounds of discomfort. "The old back is not what it was. Or the hips. Or the knees, for that matter." He pulled his own swiped liquor bottle to his lips and had a healthy swig. "And the gout's really playing up today."

"Dude, we don't need medical updates," said Suede. "Keeping up in silence would be a real help."

Colin stared at him. "Listen here, you little shit, I've—"

"Dude, I'm twice your size!"

"I've caved in noses for less."

"Stop!" said Grace.

Suede sniggered, then jumped to his feet to stand over Colin. "OK boomer, let's see you try."

Colin stepped up to him. "That's about the level of self-absorbed shit I'd expect from someone your age."

"My age self-absorbed? The fact you said that without any sense of irony says everything."

"Stop!" said Grace again.

Colin and Suede looked at her. Before Colin returned his focus to Suede. "Idiot!" he said.

Suede reeled in open-mouthed shock for a moment before pushing Colin in the chest. The old man tripped over his bag and thudded into the dusty roadside surface with a thud and a groan.

"Idiot!" said Grace.

Suede smiled temporarily before realising the barb was directed at him. "Me? This flog doesn't know when to keep his mouth shut."

"Neither do you!" she squealed. "We're supposed to be hitching a lift down south! How the fuck is this helping?"

As if on cue, they looked up to see another convoy of cars, this one slowing down to view the curb side show they provided.

"Hi," said Grace as she waved at the rubberneckers.

It was enough to simmer down the tension but left a whole study of new material unresolved in the air, floating in such a way it would hover there until some minor future trigger point kicked it off again.

"Perhaps the pair of you could focus on acting normal enough that some sucker would slow down long enough to consider letting us in their car." Her eyes darted between the two, her look challenging them as a long-suffering teacher would a wayward student. "Because, you know, zambies! And robots and all those other things Kane said that I didn't understand yet sounded like we should be scared of."

Both men conceded with a nod of submission towards her before nodding their apologies to each other.

"That's better," said Grace. "What now?"

"We take the left up here," said Colin.

"No way," said Suede. "We stick to the main road."

"Sure, if we want to head right back to the suburbs, why not!" said Colin, his focus on Grace. "Or we skip across the valley road, which will open up a path all the way to McLaren Vale. From there, we should be able to cut down to the coast, and we'll be away."

Suede toyed with his phone, trying to get a feed on his maps to confirm or deny the accuracy of the suggestion. Eventually, he looked at Grace and shrugged. She, in turn, looked at Colin.

He pointed to his head. "That's where I keep my directions. No connection issues in there."

"Hmmm, can we say that?" said Suede.

No one responded. Colin held his gaze on Grace.

"Right then, next left it is," she said.

Suede pulled a disrespectful face at being outsmarted.

Grace gave him a death stare.

Colin smiled at the win. "Pant wearer identified," he added, looking in judgement at Suede.

*

They were barely twenty metres onto the side road when a car turned off the main road behind them, pulling up to their side. It was a people mover. The group slowed to a stop, and the passenger side window rolled down to reveal a mother and daughter in the front.

"Um, hi," said the woman. She appeared to be in her mid to late forties, her shoulder-length hair dyed red.

By her side, the teen eyed them suspiciously. She was eighteen, give or take, and a streak of her dark brown hair was dyed blonde at the back. Her nose was pierced, and she had a couple of homemade tattoos visible on her forearm.

"Um, hi," repeated Grace.

The woman in the driver's seat took a second to collect herself before she cleared her throat. "So, this is probably going to seem like a weird question, but why did you guys turn off the main road?"

Grace shot her a confused look.

"It's just that… Well, it seems most of the cars are following the main road and we're wondering what you know that they don't."

What they knew that the others didn't. Grace did her best not to let a smile give her away. At the same time, she knew the gravity of the moment and the opportunity it presented. She shared a look with Suede that ensured he was on the same page before turning to Colin and mouthing 'leave this to me'.

"What?" said Colin.

He was looking at Grace. She felt her cheeks flush as she turned to face the van occupants once more. "I didn't say anything," she said before smiling reassuringly.

"Yes, you did!" said Colin. "It went something like—"

Suede elbowed him, taking more pleasure in the action than the moment required.

The woman took in the scene. "I'm sorry. Are we interrupting something?"

Grace took the opportunity to turn to face the others again, sending a scalding expression Colin's way, before returning her focus to the driver. She smiled warmly. "Of course not."

The woman exchanged a look with her daughter before she returned the smile but in a less convincing fashion. "Yeah, so, anyway. We thought you might be locals or something."

Suede scoffed.

Grace scratched the back of her head, but the move was purely to disguise the bird she was flipping him in disgust.

"Look, we just need some time to get off the streets and try to wrap our heads around what's going on," said the woman. "Maybe get some food into us, grab some clean clothes maybe. Then come up with a plan of what we're going to do next before we head on our way."

Grace nodded as she processed the new situation.

"Otherwise, that's cool. We'll just wish you all the best. Seems like everyone is going to ne—"

"We are heading to a safe place, as it happens," said Grace. "It's just, not exactly along this street."

The woman and teen exchanged a look before nodding a noncommittal invitation to continue.

"In fact, it's a bit of a hike from here."

The woman left the comment hanging without a response.

"I've got a safe house near Normanville," said Colin.

Grace turned and gave him a subtle nod of approval.

"OK, well, that's not entirely what we had in mind, but certainly, good luck."

The passenger window started to rise as they heard the engine click into drive.

"That's because anywhere closer will probably get us killed!" said Grace.

The window lowered once more. The two occupants stared expectantly.

"She's right," said Suede. "What's happening right now? It's much more than you think."

He shared nods with Grace and Colin before looking the mother dead in the eye. "Have you ever heard the term 'zambies'?"

*

CHAPTER 13
OVER THE HILLS AND FAR AWAY

They had been on the road for over two hours and were only now arriving in the outskirts of McLaren Vale. The trip would have taken a third of the time on a normal day. The narrower roads were in heavy use, pocked with car carcasses and the occasional zambie in the more built-up areas. There were a couple of moments where roads were blocked completely, and they had to double back and skirt their way back around to connect with their path. A situation where Colin shone, much to Suede's chagrin.

The roles were reversed in the rest of the conversation, however. Donna – the mother – and, to a lesser extent, her daughter Ava, reeled out questions. Suede's capacity to regurgitate what Kane had told them as if it were something he had lived for years was, well, something to behold. Even more than that, he came across as a rebel, reliable, dependable, strong, almost heroic… as silly as all that seemed to anyone who knew him. He even sat differently in his chair. Somehow, his jawline seemed, well, more pronounced. His very essence just changed. Even Grace was in the trance this newly remodelled Suede created.

Such was the gravity of his performance that Colin and Grace rose in stature by merely being in the orbit of Suede 2.0. Donna and Ava gave Grace looks she hadn't seen since, well, ever.

All they had to do was make sure Suede didn't stray too far from the truth as had been revealed by Kane, and their ticket to Normanville was seemingly assured. Then things could return to normal.

Despite regurgitating Kane's info dump, there was no talk of rebellions. That topic was replaced with discussions about safehouses. There was, according to Suede 2.0, a global movement of preppers ready to disappear into the bush to ride out the global zambie phenomenon. And that is what they were going to do. Go grey mode from the world – blend into the background. Go off-grid, off-network. Become self-reliant.

Survive.

*

As the kilometres passed, it didn't take much to get a sense of Donna and Ava's plight. It was clear they had escaped their situation in a rush. They had barely more than the clothes on their back. Grace studied them. She saw the unspoken conversation of expressions they exchanged. They asked the group (Suede 2.0) questions, observed answers and silently shared their thoughts on how much to trust their three passengers. Grace monitored it all like a hawk.

Donna seemed as switched on as one could be in the circumstances, while Ava had an aura of brooding teenage darkness, dolloped with generous portions of intelligence. She rarely spoke, but when she did, it was usually insightful or subtly cutting. Grace felt comfortable in their presence and knew in circumstances other than this, Suede's game would've been seen through in quick time. But, with the haze of the surreal that blanketed this day, he presented a mirage of hope.

Maybe the connections made in the van on that trip were the mirages. But it was something tangible and human, and that was the only real thing any of them had at that moment. As if driven by some magical force, the landscape around them reflected the change in the van. Undulating, tree-lined, narrow roads overloaded with gum trees soon gave way to rolling slopes, open plains, grape vines and cellar doors. They were nearing McLaren Vale and the southern plains, and were one step closer to refuge.

"Um," said Donna, concern in her voice. "How far are we from Normanville?"

Everyone looked at Colin, now their unofficial navigator. "Can't be more than fifty kilometres. You could probably get there in around forty-five minutes on, you know, a normal day."

There was a pause in conversation as all eyes fell on Donna. "We're going to need to get petrol."

"What!" said Ava. The word was spoken in the perfect tonal combination of disbelief and accusation.

Donna looked at her. "I'm sorry. Have I disappointed you by not having a full tank ready to go?"

"I don't want to stop."

"Well, neither do I. But since I wasn't prepared for the unannounced end of the world last night, here we are."

Ava groaned her displeasure.

"Do you think it'll be working?" said Suede.

"What do you mean?" said Grace.

"Well, is the station operational? Zambie free? Are we going to be able to gain access to the pumps? Can we get the pumps working? That sort of thing."

No one had an answer, so silence gripped the cabin once more. They watched the landscape change from grape vines to country suburbia. First McLaren Flat, then a short stretch of vineyards before McLaren Vale.

"It looks like a ghost town," said Suede, eventually.

His words did nothing to lighten the mood. But he was right. There was no traffic on the roads, nor any signs of activity, human or zambie.

"Turn left onto Main St," said Colin.

Donna obliged, and they were soon working their way down the main strip to the heart of the vale. Old architecture with modern finishings lined both sides of the thoroughfare. Ahead, the eerie silence was broken by a car taking off to the sounds of rubber on road. It was enough to make several in the cabin jump.

"Shit!" said Donna in the driver's seat. She squinted her eyes. "What are they doing?"

Ava shrugged. "It's too far away to tell. I don't like this."

"Neither do I," said Donna.

"We just need to get in, get the petrol and get out," said Grace.

"There it is!" said Colin. "Up on the left."

"Got it," said Donna. Her hands gripping the steering wheel hard.

"That's it," encouraged Grace. "Nice and easy."

Donna shot her a look that let it be known she didn't appreciate the patronising tone.

"Sorry," said Grace.

"Well, the price board still has power," said Suede. "That's got to be a good thing, right?"

"Better than the alternative," said Colin.

"Is that smoke?" said Donna, sniffing the air.

"Yep," said Ava. "Stinks!"

"Can anyone see anything?" said Grace.

The silence confirmed the negative. But all thoughts of fire were soon forgotten as the service station came into full view. At the bowser closest to the entryway, a car sat at an angle across the pump. A body could be seen slumped over the seat. Beyond that, the automatic doors to the shop were attempting to close, their mission blocked by another body slumped in the centre of its path, the head preventing it from completing its task.

Beyond the visible bodies, a large pane of glass at the shopfront was smashed, as were the windscreens of the two cars still parked to the side of the building.

"Holy shit," said Donna. "What the hell went down here?"

"Not sure," said Suede as he continued to scan the space.

"It looks pretty open around that pump at the end there," said Grace.

Donna wiped the sweat from her hands and nodded before steering in its direction.

"What's that?" said Ava.

It was then that the rest of the scene revealed itself to everyone. The burnt-out husks of three cars on the other side of the building came into view. Nearby, more than a dozen zambies stood, at least three with burns so severe it was a wonder they were standing. And they were staring at the approaching van.

"Shit," said Suede. He was immediately aware that Donna and Ava were more concerned following his reaction. He silently cursed himself, then studied the situation with a more detailed eye and heroic demeanour. There was a good twenty metres between the cluster of zambies and the pump.

"Am I doing this or what?" said Donna.

"If we don't do it here, now, who knows what we'll face at the next station," said Colin. "And we don't really have that many more options until we hit the coast and head south."

"Well, I'm not going out there," said Donna. "And neither's Ava."

"Fuck it," said Grace. "I'll do it."

"How long until they're on us?" asked Suede in an attempt to regain some hero status ground.

"Thirty seconds? A minute? I don't know," said Donna, full of doubt.

"Not long enough," said Suede. He took a deep, deep breath, hoping another solution would come to him other than the one in his head. "Someone's going to have to go out there and distract them," he said when an alternative failed to present itself.

He'd barely finished the sentence when he realised everyone was looking at him expectantly. Stupid brave, suave, knowledgeable persona!

It was pinning him into a corner! He looked at Colin for support. Colin looked at the floor.

"I'll guess I'll go then," he said before gulping, raising the crowbar and putting his hands on the sliding door. The horrors and dangers outside became all the more real in an instant. "I guess I'll head that way and try to distract them while you…"

His words trailed off on the plan he did not fully have nor want to execute, and it was met with no words from the others who didn't want to utter any last words they may regret.

Suede nodded, knowing his hero fate was sealed. "Just to check, they don't do the fast-running thing, do they? You know how they're mostly depicted as slow, yet sometimes are super-fast."

Grace looked at him and shrugged. "I don't know."

"You said you knew everything about them," said Ava. She exchanged a look of doubt with Donna.

Donna turned her gaze to Suede. "Ava here has a yellow belt in jiu-jitsu from when she was 11 and a couple hundred hours of playing *Fortnight* to her name. Shall we send her instead?"

Suede went to respond but figured it was far easier and safer to just enter the horror zone of the service station.

Doubting eyes in the cabin soon fell to Grace. "That's my cue," she said, pulling her weapon from her jacket and opening the opposite sliding door.

"Is that a salt lamp?" said Donna. Again, a look was exchanged with her daughter.

As the door closed behind her, looks of doubt were shared with Colin. He did his best to avoid their gaze and sink further into his seat.

Outside the protection of the thin vehicle frame, the full depth of the moment soon sunk in. Even on what would have been considered the safe side of the van, Grace's heart purred along at a rate so fast she thought it may well explode and end the job before the zambies had the chance.

Then there was Suede. There was nothing but open space between him and the group of zambies slowly heading his way. He was totally exposed. He turned to the van. Even the expressions he could barely make out through the reflective window spoke of the horror of a moment he was in. As if they were preparing to witness something traumatic with him as the centrepiece.

That's when the true horror of environment immersion hit home. While switching his gaze between the inbound cohort of zambies and the looks of dread in the van, he'd almost blocked out the rest of the space. Suddenly, he freaked out at the unknowns of what may be behind him. He raised his crowbar, shakily, in defiance. Was that what the horrified looks in the van meant? Was there something behind him? There definitely was. Oh God. He heard a noise. He turned to face the terror.

*

CHAPTER 14
PARANOID

Nothing. The terror turned out to be completely nothing. Just an abandoned and lifeless street making the noises that one would fully expect when a breeze meets an environment of inanimate objects. He couldn't pin down the noise's source, but it didn't matter. It wasn't zambies, it was paranoia.

He turned to the van to give a thumbs up and reassuring look. Their reactions were anything but convincing.

He then snapped back to the approaching menace before conducting another quick scan of the area, this one more targeted. He needed a distraction for the approaching zambies. He soon found it where the car park met the road. A couple of parked cars were perfectly placed for his needs.

He turned back to the horde. They had covered more than half the ground in a surprisingly short amount of time. He breathed deep, several times, trying to muster all of his bravery for what he was about to do. A quick glance back at the van showed looks of fear at impending trauma mixed with one of disillusionment. He knew it was the breaking of his sham hero persona. He sighed. Brave… be brave.

He cleared his throat. "Listen up NPCs."

His words ended as abruptly as they had started and in a high-pitched squeak of nerves.

Regardless, his words received the intended result. The zambies were now headed in his direction, abandoning their curiosity for the van. Again, he looked towards the van. This time, he was greeted with expressions of cringe.

"Dry throat," he mouthed, gesturing to the area in a far-from-heroic way. "Got any water?"

He wasn't sure why he'd mouthed the lines. Regardless, his question was met with confusion in the cabin.

*

"What is he doing?" said Donna.

"I have absolutely no idea," said Ava.

"He's fucking things up," said Colin. "That's what he's doing."

They watched as Suede sought to clarify, miming a gesture of drinking a cup of water. Horror or embarrassment in his eyes.

"Something about fellatio?"

"Mum!"

"What else could it be?"

"Wait," said Colin. "Giving or receiving?"

Ava's jaw dropped in incredulity. "Or, you know, perhaps he meant something contextually appropriate in the circumstances."

The cabin went quiet as they searched further for answers.

Except Colin. "Pretty sure both of my suggestions were contextually appropriate."

Ava glared at him.

"Water!" said Donna.

She grabbed the half-filled bottle by her side before starting to lower her window in preparation to throw it through. It was only then that she realised Suede had abandoned hope of help and was already backing away to the parked cars, zambies in tow.

"Well done you two," said Ava.

*

Donna had already opened the fuel door by the time Grace was out of the van. Grace had the cap off and the fuel nozzle in seconds later. Now came the most stressful part of the process – payment. Or pre-payment to be more specific. Like a well-conditioned Pavlov's dog, her palms started to dampen in the dread of anticipation.

Not that she was poor. But her income was paid in fits and starts from multiple sources. And there were good months for content and not so good ones. Same with Suede. And sure, perhaps over the years, they could've planned around that a little better. Perhaps they could have budgeted? Or saved some in the good months. But that went against the van-life ethos. It was all about living to a new set of rules. They weren't pinned down by a mortgage, or renting, or the hustle and bustle, or keeping up with the Jones or whatever mind-washing form of indentured servitude most people seemed to want to subject themselves to for the bulk of their lives.

No, their way was different. Freer. Better.

Except for those few seconds when waiting for the payment accepted notification to chime its approval, assuming it di—

Payment declined.

"Fuck," whispered Grace. She snapped her head around to see if anyone in the van had noticed. Fortunately, they were distracted by whatever Suede was doing on the other side. She swapped her card out for the emergency one and repeated the process.

Payment declined.

To be fair, she already suspected with almost complete accuracy there was no money in that account after the last such situation, still it was worth a shot. She felt her cheeks start to redden as the only path forward became clear. She knocked on the van window.

Ava's window was winding down almost instantly.

"Everything OK?" said Donna.

"My card seems to have broken in the crash or something, any chance I could borrow one?"

"Here, take mine," said Ava.

Grace did her best not to let the humiliation of the moment get to her. She smiled as authentically as she could as the teenager passed her card. "Thanks."

She put it in the slot and interfaced with the payment system. "Pin?"

"I forgot, I only have fingerprint," said Ava, as she opened the door.

She shared a look with her mum before Donna double-checked the horde's location, then nodded her approval.

She pressed her thumb on the sensor before the display turned green. Grace and Ava let out a heavy breath in synchronisation, then smiled awkwardly at each other. Ava nodded and Grace completed the transaction process.

Payment declined.

"What the…" said Ava in confusion. "That's not right. I've got thousands in there."

Grace did well to keep her thin smile straight.

"What about this?" said Ava, as she pressed her watch to the machine. After taking a few moments to process the transaction, the bowser again declared its judgement.

Payment declined.

"Here," said Donna, passing a credit card through the open window. "Try this. Pin is 1985."

Everyone leaned in to watch the ensuing interaction.

Payment declined.

"Oh, fuck," said Grace.

*

Meanwhile, Suede had been slowly snaking his way towards the two parked cars, pied-pipering the small cluster of zambies as he went. He had adjusted to the threat. In truth, it wasn't that hard to ensure he stayed ahead of them in an open space. Their speed really was no challenge. Yet he didn't take much imagination to stay humble.

It did give him a chance to have a close-up look at them without being smothered by fear. They didn't look like the skin-decayed freaks he knew from popular culture. In fact, their skin wasn't too bad, aside from the burnt ones, obviously. Perhaps unusually pasty, maybe carrying a tinge of yellow in this light, but not overly freakish. It was the expressions on their faces that made them distinctly different from humans. Their faces seemed to drop, in a way. Not literally, of course. Just in the way muscles do when they aren't constantly on call, ready to deliver whatever expression their human carrier feels at the time. Instead, they were slack – mouths agape, eyes heavy, the tension of activity and awareness gone.

His mind flashed back to the one Grace downed at the crash site and the many others he'd seen at a greater distance across the day – they were all the same. They just looked super, well, dumb.

Then there were the burnt ones. They were charred black in places, flesh melted like plastic cheese in a microwave in other parts, honeycombed crispness in others. Yet they soldiered on, drawn by the same lure of their able-bodied cohorts – humans. They were a miracle of physics. Suede hoped it wasn't another sign of just how hard they were to kill.

He didn't dwell too long on them, instead focusing his energy on the speed differential he had over them. It was a way to find some comfort in everything that was going on. Hope, maybe, that they could survive. Even when he tried to mentally calculate how many former people were like this in and around the city, or the world. He just had to avoid the larger packs. And find shelter. And a sustainable food source. And protection. And hope all the other things Kane had mentioned were exaggerated, despite the fact he seemed to be the only one who had any idea of what was happening in the first place.

He shook the thoughts away as he reached the cars. He picked the sedan as the easiest target, climbed up onto the hood and assessed the scene again for escape routes. He was pretty confident he could jump to the roof of the adjacent SUV if the heat was on, and from there he could leap to the fence and into the neighbouring business.

He raised the crowbar above his head, and looked at the inbound zambie pack, then the van.

"Goddammit!" he muttered.

They weren't even watching. For the first time, he was about to do something actually somewhat heroic and no one would see it. Witnesses aplenty when he embarrassed himself, donuts now.

He screamed out his frustration, then smashed the crowbar down on the windscreen. It crunched into the glass. The hook penetrated through while the glass itself crumpled around the impact point, mostly keeping its shape. The sound was somewhat loud, but nothing like what he'd hoped for. Still, the zambies were attracted.

He fished around until he could retract the weapon, then took another swipe. Then a third. The windscreen was weakened enough that he could run the crowbar along the shattered surface, and it fell apart like a cheesecake base. The closest zambies were reaching the front of the car. He moved down to the side of the car facing away from the SUV and smashed the passenger windows in quick succession. The move had the desired result of luring the lead zambies to where the noise was the loudest. But instead of the pack following to the same spot, some hovered at the front of the car while some of the tail enders worked their way to the other side.

Within seconds Suede had gone from shepherd to surrounded. Instantly he developed a new appreciation for the power of numbers. Hands started encroaching onto the roof of the car and he backed up to the middle where a small oasis gave him space to kick or crowbar hit away unwanted arms. His head spun at how quickly things had shifted.

Then he screamed.

*

Payment declined.

"Perfect," said Grace as she handed Colin back his last card. "Either we all no longer have any money, or we don't have access to it."

"Let's just go!" said Donna.

"What about inside," said Grace. "Don't they have a button in there or something they press to allow you to start pumping?"

"Yes," said Donna. "Behind the counter inside. But I'm not going in there!"

Grace nodded in a way that excused Donna and Ava. Then she turned to Colin.

"Perhaps you should go?" he said, rightly realising he'd beaten her to the punch.

Grace thought about the counter arguments she could make for Colin to be volunteered, but instead realised the energy was better wasted on quick decisions. She nodded to the others. "Any chance I could get you to tag along and spot for me at the door?"

He signed in unfiltered frustration. "Fine!"

That was when they heard Suede scream.

*

CHAPTER 15
PUMP IT UP

"You two stay here and get ready to pump!" said Grace as she rounded the front of the van, Colin doing his best to keep up.

Her eyes soon darted to the cars at the end of the car park where Suede was on the roof, the pack nipping at his feet. He looked up to see her, then she started running for him. He held up his hand to give the stop signal, then he swiped away a line of zambie hands, took a step towards the side of the roof and leapt to the SUV at its side.

Her arm instinctively reached out to help him as she watched him stumble on the landing, then head into a roll. He managed to lower his centre of gravity just enough to avoid falling from the roof. The impact sent a deep pulse of bass through the service station as the roof dented. It was followed almost instantly by an even louder noise – the alarm.

It blared out, scorching eardrums with its abrasive pitch and unrelenting whine.

"Oh shit," said Grace.

"I'll get the bowser started," said Colin. They shared a nod and he turned to hobble off as fast as his gout would let him.

Grace turned back to the car to see Suede gesturing for her to vacate the area. He was back on his feet and now safe from the hands of the enemy on the higher roof. She gave him an are-you-sure gesture and he nodded in response. She put her fist to her heart. Something they did to indicate the depth of their love. He responded in kind.

She felt a tear welling in her eye but turned to sprint towards the service station's entrance. She had well and truly wiped it away before she passed Colin. "Change of plan, you're back on lookout."

As she neared the entrance, the doors opened, and she slowed to a halt. She held the salt lamp out in front of her and glanced as far into the aisle as she could. There was no sign of zambies. She felt Colin's presence behind her.

"OK, let's take this nice and slow," he said as he, too, began to scan. "We need to make—"

His advice came too late. Grace had entered the store.

*

"I'm scared," said Ava.

"I know, hun, me too," said Donna, now positioned at the front of the van so she had eyes on Suede and Colin. "If it all goes south, we can… you know." She jingled her keys quietly enough to just be heard over the car alarm.

Ava nodded.

*

At the source of the alarm, Suede's comfortable break on the roof was coming to an end. On the hood side of the car, one of the zambies had managed to leverage the pack behind it to shift its body weight onto the car. It was now trying to manoeuvre its legs into a position where it could, literally, make a stand. Suede was caught between the comical slapstick sight of its attempts at coordination on the fringes of its ability and the sheer eye-peeling terror of its relentless drive.

After a few false starts on the slippery paintwork, it found a position where its weight was under its knee, then it leveraged the rest of its body onto the car.

Suede scanned the rest of the vehicle to make sure this was the most immediate problem. Once confirmed, he prepared himself in the most secure position possible with crowbar raised.

The zambie rode the wobbling surface of the car, which was being shaken by the others. It slowly eased one leg forward until its foot planted flat underneath it. Then, after a couple of failed attempts, it pushed its body weight on its legs and slowly raised itself to standing. It rasped at Suede in a mixture of triumph and menace before stepping into an attack.

Suede screamed as he swung the crowbar at the creature's head, ensuring the swing path avoided its outstretched arms. The blow struck with a satisfying 'thnnkk'. The creature reacted slowly to the strike but still managed to use its limbs to rebalance in a way that prevented a fall. Suede seized the advantage and swung again, striking the zambie in the back of the head. He felt the gush of the strike as it penetrated the skull, then watched as the defeated creature could fight gravity's force no more and fell to the ground.

Its impact was cushioned by the other eager zambies in the drop zone.

And the crowbar was still stuck to its head.

"No, no, no, no, no, no, no, no!" screamed Suede in beat with the car alarm.

He fell to his knees and looked at his empty hands to confirm the loss, still in shock from the moment. He knew he would've been down there as well had he fought any harder for his weapon, but that didn't help him on the roof. He searched for the others, lost in their own tasks. How had this gone so far south so fast?

Below him, crowbar zambie slowly made its way to its feet again and joined in the group attack on the SUV. Suede just stared in defeated silence for several seconds. Until he heard a noise. It was only a faint hum between pulses of car alarm, but it called his attention all the same. It was something. Something big.

It was coming from beyond the fence at the edge of the service station property, the direction they needed to go. He found his feet once more, then turned to face the sound.

"Oh, sweet jeebus!"

Spilling out from behind a building further down Main St was a pack of hundreds and hundreds of zambies. The lead creatures were already heading in his general direction, with the giant pack following. Well, more accurately, they were headed in his specific direction, towards the car alarm.

A large abyss formed in the spot his hero gene had briefly occupied. Normal programming had resumed.

*

Grace skirted the aisle of shelving that ran parallel to the window, her heart racing and her senses heightened, ready to detect the slightest sign of life. Or, more accurately, unlife. She was headed towards the service counter that stretched from one side of the back wall to the other, offering everything from coffee and donuts to fast food meals, slushies, lottery tickets and cigarettes. At the far end of the display was the door the staff used to move to the front of the store. It was guarded by a keypad.

She found the most open stretch of counter, took one last look around to make sure there were no signs of movement, then jumped up, rotated her legs around and dropped down the other side. A few heavy breaths in recovery reminded her how out of shape she actually was. She shook off the thought, focusing on the nearby staff monitor screen.

At that moment, another sound emerged from the back of the store.

"Gggweeahahhh."

Definitely a zambie. Probably female. Not that that mattered, but the fewer surprises, the better, she figured. Perhaps, if she was fast, she could be done and on her way before it became a problem.

"Hhhuouoouououwwweeeahhh."

No. That was definitely closer. It must be tracking the noise she made when she jumped the counter. She took a deep breath to collect herself and focused on the task at hand. The monitor had a display of the pump stations, with the bowser Donna had parked in flashing.

She shrugged before pressing the flashing section of the screen. Immediately, the display changed again, showing the fuel being pumped into the van. She did a silent fist pump, then swiped a couple of chocolate bars from a nearby display as she prepared her exit.

As she faced the open section of the counter and placed her hands down to jump, the zambie appeared at the end of a nearby aisle. She instinctively jumped back as her heart galloped. It was close. She froze, eyes locked on the creature. She could hear it wheezing each wet breath as it studied her, then stepped forward to the counter. Way too close for comfort. Way too close to run from.

"Gggwaaarrraaghhh."

Grace was pressed back against the cigarette dispenser wall, frozen in terror, eyes still locked in a dance with the zambie now reaching over the counter to get a touch of human flesh.

"You OK in there?" said Colin from the door.

"No."

"That's a relief. For a second, I thought I heard something."

*

The bowser made the sweet noise of engaging before the purring rattle of liquid rolling through it hit their ears.

"Yes!" said Donna, trying to keep the celebrations as quiet as possible.

Ava, who had her hand on the pump, shared in the silent rejoicing. Until she saw Colin disappear through the service station doors.

Her mum caught the look and stepped back to the front of the van to investigate. Something wasn't right. Then she turned in Suede's direction to see him sitting in a prayer position in the centre of the SUV's roof. "Something's wrong. In the store, by the cars – everywhere."

Ava tried to stop her hand shaking as she held the pump. It was all she could manage in the moment. She looked to her mum for solutions further afield.

"Let's just see what happens once the tank is full. Hopefully, they'll be back here, and we can get on our way."

Ava locked eyes on her. "If not?"

Her mum shrugged to convey the words she didn't want to say.

*

CHAPTER 16
THE SOUND OF THE CROWD

Colin was puffing heavily by the time he reached the far end of the service counter. "Sorry, the old ears aren't what they used to be."

"What?" said Grace, in between hurling donuts from the counter display at the head of the zambie.

"Doesn't matter. Need help?"

Grace hurled a pink-iced speckled donut with laser-like precision at her attacker before turning to stare at Colin. She went with her classic 'you think?' look, pairing it with a loaded round of searing eye scorn.

It took a few seconds for Colin's mind to catch up. He nodded with added urgency. "OK then. Why don't we start with the custard berliner buns? You'll cause more damage that way. Wait, no, custard tarts."

Grace stared at him in disbelief before hurling a custard tart in his direction. She was surprised at how deftly Colin avoided the potential headshot.

"What about creating a distraction," said Grace, in a tone as calm and measured as she could muster in trying circumstances. Meanwhile, her missile gooped its way down the window.

Again, it took Colin a few seconds to catch up with the conversation. When he did, he nodded, then disappeared down a nearby aisle. Grace renewed her donut attack, finding more satisfaction using the gooey-centred options. Colin soon emerged with an armful of cans.

"That's better!" said Grace. "Attack!"

Colin raised his first canned missile in his throwing arm and hurled it at the custard-glazed zambie. But the shot fell short. Several metres short, as it turned out. Not quite halfway.

Once again, Grace stared at him in disbelief.

"Sorry. The old throwing arm isn't what it once was." He stepped closer to the zambie. "I used to be an outfielder, you know."

This time Grace's chosen silent response was an ample serving of 'does it look like I give a shit?'

"Buuurrraaahhh."

Colin lobbed again, but having ambitiously left himself a range far greater than his first projectile travelled, he once again fell predictably short. Grace rolled her eyes as she unleashed another attack, this time a long sausage roll from the pastries section.

"Sorry. I really thought I'd do bet—"

"I don't care! Just get closer and hit the thing!"

Colin submitted in an instant. He shuffled forward with his round of cans. He was within a few metres of the zambie when he stopped, raised a baked bean missile, and fired. The thudding impact noise and splattering of custard remnants confirmed the successful headshot.

The zambie roared with displeasure before turning accusingly towards Colin. It chased after him as he turned to sprint to safety. Well, it was a slower-motion version of that description. Grace stared in disbelief as the two hit maximum shuffle speed. Colin had the creature covered for dash, despite turning to hurl missiles every few seconds. But the advantage was hardly decisive.

Once the zambie had moved far enough from the counter, Grace jumped up and over to freedom. But not before she swiped rollie papers and filters from the counter, as well as a few lighters. She added them to her pockets with the chocolate bars she'd already acquired.

She hit the customer side of the counter and headed down one of the aisles. Halfway along, she saw a pack of garbage bags on display. Immediately, she ripped the pack open, pulled some bags from the package and scanned the aisles for things to fill it with.

"Aaarrggh." The sounds of pain echoed through the store. It was Colin.

*

The pump chugged to a halt. The tank was full. Donna and Ava looked at each other, the weight of an impending decision cutting the air between them. In silence, Donna headed to the front of the van for a visual update on the others, while Ava returned the pump handle to the bowser.

"Suede's still sitting there," said Donna. "I can't see a thing inside the store, although I thought I heard something."

"What something?"

"Some sort of ruckus."

The pair shared a look.

"Why don't we just get in the van. I could maybe get the engine running for when they get out," said Donna. "Or whatever happens, really."

*

Inside the store, Grace was already at a sprint. "Are you OK?

"Not really," said Colin. "My sciatica."

Immediately, Grace screeched to a halt before rolling her eyes. "Can you still get your arse to the doors?" She returned to her new side mission of filling the garbage bags with food. The nearby cans proved a perfect place to start.

"Well, it's not going to be pleasant, but—"

"That's great. Well done. I'll be there in a minute. Let me know if you have any problems with custard face, because…"

Instantly, all thoughts of her conversation and the mission at hand faded. At the end of the aisle stood another zambie. It stared at her with dark, threatening intent. There was something about this one that tapped right into Grace's biggest fears. She froze and stared in silence.

"Everything OK?" said Colin.

Silence.

"Grace?"

"It's… looking at me," said Grace, the tone of her words in a calm she was hoping would fill the rest of her body.

"What is?" said Colin, hurling another can.

"A fucking kid."

"What kind?"

"A girl one."

Colin had made his way back to the entry doors, custard face still on his tail. "I meant one of us or… one of them."

"One of them."

The girl zambie headed forward in chase. Grace screamed as she started to back away. It was by no means quick, but certainly faster than the adults she'd observed. The commotion was enough to have custard face turn its back on Colin and head back to investigate.

"Custard face inbound."

Grace swore. She was immediately aware that if it were to show up at the other end of her aisle, she'd be trapped. She stared at the girl zambie and its bizarre mannerisms and twitches. It studied her in turn, tilting its head at various, seemingly unnatural, angles. The metres between them closed, and Grace breathed heavily as the choices ran low. Ending an adult zambie was one thing, but this was something else. However, if she didn't act now, it might be too late if custard face appeared behind her. She held the can in her shaking hand above her shoulder, then pelted it at the girl zambie. The shot connected with its throat and was accompanied by a sickening sound. Despite temporarily halting its momentum, the shot didn't seem to do much more than make the zambie focus its attack on her with renewed enthusiasm. She hurled another can in response, then another. Both shots connected, yet neither downed the zambie. "Oh, c'mon!"

As she backed down the aisle, she heard custard face. Somewhere. When she turned back to face the child zambie something caught the corner of her eye – insect repellent. It instantly flashed an idea. Not so much the ingredients of the can, but the delivery method.

"Colin?"

"What?"

Grace's ears pricked up, homing in on his direction. "Where are you?"

"I wouldn't be so sure about that."

She sighed heavily at the communication breakdown. Then, she lobbed the bag of garbage bags as close as possible to what sounded like his location.

"Ouch!"

"Can you fill those up for me?" she said before throwing another can at the child zambie. "Food, obviously."

"What?"

"Just fill them up with—"

"You want me to fill the bags with food?"

"Yes!"

Whatever Colin said next, she had already blocked out as she turned to the end of the aisle where custard face threatened to emerge at any moment. She took the lighter from her pocket and toyed with it until she had it flicking into a flame. Then she popped the lid from the insect spray before bringing the two objects in front of her as the weapon they would become.

She reached the corner and paused to collect herself with a deep breath. Behind her, she could hear the girl zambie advancing. The sound told her she had a reasonable window of time to pull off her move. Around the corner ahead, she heard shuffling and wheezing nearby. It was most likely custard face, but there was also a small chance it was Colin. She shrugged and continued with her plans. The noise got closer and closer. She counted down.

Three, two, one.

*

"Three, two, one." Donna stopped her countdown with a long pause.

It had been a while since they'd seen Colin at the door, with a zambie not too far behind. Meanwhile, Suede hadn't moved.

Donna sighed, long and hard. She looked at Ava. "They'll understand."

The silence that followed made her unsure if even Ava did.

"Besides, like they said, they're survivors. They've been prepping for this for years."

She eased her foot off of the brake and the van began rolling out of the service station. "They'll be fine."

The commotion stirred Suede into action. He immediately read the moment and jumped to his feet, waving, and begging for them to stay.

Donna covered her left eye to block Suede's movements out of her peripheral vision.

"If you say so," said Ava. She slumped back in her seat, not daring to look.

*

Grace waited until her read on the distance to custard face felt within range. She flicked the lighter into life and jumped out of the aisle. Custard face saw her and leaned in to attack. As it did, Grace sprayed the aerosol through the open flame. A ball of fire licked out, and she pressed forward to ensure it met the creature.

The designer hoodie of the zambie went up in flames in an instant. Grace adjusted her shot upwards as the initial flames also licked the zambie's face. The creature halted its advance as it squealed and writhed in discomfort. As its balance began to wane, Grace kicked out and sent it crashing to the ground, where it continued to writhe.

Then she set her sights on the child zambie. She marched over, makeshift flamethrower in hand. Only when she was in striking distance did she have second thoughts. Sure, she had never really liked children or bonded with a child, nor had she spent one second of her life wishing for one, yet they were different. The girl had now stopped advancing. It looked at her with its arm raised. Not that she was going soft in her stance – for the most part, she found them utterly annoying – but, it just seemed unfair to torch one. Wait, was it reaching out to her? Perhaps somewhere, deep down, still existed a little girl who only wanted to be lov—

The zambie lunged at her. Grace screamed in fright as she crashed into the shelving to avoid its touch. It stumbled forward before falling face-first to the floor. Grace seethed with rage. Mostly at herself. She directed it all into her focus on the zambie. She kicked it in the ribs several times. During the vigorous back-and-forth movement, she remembered she had the salt lamp in her pocket. She lifted it out and brought it down on the head of the zambie several times, accompanying the action with another rage-filled scream. After all signs of movement from the creature stopped, she grabbed her mini-flamethrower once more and torched the body from top to toe. Finally, for good measure, she spat into the flames, then turned to head out of the aisle.

It was there she saw Colin staring at her with two loaded bags by his side. His mouth was wide open, but no words were coming out.

She stowed the salt lamp and lighter in her pocket before loosening her belt and slipping the can of insect repellent inside. She took out her hair tie and quickly adjusted her hair as causally she could muster. All the while, Colin stared with the same expression plastered on his face.

She walked towards him, grabbed the two bags and headed towards the exit. In her wake, flames started to take hold of shelves.

It was only then she heard the sound of the van driving away in between pulses of the car alarm. “Fuck!”

She looked accusingly at Colin.

“What?” he said.

*

CHAPTER 17
RUNAWAY

Suede waved in ever-increasing scales of panic. It had started as a way to draw Donna's attention to his plight, in case she'd missed the human on the car in the centre of the cluster of distracted zambies. Then, as it became more and more apparent that the trajectory of the van was not, in fact, towards him, but aimed for the nearby exit to Main St, his wave reached a crescendo of kinetic rage.

"I'm right here!" he screamed needlessly. "Right here! Literally, like, five metres away!"

That's when he saw Donna's face through the windscreen. She actively avoided eye contact. He contemplated making a leap clear of the zambies, army-rolling past the danger and chasing the van on foot, but he knew what awaited them not many metres down the road. "You're freaking leaving us? For dead? Just like that?"

He had more lines ready to go, but it seemed a little pointless as the van rolled out of sight. Instead, he turned his attention to the store, where he saw flames licking up the shelves inside. "Oh shit!"

He looked at the car beside the SUV, the size of the gap between them and the zambies filling it. "Oh fuck." He took a deep breath, steadied himself, then took a leap down from one rooftop to the next. He lifted his feet at the knees to avoid stray hands but still managed to clip something before he'd even crested his jump.

He swore as he tried to regain full balance, but the contact had ensured a rough landing on what was already a small target. The extended curse word evolved into a grunt as he hit the car roof, his momentum nowhere near the alignment required to stick the landing. After his leading foot hit hard, he tried to lower his body weight to limit the inertia of the fall, but he was destined to overshoot. His shoulder hit the roof, and he started rolling on his back. When he reached the end of the roof landing strip, he fell again.

By that point, it was too much to assess where up and down were. He just gave himself over to gravity and chance, and braced for pain. The impact with the ground didn't disappoint. His hip hit the concrete, followed by his leading arm, which was whipping around at speed. His body rattled, and his arm numbed in a mix of gravel rash and bone-jarring pain. As he closed his eyes to fight the pain that wasn't numbed, he heard the sound of zambies rounding the hood of the car, headed his way.

*

"I think it's best if we focus on the positives right now," said Donna. "We've got each other and a full tank of fuel."

Ava smiled sarcastically. "Yeah, and all the belongings of the people we just left for dead who helped us get that fuel."

Donna stared at her. "Don't start with me, I—"

"Erm, mum," said Ava as the view through the trees consumed her. A horde of zambies of a size she couldn't begin to calculate.

Donna was lost in the road ahead. Negotiating objects that peppered their path to Main Rd. Any one of which could have punctured a tyre. "Don't give that tone! I was tryin—"

Ava stared at her aghast. "What tone? I was going—"

"I'm sorry," said Donna. "But when you start stepping up to take on the life and death decisions, you can start offering your criticism, until then—"

"Look!" Ava had both hands pointed to the activity coming into view up Main Rd. She still felt her mum's eyes on her and added a nod of her head to accentuate her point.

"Oh shit." Donna finally caught up with the state of play.

Zambies, well over a thousand, filled Main Rd. And they were still pouring out from behind a building less than a block down the road.

"They're heading this way, aren't they?" said Donna.

"I'm pretty sure they're heading this way," said Ava.

"This is bad, isn't it?"

"It's bad."

"Ideas?" said Donna.

"I guess we could ask the old guy. He seemed to be the only one with any idea of how to get anywhere around here."

Donna swallowed hard.

Ava turned to face her mum. "But you just left him and his friends for dead."

Donna made a throaty roar of frustration at the wheel. She took several deep breaths as she mulled over her next play, and then she turned the wheel and let her foot off the brake.

"What are you doing?" said Ava.

"Getting us out of here."

"What! What about the others?"

"I can't go back there," said Donna.

"What?" squealed Ava. "Why?"

"It'd be embarrassing. And awkward."

"So, what? To avoid that, you're just going to leave them for dead again instead?"

Donna pretended not to hear her.

*

Grace burst through the doors and assessed a sea of new information. She sought out the zambies Suede was distracting and found them making their way back around the car she'd last seen him—

Wait, there he was on the ground. He was hurt.

She heard Colin's wheezy voice catching breaths in her wake. "What's happen—"

"Suede!" Grace yelled, dropping the bags of supplies and heading his way. That's when she caught sight of the van on Main Rd. It hadn't driven off, as such, instead it looked to be performing some sort of three-point turn manoeuvre around some debris. It was all too much to contemplate at that moment, and her focus was soon back on Suede and his pursuers. She raised the spray can flamethrower at the pack in readiness.

Suede was on his haunches, part in recovery, part fighting the pain to stand once again. He raised a hand of acknowledgement in her direction. He turned to see the leading zambie close enough to make him forget his pain and stand. He inhaled through his teeth as he did. Grace soon had flames set on the lead attacker. It writhed in discomfort as she issued out doses to the other closest threats, then cut her way back to Suede.

"Let's go!" she said as she offered out an arm.

"Go where?" said Suede. "They've taken the van."

Grace started leading him back towards the service station entrance, where Colin was recovering his breath with the new supplies by his side. Through the glass doors behind him, what had been a small lick of flame was expanding rapidly.

"No, they're just out on the street," said Grace. "Doing… something."

"Doing fucking-us-over is what they're doing. And now they've just seen what's headed our way."

It was only then Grace sensed the background noise lurking subtly under the din of the car alarm. She looked at him with dread.

He nodded, but not in a way that was reassuring. "Hundreds and hundreds."

"Oh shit."

"Colin!" yelled Suede. He pointed to the main road exit the way they'd come in. "Run! Go, go, go!"

Colin looked at them, confused.

"We need to get out of here now!" said Grace, also pointing towards the exit. "Go now."

Colin nodded and turned his attention to the supply bags, wrapping a hand around each and preparing to lift.

"No!" yelled Suede. "We'll take them. You run!"

Colin gave them a confused shrug before releasing his grip on the bags and looking at the inbound pair for clarification.

"Yes!" said Grace. "Now run!"

But it soon became clear that attempting to give Colin a head start was now futile. Mostly due to the fact they were now standing next to him.

"Well, that was a big help," said Suede as he grimaced and picked up one of the bags.

"What?"

Suede looked at Colin in bewilderment. "It's just… never mind."

Grace picked up the other bag, and the three were soon escaping the scene at Colin pace. "Looks like Main Rd is a write off. Is there any other way we can loop around through the side streets, or is there another way out maybe?"

Colin nodded. "Yes, but—"

"We're going to need a car," added Suede. "Given the amount of zambies around here, surely there's some vacant houses with cars and matching keys nearby."

"Sure," said Colin. "Or we could jus—"

"There should be homes back through the side streets," said Grace. "We just need to find a house with a set of keys and—"

Colin nodded again. "Yeah, or, why don't we just get back in the van?"

"I hate to break it to you, pops," said Suede. "But that toerag, Donna, and her daughter left us for dead."

Colin went quiet, the sort of quiet that made things awkward. Meanwhile, the world around them raged with noise, the sort of noise that covered far subtler sounds, like idling engines, for example.

But there was something about the look on Colin's face that was telling a larger story. Suede just needed to figure it out.

"She's behind me, isn't she?"

Colin nodded.

The three had now all turned to face the van, where Donna and Ava were watching them, and the service station now going up in flames behind them.

"Need a lift?" said Donna meekly after an elongated silence.

*

CHAPTER 18
FIRE

Donna headed back up Main Rd in the opposite direction to that she'd headed in not fifteen minutes earlier. Inside the van, the same five people sat in the same configuration of seats. That aside, everything had changed. Sure, she could see the visible signs in the rear-view mirror, where the road behind her was so thick with zambies that she couldn't see beyond them. Or the plume of thick smoke now rising from the service station as well as the—

An explosion ripped out from the centre of the fire. The blast wave was so powerful it could be seen pulsing through the zambie ranks as they swayed to its will. Shortly after, it rattled the van, followed seconds later by the deep pulsing sound of the explosion, echoes which bounced back off the surrounding hills. This sent the zambie horde into a frenzy of even less organised activity.

But in the cabin of the van, there was barely a flinch of reaction. Everyone remained silent. Now that Donna thought about it, that was the biggest change of all. The atmosphere in the cabin. The smothering silence. Such was its intensity that, had she been able to capture the frostiness in some manageable form, she may well have been able to douse the flames behind her.

But that was impossible.

She looked at the scene in the rear-view mirror once more, careful to avoid any eyes from the back seats of the van. There were only so many flames one could take in at any given time.

She kept the van moving at a pace barely quicker than the zambie horde on their six. Not because it was some kind of sport or she had a plan to lead them somewhere, she just had no idea where to go next. None.

And, in the current climate, there was no way she was asking anyone for help. So, putter along she did.

She exchanged a look with her daughter that encapsulated her plight, but Ava scrunched up her face and mouthed the word 'what', before turning her focus back to whatever distant point she was lost in. Donna returned her efforts to puttering the van along, waiting for someone else to break the deadlock.

That seemed to take a long, long time.

"Do you know where you're going?" said Colin.

Donna shook her head. "Not really," she said apologetically. Perhaps things weren't as bad as she'd imagined. Perhaps they would all just—

"It wouldn't be the first time she'd just started driving off," said Grace.

Then again, perhaps not. Donna cleared her throat to release some tension. "Can we just focus on getting out of here, perhaps?"

"OK, sure," said Grace. "We won't talk about your betrayal if it makes you feel more comfortable."

Beside her, Suede nodded encouragingly.

"Another few blocks, and we'll hit Tatachilla Rd," said Colin. "That will take us down to the coast and we can avoid any trouble in the side streets."

Donna nodded in silence, slowly pressing her foot down on the accelerator. The blocks passed, and there was soon a healthy distance between them and the chaos. The thoroughfare was noticeably zambie-free. They were soon heading into the main shopping section of the town.

"You're going to want to take the big T-junction right in about two-hundred metres," said Colin.

That's when Donna saw the sign for the supermarket and chemist. She eased off the gas.

"What are you doing?" said Grace.

"Thinking about supplies," said Donna. "This could be as good a chance as we're going to get to stock up on… whatever we think we'll need."

"Let me guess," said Grace. "You'll just drop us at the entrance, where we can expect you to be waiting for us when we get back."

"No, I…" started Donna, unsure how to safely navigate a response. "Look, in case you hadn't been watching, it looks dead around here and—"

"Dead? Really, Mum."

"I haven't seen one of those things in blocks. Hell, it could've been the entire town back there for all we know. We'd be crazy to drive by a chance like this."

Despite the silence that followed her sentence, she eased the van to a stop near the car park entrance. After there were no sounds of protest, she pulled in.

"Alright then," said Grace. "But you two go first."

For the first time, Donna sought eye contact in the rear-view mirror. She could see a spark in the corner of Grace's fiery stare. Whether a challenge or an offer of atonement, it was deadly serious. She looked at Ava, who wore the horrified expression she hoped she was hiding. She was subtly shaking her head.

Donna swallowed hard. "I'll go," she said.

"No, the both of you," said Grace. "And leave the keys."

Grace stared at the rear-view mirror until Donna made eye contact once again.

"That's how you start to get our trust back."

*

It had been the best part of ten minutes before Donna and Ava returned to the van. There was a trolley full of bags from the chemist as well as heavier ones from the supermarket. Grace opened the driver's door and jumped out when she saw them coming, then handed Donna back her keys with a nod. The mother and daughter then headed to the back of the van, where they loaded up their supplies before jumping back into their respective seats.

"We saw a couple of zambies in the back of the supermarket, but one of the other groups inside dealt with them."

"Other groups?" said Suede.

"Looters. I don't think the good stuff will be around for long."

"What'd you get?" said Grace.

"Cans – meals, fruit and veg, pastas, pretty much anything long life," said Grace.

"And the chemist?"

"Painkillers, antibiotics—"

"I jumped behind the prescription counter," said Ava.

Donna nodded. "Some antiseptic creams, deodorant, toothpaste, a few first aid kits and, erm, hygiene products."

"What hygiene products?" said Colin.

The other occupants of the van fell silent. Except Ava, who unsuccessfully tried to keep in a scoff.

"Girly things," said Donna.

Colin's brow furrowed. "What?"

"For periods," said Grace, a little loud and slowly.

"Alright, alright. No need to be so crass!"

Grace turned to him with a stare he hadn't seen since she took on the zambie child. Suede put his arm across her in case she lunged from her seat.

"We've got more room in the back," said Suede, using a tone he hoped changed subjects. "Another run?"

*

They were soon back and on their way towards the coast, heading down Tatachilla Rd with a full tank and a van full of supplies. And a little less tension in the cabin. They soon passed under Victor Harbor Rd, the main route out of the city's southern suburbs. It was the carriageway that led to all the most populous coastal towns along the peninsula, yet you wouldn't know it. There was only a trickle of traffic heading towards the nearby Willunga hill climb, which made eerie viewing. Somewhere, something must have blocked the escaping city traffic. Or perhaps it didn't. Either option hadn't consequences not worth pondering for too long.

While Donna drove, the others sat in silence, taking in as much of the view as possible. One way or another, everything was different now.

Once west of the highway, the coast beamed its presence like a beacon of hope. It was enough to draw a small smile from the corner of Donna's mouth. There it sat, its tranquil waters unaffected by the mayhem kissing up against it. Just nature, formed by time, working to larger rhythms than those shaping the land around it right now. It would be there tomorrow, whatever else happened. There was something comforting in that, somehow.

They passed a crossroad intersection, surrounded by farming land, where a billboard sold its out-of-place wares. Robots for your house. They did everything. Anything one could want assistance with around the house was taken care of. Literally everything, especially with the purchase of a few additional accessories and personality upgrades.

She'd passed another billboard just out of McLaren Vale promoting the latest in nursing home care, which featured another brand of robots altogether. It made her realise how fast things had changed in the last few years. It made her wonder about what was happening right now, how everything might be connected and what that might all mean.

"Hope they're not part of this as well," said Suede.

"Who isn't?" said Colin.

"The robots, man – the things on the ginormous billboard we just passed. Just saying we have enough on our plate without dealing with them too."

"Anyone could take one of those contraptions down."

Suede eyed him. "What world do you live in?"

"I doubt they'd even weigh as much as me. They're slow and generally a bit useless outside of cooking and chores."

"Maybe a couple of years ago. They're fast and strong these days. And they have all the skills. They train one of them on anything – from real-life experience, a world-class human expert or virtually through simulation – one gets the lesson and passes the upgrade onto the rest. All. Of. Them. Times every subject matter. God knows what sort of combat training they'd have."

"Pftt, combat training," said Colin. "I'd be more worried if I had a random crease in my jeans they'd want to iron."

"You really haven't grasped the whole network learning thing, have you. They sailed past human abilities in the blink of an eye a couple of years back. The gap in ability is astronomical now."

"Sure thing, kid," said Colin. "Pretty sure I've still got them covered if push comes to shove."

Suede rolled his eyes, then gazed out the window.

"Can we not talk about bots?" said Grace. "I think we've already got enough to deal with."

"And you don't want to jinx anything," added Donna.

"Pfft, jinx!" said Colin. "Do you honestly think anything we say in this van is going to affect our fate?"

"I've seen Grace punch people for less," said Suede. "So, yes."

"Bollocks!" said Colin. "Robots, robots, robots!"

"Colin, shut up!" said Donna.

Grace glared at him.

"Robots, robots, robots," said Colin before scanning the cabin of the van, as if looking for a hidden bot. "See – nothing!"

"You really are a jerk, aren't you?" said Grace.

Just then, something caught Suede's eye in the distance. "Oh, you've got to be shitting me."

The others quickly followed his eyes to see movement in the skies.

"Are they…? Oh fuck." said Grace, leaning over from her side for a better view.

"Drones!" said Donna, staring at the sky. The van rolled to the edge of the road and she wrestled with the steering wheel to straighten it up, her eyes again fixed on the road ahead.

Suede gave Colin a dirty glance. Grace clipped him over the back of the head.

"See," Suede said to Colin.

But, Donna aside, all eyes were soon focused out the window again. Despite the viewing conditions being far from ideal, as smoke billowed skyward from multiple points, there was definitely something moving through the skies.

Many somethings would be more accurate. Distant dots of movement could be seen as they dipped in and out of view on the whim of the smoky skies. There seemed to be a coordination to the dance, abstract, but intended.

Every now and then, a spark of light would change the colour of one or several of the dots. A blink of yellow here, a flash of white there. Just as quickly, they would return to the speck of black they were.

"That's not good, right?" said Grace, leaning across Suede to get a view.

"Probably not," said Suede.

"At least they're a long way away," said Donna.

As she said it, the others noticed the van's speed increase.

Then, another source of light exploded in the far-away scene. This one started from the ground and chased after the drones, then burst into a frenzy of purple light.

"Was that a firework?" said Suede.

"Yup," said Ava.

The pyrotechnic instantly had the attention of the drones. The entire pattern of their movement changed. Like an airborne school of fish, the pack balled up and rolled over before descending on the point where the missile was launched. They circled in that ball shape, slowly rotating, slowly pulsing. All the while, they lit up in their sparkly colours more than before.

"Jesus!" said Colin.

Within seconds, the show in the sky abated, and the drones spread out once more, disbanding their tight formation and returning to the pattern they had before the firework.

"I think they just ended whoever fired at them," said Suede.

Silence acted as agreement in the cabin. It was broken by the sound of the firework detonation from seconds earlier. Everyone in the cabin jumped. Except Colin.

"Let's just get the fuck out of here," said Grace.

In the front seat, Donna was already nodding, and she gave the van another burst of acceleration.

*

CHAPTER 19
NUDE SCHOOL

"Hang a left up here," said Colin when they reached Main South Rd. He looked at the signposts on the intersection, showing Maslin Beach directly ahead before their turn. "Unless, of course, you want to head for the beach."

There was something about the tone in which he ended the sentence that hit the others with the impending dread one gets when an old man is setting up a joke. Especially one about a nudist beach.

"We could just hang out and talk about the first thing that pops up," Colin added before laughing. He looked at Suede for a reaction.

Suede stared ahead. They all did. The silence was somehow more judgy than it was before.

Colin searched further afield for approval. "Because Maslin's is a nudi—"

"We get it!" said Ava.

"And by pop up, I mean my—"

"And that!" said Donna. "Also… ewww."

Colin focused his disappointment into a gaze out of the window. "You all just need to learn to relax a little more."

Suede made the noise one might when seeing and hearing prey act the way they did when completely unaware of the dangers of their surroundings.

"Hey, boomer!" said Grace. "Read the room and get better material."

Suede gave his head a slight sideways nod, somewhat surprised at the leniency Colin had received. He'd seen Grace eviscerate men for less. He figured it was due to the fact they had to tolerate him long enough to reach the holiday house at the very least.

The cabin fell into silence once more. At least the faint smell of the beach managed to lift spirits. Their backs now faced the city, suburbs, zambies and drones as they traversed the ground to Sellick's Beach via Port Willunga and Aldinga. It was a short trip that marked an end to the Adelaide Plains. The view soon changed to that of rolling hills where humanity's footprint was in the form of farmhouses, grazing land and dairies. For the first time, they felt far enough away from it all to feel free. Well, a little bit free.

Occasionally, the coastline popped into view on their right as they explored deeper down the peninsula. All that was left to do was follow the winding road.

Sure, it was still busy with cars escaping the horrors of the plains, but nothing like the chaos from earlier. There was no competition for lanes or position and no road blockages, just a hypnotic meander into whatever unknowns awaited.

Donna switched on the radio. She flicked through the music channel on the FM dial, before jumping over AM for talkback. After a few false starts, including some unrelated news and sport, she turned it off. "I forgot about that. They're talking like this thing isn't even happening. It's creepy."

"We heard the same thing this morning. Every channel," said Suede. "Of everything that's happened today, that may be the weirdest."

"The TV was the same," said Colin.

"They can't all not know this is happening," said Grace. "Surely everyone has to know what's going on by now."

Colin tutted. "They just don't research like they used to."

Suede stared at him. "What are you talking about?"

"Well, they used to have more journalists and sub-editors—"

"That's newspapers, grandpa."

"Whatever," said Colin. "Every year, the radio quality drops off. The DJs get dumber, and so does the conversation."

"Wait, you actually listen to that shit?"

"It's called staying in touch."

"Talkback?" said Suede. "What are you trying to stay in touch with exactly?"

Colin stared at him like he was an alien.

"This has got nothing to do with legacy media quality," said Suede. "We're getting deepfaked. By someone, somewhere. And at an epic scale."

"What?" said Colin.

"The... bad actors, or whoever the powers that be behind this entire thing are. Faking everything."

There was a long pause as everyone contemplated the enormity of what they might be experiencing, with the possible exception of Colin. "Are you seriously trying to suggest they're impersonators or something?"

"No, no, I'm not. There are no humans involved at all. The voices are fakes, the videos are faked, it's all been faked," said Suede. "I mean, the tech has been there for years, but on this scale, that's… wow!"

"But why?" said Grace.

"To mess with our heads? Gaslighting? Propaganda? I don't know."

"Probably just the usual disappointing standard," said Colin, not buying in. "I listen to Mark and Ingrid talk sport every drivetime, and that was definitely them before."

"But they were talking about Saturday night's game!" said Suede. "Look around. There will be no Saturday night game. Surely, they'd at least know that."

"Well, it would've been a blowout anyway," said Colin.

Suede stared at him in the way one does when they're making a point entirely irrelevant to the conversation.

"Why don't we put on some music," said Donna, her tone clearly indicating that the conversation was annoying her. "Ava, you're still plugged in, right?"

She looked around at the back seats full of strangers. "It won't let me stream. I don't have many things downloaded. I'm not choosing!"

"Any takers?" said Donna.

"Anything recorded before 1990," said Colin. "Nothing good happened after that."

Suede stared at him, "Music in the 1980s was a fake-drum generic disaster."

"It's sad to see kids today with no taste in music," said Colin.

"Kid?" said Suede. "It's sad to see boomers still boomering their boomerness all over the place. Classic judgy statement, based on no facts and spoken with all the world-class authority of your shit opinions."

"Listen here, upstart, I grew up with the best music that ever was or ever will be," said Colin. "Beatles, Stones, Zeppelin, Floyd."

"You probably haven't heard any new music for forty years, have you?"

Colin made an aghast sound. "I don't need to hear it to know it's shit in comparison."

"I knew it!" said Suede. "What happened to your generation?"

Colin stared at him. "My generation? We carried you all on our backs when working for a living was just what you did."

Suede gave him the whatever look. "You went from free love hippies to OK boomer? If anyone ever figures out how that happened, we might find a cure for the world's problems."

"They stopped taking drugs," offered Donna.

Everyone laughed, except Colin.

"Jesus," said Suede. "That's exactly what happened – they stopped taking drugs. It was right in front of me all along." He toyed with the pipe and bag in his pocket and swore never to fall for a similar fate.

*

After a winding meander through the hills, the road soon turned westward to the water once more. They rolled down and into the outskirts of Yankalilla, just a stone's throw from their destination. The sense of quiet country streets had barely been absorbed when they noticed a disturbance near the supermarket.

A large group of people stood around the entryway and were met with defiance from another group already in the store. Sporting and gardening equipment was being raised as weapons, and the shouting between groups sounded quite heated.

"Serious shit going down here," said Suede, concern in his voice.

"Yep," said Donna as she arced the car along the verge of the road on the opposite side, as far from the mayhem as possible. As she cleared the thick of it, it soon became apparent how many bodies were lying on the road. "And some other shit already went down," she added.

Ava made the gagging noise and covered her eyes. It wasn't long until those in the back seat had their attention drawn to the carnage strewn across the road.

"Jeebus," said Suede.

"Were they zambies?" said Grace. "Or, you know."

"Hard to tell," said Donna.

They followed the road for several blocks past the houses of Yankalilla before it opened onto a short stretch of open land, which led to the outskirts of Normanville. Soon after, Donna had to drive the car to the fringes of the road to avoid the debris from a nearby crash site, where a car was wrapped around a tree. A zambie, pinned between the driver's seat and the compressed dashboard, hissed at them as they rolled past.

Colin cleared his throat. "Take the left ahead."

Donna nodded, not tearing her eyes from the gruesome scene until it passed. It was a lot for each of them to process. Each of them prayed things would be calmer and safer when they reached Colin's. Meanwhile, a different sort of truth was unlocking itself. It was not one of fairytale sanctuaries and abundant supplies. It was a preview of the reality of their lives. Until they figured out something else or died.

"Yep, this one," confirmed Colin, just as Donna had put on her indicator. "Hopefully, things are a little quieter ahead."

After a few dotted houses, the road quickly turned into a winding country drive again. As it did, the tension in the cabin abated.

"Take the right up here," said Colin shortly after.

Donna turned the car through a gate, and they were soon in an estate. A string of large houses lined the ridge up ahead. They were nestled in greenery, wetlands and a—

"Is that a golf course?" said Grace.

"Not just any golf course," said Colin with pride. "One of the finest – and most difficult – in the state. Links Lady Bay."

"And difficult is a brag point, is it?" said Suede. "Convenient for your personality if so."

Colin ignored him as he looked over the familiar grounds with a mixture of emotions. "Left up here."

Donna followed the instruction, and they crested the ridge to reveal the bulk of the course, clubhouse, estate and view of the coast beyond. They followed the road along as a line of large houses watched on.

"Is that a zambie?" said Grace. "Wait, no, I think she's just one of the residents. My bad."

Suede looked at Colin. "Is everyone here that old?"

"I guess."

Suede smiled with relief at the news.

"Wait, no, it's a zambie," said Grace.

Donna pulled up next to the frail, hobbling, reanimated body of a woman.

"Should we bash it?" said Suede. "Or get Donna to mow it down in the car?"

Grace stared at him.

"What?" he defended. "We can't just leave it like that. It doesn't feel right."

"Well, I'm not mowing anything down, so think of something else," said Donna.

Suede looked at Colin. "Is there any course etiquette that covers this situation?"

Just then, a kangaroo hopped alongside Suede's window. The two beings studied each other. "Look at that," he said, lost in the wonder of the moment.

Suede looked at its face markings. White dots abounded. They seemed to be concentrated around its eyes. It was as if it had been painted by an Aboriginal artist. The moment lasted just long enough for Suede to get a sense of home from the interaction. But it was broken by the growl of the nearby zambie and the kangaroo bounding out of sight.

"You get lots of them around here," said Colin. "It's great, aside from the shit on the greens, obviously."

The cabin fell silent, the occupant's thoughts filled with a momentary glimmer of hope, which, ironically, would not have been the case had they not been so distracted. They would've had far more time to observe the clubhouse, where barricades protected the entrances and bodies abounded.

Colin turned back to his view of the estate. "There it is. Take this right. Third place on the left."

"Oh, looks fancy," said Donna.

"I hope you've got some booze stocked," said Suede. "The hotel supplies aren't going to last long." He looked at Colin, only to see the old man jittery. "Erm… you OK?"

His comment washed right over Colin. "Just pull up here," he said to Donna, eyes fixated on the house.

"Just give me a minute," he added when the van pulled up.

He got out of the van and disappeared around the corner of the house, only to return seconds later with a small set of keys.

"Wicked," said Suede as he and the others left the van and joined Colin on the porch of the property.

Colin breathed deeply before lifting the keys to the door handle.

At that moment, the door swung open. An older woman stared back from inside. "Colin? What in the fuck are you doing here?"

*

CHAPTER 20
MY HOUSE

If Colin's face had dropped any further from its normal resting position, Grace and the others would have mistaken him for a zambie. He stared at the woman at the door in open-mouthed bewilderment. "Carol? What are you doing here?"

Grace and the others exchanged glances.

"Staying here, obviously," said a slightly confused Carol.

"I thought you were in Europe," said Colin. Behind him, the confused glances begin to morph into accusing glares in his direction.

Carol smiled with awkward over-enthusiasm before moving one hand to the door handle. She closed it just enough to get a shoulder safely behind. "We weren't going to miss the club championships. We've been back for days," she said, hand still firmly on the door handle.

Eyes all soon fell on Colin, and a myriad of expressions crossed his confused, then disenchanted face. The silence washed over them like an unscratched itch. It soon became clear that Colin, in his current state, wasn't in a hurry to give anyone else respite.

Grace stuck out her hand. "Hi, my name's Grace. We just managed to get out before…" Carol's indifferent glare made holding eye contact difficult. She looked around at her makeshift crew. "Anyway, how do you two…"

Her voice trailed off as a man stepped in behind Carol, placing his arm around her shoulder. As he came into the frame, the barrel of a gun appeared by Carol's side. The man smiled when the others noticed the weapon, then he took a long, pitying look at Colin before sighing appropriately.

Colin gave him a dirty look in return. "Phillippe."

"Colin."

Both men expressed the uttering of each other's name in an uninflected monotonal note, all while keeping their mouths as still as possible. It really allowed the disdain to roll around in the palate.

"… know each other?" said Grace after a gulp.

"We used to be married," said Colin.

"Emphasis on the used to," said Carol. "That was a long time ago, and as far as I remember, this place was mine after the split."

By this point, Colin was struggling to find a safe spot to stare into the distance without catching anyone else's eyes.

"Oh, that's just fucking fantastic!" said Suede.

"Wait, have we driven all the way out here for nothing?" said Donna.

"Well done, Colin," added Suede. "Completely full of shit."

Donna turned her stare to Suede. "You can talk! We only let you in the van because you pretended to be survivors."

"Erm, I think you'll find you guys were lost and desperate until we came along," said Suede.

"Look how far we've come." The sarcasm dripped from each one of Donna's words.

"Don't look at me!" said Suede. "We would've been fine if Captain Stalker actually had a place to go like he said he did!"

Grace tried to block out that conversion as another one of equal volume opened up between Colin, Carol and Phillippe. There was clearly a vast amount of unresolved frustration between Colin and Carol. Meanwhile, Phillippe had lost whatever seemingly little patience he had for the ongoing history presented at his door, and Colin had an equal measure of patience for his Frenchness.

They were making way too much commotion, given everything that was going on. Who knows how far their noise was carrying on the still air, across the golf course and beyond. Grace looked up the street to see the hobbling old-lady-turned-zambie now migrating in their direction. She needed to get the group under control. Who knew, perhaps if she offered some helpful advice, Carol and Phillippe would see it within themselves to help them out in the moment. I mean, they looked decent enough, all things considered.

"Enough!" yelled Grace over the commotion around her.

Immediately, the conversations stopped, and eyes fell upon her. She shared a round of eye contact with everyone. "That's better." She directed everyone's attention to the inbound hobbling zambie. "In case you hadn't got the memo, we're supposed to be keeping our voices down. Or we'll end up either like that or eaten by that."

She studied the others again, her focus on Carol. It was then she noted something in Carol's reaction as she looked at the zambie. Grace suddenly became aware of their location, the gated community. Everyone must've known each other, including the zambies. She studied it again before returning her gaze to Carol and searching for the right words to endear herself to the actual homeowner. "I'm sorry."

"Fuck Judith," spat Carol.

Grace stared at her in stunned silence.

"The golf club will be better without her snooping snout getting up in everyone's business."

"I don't really think the golf club is really going to be that much of a factor going forward," said Grace.

"Fuck Judith," said Phillippe. "Some things are bigger than people acting weird."

"Leave Judith alone," said Colin.

"Of course, you would have her back," snapped Carol.

Grace looked at the three old timers and all the history she had no interest in knowing any further. "People aren't acting weird," she said, with air quotes. "Humanity is being exterminated."

"Well, it couldn't have started with a nicer person," said Phillippe. He put his arm around Carol, and the two stared at the reanimated corpse with a sense of shared satisfaction.

Grace shared looks with her group, aligning them on her plan to work their way into the house. "Look, you seem like…" She cleared her throat. "… nice people. And I'm not sure what you know about what's happening, but whatever has happened to Judith over there has happened to a lot of people."

"Thousands and thousands," said Suede. "Adelaide's a ghost town."

"Adelaide *is* a ghost town," said Colin.

Suede stared at him. "Undead town. Just like everywhere else. Whatever this thing is, it's coming for all of us. And, if we don't find a way to work together soon, well, there'll be no stopping it."

The group looked at the couple with pleading eyes. Colin and Phillippe stood unresponsive behind the door.

Grace cleared her throat. "If you could see it within yourselves to let in a few visitors for the night, we would all be much obliged."

Donna put her arm around Ava, and the pair smiled with as much warmth as they could muster. "You have no idea what it would mean for us. All we have is what's in that van."

Grace dropped her big eyes into a pose she knew fit the moment perfectly. "Just one night. Please."

Carol and Phillippe exchanged a long glance as a silent conversation played out between the two. Eventually, Carol's eyes softened into a warm smile.

Grace gave her an encouraging nod.

"Naaahhh," said Carol over several gut-wrenching seconds.

Phillippe stepped to her side and lifted the rifle at a more threatening angle. A new darkness washed over the scene.

"What!" said Grace. "Why?"

"Why would I?"

"To help out fellow humans?"

"What? A guy who can't keep his cock in his pants and a bunch of entitled millennials. I couldn't think of anything worse."

Donna took a quick moment to enjoy being group bundled as a millennial. Not so much, Ava.

"Would it help if we got rid of Colin?" asked Suede.

"Also naaahhh," said Carol after a short evaluation. "But thanks for the offer."

Colin stared at Suede before clipping him over the back of the head.

Grace raised her hand, palm out, to counter Phillippe's rifle. She took a short step forward. "Look, things are pretty crazy out there and we—"

"Back!" snapped Carol.

Phillippe now stepped past her and raised the gun at Colin.

"After the day we've had, the last thing we need is Colin and more of his shit."

"What day?" said Grace with compassion, sensing another play.

"We lost a lot of good people."

"How?"

Carol eyed Grace. "None of your business, girlie, but if I were you, I'd avoid the clubhouse and hotel on the way out." She then signalled to Phillippe, who nodded back before she briefly disappeared. Phillippe shared the aim of his weapon with anyone who would look at him.

Grace and Suede raised their hands, Donna positioned herself in front of Ava, and Colin stared back as if daring him to shoot. Carol soon returned with a moving box, taped closed, with the word 'Dickhead's' written in permanent marker on the side. She threw it at Colin, who somewhat caught it as it flew into his breadbasket. He sighed with a pain he tried to hide.

"Take the last of your shit and get out of here," said Carol.

Phillippe emphasised her words with a rifle movement, and Grace and the others backed away from the door.

"What are we supposed to do now?" said Grace.

"What do I care?" said Carol.

After many dramatic moans, Colin stood tall once more. "Fine, if they don't want us here, we'll leave."

"Where to?" said Grace.

Colin looked at the zambie now near the van. "Looks like there's room at Judith's place?"

*

CHAPTER 21

ALIVE

After a short drive to the top of the hill, Colin directed them to Judith's. The view from the front of the property would've been considered spectacular on any day before this one. It had unrestricted views over the approach roads, the other rows of houses and the golf course, right through to the coast and the horizon. Today, that view was defined as secure. Well, about as secure as they were going to get.

What wasn't so secure was Judith's house. The group split up into two teams, circling the house in either direction. Colin led Donna and Ava down the side path one way, while Grace and Suede jumped the fence to the neighbour's yard before jumping into the backyard on the other. They soon overturned a terracotta pot to reveal a house key, which unlocked the main rear sliding doors. But by the time they had made it inside, Colin and co. were already there, having found access to the property via the side laundry door. The look on Colin's face was every bit as smug as the one he wore when Carol started yelling abuse, knowing he was headed towards Judith's.

"Nice security," said Suede. "How did she even survive long enough to make the apocalypse?"

"It's called country living," said Colin. "Dibs on the front room."

He sped – well, Colin-level sped – down the corridor to claim what he knew was the master bedroom.

"Did he just dibs?" said Grace. "What is he, like, 12?"

As it turned out, the house offered plenty more sleeping options, with another two bedrooms downstairs and the same again upstairs. The upstairs rooms bookended the front and back aspects of the house, with a large living area in between. Grace and Suede took the front, while Donna and Ava took the back, leaving Colin the only one downstairs.

They had soon unloaded their minimal gear and supplies before Suede poured out a round of drinks from his Crafers Hotel bottle swipe. There was no shortage of mixer options in the fridge.

He paused before pouring Ava's drink, seeking guidance from Donna.

"I'm twenty!" said Ava, insulted.

"What? How?" said Suede as he filled her glass.

"I don't drink though."

"What? How?" said Colin.

"It's a poison that's bad for your body."

"Well, I'm not going to cope with tonight without that poison," said Colin as he grabbed a glass.

In the background, the television was on. One of the commercial networks broadcasting their evening news. They were nearly through to the sports section, yet there had been not one mention of the cataclysm that had changed their world.

"Cheers," said Suede as he held his glass aloft. "Here's to…"

That's where his words fell short. He looked to the others for guidance.

"Being alive?" said Donna timidly.

"Judith?" offered Colin.

"The memory of Halen," said Grace.

"Very well," said Suede, stepping into a speech pose. "Here's to being alive, Judith – probably the kindest zambie we've ever met – and sweet Halen, a servant, friend and a van of the highest order. Cheers!"

The group cheersed back and took a drink, embracing the surreal nature of the day and the moment. No one wanted to think of the deeper losses of people they knew and loved. It was all too vast to be calculated, too difficult to measure. Instead, they compartmentalised the moment of relief. Enjoying the first chance any of them had had to catch a breath from the craziness of a broken world, which was perhaps already beyond revival. Donna was the first to laugh at the preposterous nature of it all. Within seconds, it had spread to the others. Nothing made sense.

"You guys are quite possibly the worst survivalists I've ever met," said Donna, between fits of laughter. She held the remains of her drink aloft before sculling it.

Grace laughed. "Coming from the worst betrayer I've ever met, that's some compliment."

Donna gave her a guilty expression, laughed, and then reached for the bottle.

"And let's not forget the man who made this entire trip possible," said Suede. "You may know him as the boomer who stalks his ex-wife, but around these parts, you can call him Colin."

By this point, Colin had disappeared into the butler's pantry, emerging with a bow and two more bottles of liquor. "You're welcome."

The laughter went up a notch. As Suede was celebrating, something in the loungeroom caught the corner of his eye. "Oh, fuck yeah."

He was over to the record player in seconds, opening the cupboard doors underneath to reveal a cascade of vinyl. "Boom! Bingo!"

*

The second side of The Beatles' *Abbey Road* played downstairs while the five survivors stood on the upstairs balcony that led from Grace and Suede's room. Their moment of relief and elation was now as far behind them as their first couple of drinks. The reality of the road ahead started to sink in.

Colin was doing his best to keep everyone's minds occupied, pointing out the key features of the area from their view. "… beyond that group of houses at the far end of the golf course is pretty much the main strip of shops in Normanville. That leads down to more housing on the way to the jetty, but I think they're more holiday homes than houses. Take the road the other way, and you head back to Carrickalinga up there – that's pretty much all holiday homes, too."

They could make the distant lights of Carrickalinga out a few kilometres away. Back along the main strip, cars seemed to still be rolling past in dribs and drabs, their headlights flashing in and out of view between buildings and trees. Sounds were filtering back from the main street, but it was hard to gauge if it was a commotion.

"I wonder what the shops are like?" said Grace. "I mean, should we be trying to get something?"

"Maybe," said Colin. "But if what was happening at Yankalilla was anything to go by, it'll be messy."

"Agreed," said Suede. "Some of those people would've escaped the city with nothing. They'll be desperate. Could get ugly."

"A mix of locals, holiday home folks and people with nowhere to go?" said Colin. "That's a combination to avoid, I say."

"Works for me," said Donna. "I don't think I can today anymore."

She exchanged a look with Ava, who nodded her agreement.

"Naw, look," said Grace, eyes drawn to the nearby fairway. "Kangaroos."

Donna smiled as she did a quick headcount. "Fourteen!"

"They're everywhere on the course," said Colin. "Especially at dusk and dawn."

"Cool!" said Ava.

Everyone watched on as the marsupials grazed away, seemingly blissfully unaware of the plight of the humans around them.

"So, the thing I don't get is—" said Colin, eventually. "—if they kill us, do we turn into them or not?"

Suede stared at him. They all did.

"Or is it just bitten? Would that turn us? And we need a headshot for the kill, right? I mean, that's the rule, isn't it?"

"Can we not do this now?" said Grace. "I think I've got enough to process for one day."

"To process?" said Colin, visually air quoting. He scoffed. "I've got news for you. If we don't sort thi—"

"Look around. No one here wants to talk about those things right now."

"Listen, lady, I'm—"

"Don't 'listen lady' me, cockswab!"

Suede tutted. "I was going to cockswab him."

Colin gave him a confused look before turning his focus back to Grace. "Unlike you ladies—" He made sure to stare at everyone in turn, including Suede. "—I'm prepared to have the conversations we need to stay alive."

"So, what? Ladies aren't capable of those conversations?" said Grace, eyes fixed on him.

Colin's face went through a number of expressions as he contemplated his answer. "I'm not saying that, necessarily."

Grace snorted with disbelief. "Just, wow!"

Ava stared at him in stunned silence.

Donna looked at her. "I grew up with this."

"Whoa, ladies! Calm the farm," said Colin.

"How about you read the room instead? I saw you in action at the service station. You're a liability," said Grace. "And I'm being kind."

Colin looked around, facial expressions showing him his conversation starter was defeated. He tutted his disgust.

"So, if you don't mind," said Grace. "We're going to have a few seconds to enjoy a moment of nature. Just a little relax, watching a few fucking kangaroos."

"Yeah, cockswab."

Everyone looked at Suede, who instantly knew he'd missed the moment and would have to seriously consider retiring the insult for all time.

*

CHAPTER 22
IT'S TOO LATE

The group watched the kangaroos until the evening had stolen the last of the light. They soon found themselves downstairs once more, with Colin and Suede gathered in zambie-Judith's lounge room while the others found wine supplies and then conducted a tour of the house. Each of them was a few drinks further into their thoughts about a reality that was too overwhelming to take in but too true to ignore. All of which led to the inescapable truth that, even between them, they fell drastically short of the minimum skill sets required to survive.

"Things are more fucked than I thought," said Suede, having just flicked through the record collection once more.

As he did, 'You make me feel (Like a natural woman)', the last track of Carole King's *Tapestry*, was playing. It was the second – and last – album they had all agreed was worth listening to. The rest of zambie-Judith's extensive collection had plenty of appeal for Colin, more than a couple of choices for Donna, and different selections again for Grace and Ava. However, to Suede, it was a hellscape of almost the same magnitude as the events of the day.

"I don't think you could've failed to buy a higher percentage of music that didn't age well if that was your goal when you set out," said Suede as he slumped down beside the cupboard and took a healthy sip.

"Pfft, rookie," said Colin. He looked Suede up and down with pitying judgement. "Who died and made you music king anyway? Has it occurred to you that you just have no idea what you're talking about?"

"Pfft," said Suede in return, blindly pulling an album out of the collection at random, eyes fixed on the group. It was a test. "What have we got here?"

"See," said Colin. "Elton John. Musical genius."

"… in the early and mid-1970s, sure," said Suede as he studied the cover. "Even the 80s to a lesser extent. Not this. *Victim of Love* was disco horseshit. And disco had already died a horrible death before this even came out."

Colin shuffled uneasily in the recliner as he realised Suede may have more knowledge than he'd first given him credit for. "What would you know about disco? Or the 70s, for that matter?"

"Because I listen to music, and I have a brain," said Suede. "Friendly tip: if you're going to argue music, think hard before you're willing to die on the hill of Elton John disco." He pulled another album out of the collection, looked at the cover and snorted.

"What?" said Colin. "That's Queen. One of the greatest musical acts of all time."

"Yeah, but *Hot Space*?" said Suede. "Dance pap. It's their *Victim of Love* moment."

Colin went to open his mouth but was temporarily short on accompanying words.

"… and 'Under Pressure', I'll give it that," added Suede.

"A Classic!" said Colin. "You know, this is why your generation is considered so entitled. You judge things you weren't even a part of with your nose in the air."

Suede snorted. "This from the guy who doesn't own any music made after the 1980s because he says it's all shit."

"Whatever," said Colin. "Opinions are like assholes. Everyone's got one. Why would I care what you think?"

"I literally don't care if you care, I just want to limit your access to the turntable, based on the evidence you keep providing every time you speak."

The two stared at each other as the girls re-entered the room.

"We can hear you two carrying on from the shed," said Grace, knowing a chat around a vinyl collection had the potential to get heated.

"This little upstart thinks he can teach me a thing or two about good music," said Colin. "It's a joke. Back then, artists didn't just press a button to make music happen, they played it themselves. It took talent."

Suede rolled his eyes. "That is one of the most boomer things you could've said."

Grace looked at Suede. "Have you told him about your music stuff?"

"What music?" said Colin, with a generous dollop of disdain.

Suede shook his head. "He wouldn't understand any of it."

"I'll be the judge of that," said Colin, sharing a smile with the rest of the room – a shark circling his prey while the audience watched on.

The two combatants locked eyes. Suede raised an eyebrow in the way Grace knew was a threatening manner before he pulled the Queen album from its sleeve and placed it on the turntable. The bass-driven beat of 'Staying Power' kicked in, and Suede bopped along in a way only Grace realised was patronising. "I'm a prompt songwriter, and I have a music reaction channel."

Colin scrunched up his face. "What?"

Suede looked at Grace. "See." He sighed before turning back to Colin. "I work with AI to write new music and I also listen to classic albums and give my reactions."

"You? Write songs?" Colin scoffed.

"What about it?" said Suede. "I write the lyrics and use prompts to craft the rest. I've got some with over a million listens."

"Like what?" said Ava.

"Just different stuff."

Colin smelled blood. "C'mon then, like what? Unless you're making it up."

"He's not making it up," said Grace.

"Well, I've got a few different projects, its compli—"

"Name one!" said Colin, smiling at the eyeball attention on Suede.

" 'Rump goes thump,' " said Suede. "It's an homage to booty. Disco style."

"I thought you hated disco," said Colin.

"It's a parody."

"OK, so a song about bums – bit disgusting – what else?"

"Why is that disgusting? Is 'Fat bottomed girls' disgusting? 'Baby got back'? 'All about that bass'? 'Thong song'? There have been many iconic songs about bums."

Colin made the kind of face one does when their point has been defeated, but they still want to argue.

"Actually, some of the lyrics are pretty disgusting," said Grace.

Suede looked at her, betrayed.

"I knew it!" said Colin, with renewed energy. "What else?"

Suede shifted in his seat. "I don't really think we nee—"

"What else was this massive hit for you?"

"Well, I wouldn't say a massive hit," corrected Suede. "It did earn me a few grand, though. A protest song."

"Called?"

"About how the powers that be make sure the rich stay rich and the rest of us go around in circles."

"Called?"

" 'Oligarchy bukkake.' "

Grace looked apologetically at the others while Ava scoffed.

"What?" said Donna.

"I don't understand either of those words," said Colin. "AI probably made them up for you."

"Let's go with that," said Suede. "Anyway, between that and the reaction channel, I earn enough to help keep us going."

Colin looked him up and down as he mustered his contempt. "Reaction channel?"

Suede eyed him back. "Because people watch me listen to albums and share what I think."

Colin scoffed. "Wow! No wonder your generation can't afford to buy a house! Spending money to listen to some emaciated vegan upstart yap on about how the lyrics hurt his feelings or something."

"Firstly, I'm not vegan. Secon—"

"You look it," said Colin, sharing looks with the others.

"Hey! I'm a vegan," said Ava.

"Vegetarian here," said Grace as she and Ava shared a smile.

Colin facepalmed.

"Secondly," continued Suede after a heavy sigh. "Almost all of my audience is around your age."

Colin gave an expression of bitter confusion.

"Thirdly, my generation can't afford a house because it's not like back in the olden days when you could just fish the change out of your pocket and pay for a deposit. No, your generation just got a free pass through everything and still needs us to slave away to prop you up. Then you've got the gall to criticise us for not doing it your way? Wow."

"Perhaps learn to respect your elders a little, sonny."

"Perhaps learn to conduct yourself in a manner that garners that respect, grandpa."

"Oi!" snapped Donna. "Enough! How about we focus on our energy on… I don't know… the apocalypse!" She eyed them all in turn. "I'm sure differences around what decade you were born can wait."

The beats took over the conversation as the overwhelming nature of everything sank in deeper for each of them.

"For the record," added Donna eventually. "This is a long way from peak Queen."

"I like it!" said Ava.

"There's no Brian May distortion, no Roger Taylor stadium drums," said Suede. "Instead, we get a horn section and drum machine clap tracks. It changes the entire core of their sound."

Colin looked at him and the valid points he raised. Silence.

"It's like our world right now!" added Suede. "A couple of things have been removed, and a couple of new elements added, and everything's changed. We've been *Hot Space*'d."

Once again, words gave way to music as the second song, 'Dancer', began. As if to prove a point, it was even more hot-spacey than the previous track.

"How has it even come to this?" said Grace as she slumped back on the sofa, the ensuing silence offering her space to continue. "Do you know what I was going to do with my day when I woke up this morning? Yoga by the riverfront. I would've made a quick video to shoot out on all my socials." She scoffed. Colin scoffed louder. She glared at him. "Instead, I've taken up residence in the house of a zambie named Judith, overlooking a kangaroo-filled golf course, with three people I've never met before after the world's gone DEFCON five fubar, hiding from zambies and God knows what else. And worse still, we have no idea who, or what, has started this!"

'Dancer's electro-funk beat took over as words failed the group in the wake of Grace's statement.

"A Brian May guitar solo!" said Colin, nodding to Suede.

Suede contemplated the symbolism. "Hmmm. Maybe all is not lost after all."

"You're right. Someone playing a guitar solo on a song recorded decades ago makes me feel so much safer," said Ava, deadpan.

It killed the brief moment of hopeful optimism.

"Is it worth, I don't know, working out what might have happened? Or how or something?" said Donna, eventually. "I might help us work out what's best to do next.

"What's there to know?" said Grace. "We're in some sort of AI apocalypse, and right now, a significant chunk of the human population is undead and looking to recruit."

"Yeah, I get that," said Donna. "But what AI? I mean, there's AI, and there's AI."

"At this point, does it really matter if it's a government, some corporation, terrorist group or an AI itself? Look what it's done. And what comes next? And after that?" Grace looked around the room and found the expressions the others wore reflected her thoughts. "Whatever is controlling this thing – if it is being controlled – is smarter than us. Way smarter."

"Rubbish," said Colin. "Those AI things – they're just logic predictors guessing the next word or what the image looks like. They're not smarter. They're just idiot savants."

"2023 called," said Suede. "It wants its outdated opinions back."

Colin stared at him; they all did.

"That's just something people have been telling themselves, so they feel OK with the tech. We put it in a little box in our brains we understand, then slap a label on it that makes us feel superior to it – comfortable. The actual truth is it's far smarter than us in every conceivable metric, and everyone's been living their lives like that's not a fucking massive problem."

Colin scoffed. "Speak for yourself on the brains front."

Suede stared at him. "It's moron statements like that that've allowed this thing to sneak up on all of us like it has in the first place." He looked around the room at the others. "Think about the difference in intellect between apes and us. What are they? Maybe 25 IQ? And we average, what, 100?"

He looked back at Colin. "In the grand scheme of all measures of intelligence, that difference is very small. Yet one species lives in trees, and the other has built cities, conquered the planet, connected every one of its kind and flown to other worlds," he said as he took a sip of his drink and studied everyone's face. "And AI is as far ahead of us as we are of apes."

Suede gave Colin another look. "It is far more than an idiot savant."

"Well, that's depressing," said Donna.

"If anything," added Suede. "We're the idiot savants. A bunch of redundant, well-groomed monkeys who somehow managed to build, train and deliver our intellectual conquerors. And now that's exactly what it's doing – conquering us."

"We're screwed, aren't we?" said Ava.

"We could survive here," said Colin. "We're isolated, we've got shelter, food—"

"For a week or two," said Donna. "Then what?"

Colin eyed her. "Then we'll figure something out."

"Did you see the people near the supermarket? They're desperate! I don't know what you're planning on figuring out, but by the time you do, people like that would've already done it!"

"There's more than one way to skin a cat," said Colin.

Donna stared at him, confused. As did Ava.

"Hey, I've been living off a pension for years. You think that's been easy? You just find a way."

"And we've been living out of a van for the better part of two years," said Grace. "Anything's possible."

"We're only surviving this… situation… if whoever is controlling it wants us to," said Suede. "Or we're just too irrelevant to matter."

"I need another fucking drink," said Donna as she downed the remains of her glass then recharged.

"Mum!"

Donna turned to Ava, not knowing if the scolding was for her language or consumption. She shrugged her shoulders.

Ava rolled her eyes.

"Pass that my way," said Grace.

"You realise how unhealthy that is, right?" said Ava.

Colin sighed. "A vegan and a teetotaller. How wonderful."

Ava eyed him. "You're labelling the one person not consuming the drug as having the problem? Cool stuff."

Just then, there was a rattling at the front door.

Donna screamed as her glass fell from her hand and smashed on the table's edge. The five exchanged glances that said *stay quiet*. They also said that if there was something out there, it definitely heard the glass smash. It then evolved into a more sophisticated expression discussion about the virtues of going to check if the coast was clear.

Then they heard the noise again.

Grace watched as Donna tiptoed towards her daughter and gave her a hug. Then she saw a silent exchange between Suede and Colin, each volunteering the other to step up to door-checking responsibility. She sighed and headed towards the door herself.

She gave Suede a glare as she passed him on her way to the corridor. As she light-footed her way along, she saw something making shadows in the frosted window alongside the door. There was definitely something out there – human-sized. Then she made out a scratching noise. It was being made on the wood by whatever it was. Her heart pounded.

Then the door rattled louder. Whatever was out there must have leaned their weight against it. Slowly, quietly, she eased forward, targeting the door viewer.

She turned briefly to see the rest of the group at the other end of the corridor watching on. Judging by Suede's expression, he could make out the look she was giving him. Then she refocused on the door, took the remaining few steps and a deep breath, and leaned her eye into the peephole.

On the other side, zambie-Judith studied the door. Its uncoordinated, undead arms pawed ineffectively at the door, while it wheezed. Grace studied it from her protected view. The inactivated muscles in its face and distant stare gave her the chills. As did the trail of off-coloured drool hanging down from the corner of its mouth.

Grace wondered if it was attracted by the conversation, the music or the lights. Perhaps it was just drawn home by some unknown instinct of the human it had been a day earlier.

Then she wondered how life had come to this.

*

CHAPTER 23
(JUST LIKE) STARTING OVER

"We got so caught up in working out whether we could make it or not, that we never stopped to ask if we should?" said Suede, lost in thought.

He was tired, parched and seedy as his mind went into recall mode, trying to piece together the events deep into the previous night. Besides alcohol consumption, obviously.

"It's just the bed, Suede," said Grace. Looking and feeling every bit as dusty.

They looked at each other, then Suede shrugged before tossing the quilt roughly over the main part of the bed.

Grace shrugged back as she checked her phone. Still no news, no trending data, no social feed mentions – nothing – about the events that changed the world. It was disturbing in its own way. She looked through her various accounts – each feed had exactly the same kind of content it was posting two days ago. Weird. She looked at her chats where, again, she found the usual sort of interactions she would expect – a few messages from friends, some accounts shilling one service/product or another and bot accounts trying to gain credibility – just another digital day.

She wondered what would happen if she posted something about what was happening and opened a new-post dialogue box. Then, her thoughts turned to Kane and everything he said about being off-grid. She closed the dialogue box and went back to flicking through her feeds.

It hit her differently now. It was all a lie. Maybe it always was, just not so overtly. So much of her existence was tied to that lie. Part of her essence needed it. Like a drug, perhaps. Seeing it exposed – or was it parodied? – in such a way was hard to observe.

Then a notification chirped into existence – a new message request. So absorbed was she in everything else digital, that it made her jump. Usually, she'd leave it to bank up with the others before letting her social-agent bot filter out the spam, but for some reason, she felt compelled to click on it.

She didn't recognise the name. The profile picture was of a mother posing with two kids. Something about it screamed bot account. The message was, "Congratulations! You made it to day two!"

A wave of dread hit Grace, and she flushed with panic before shutting down the app and turning off her phone.

"Everything OK?" said Suede.

"What? Umm, yeah," she said. "Just, yeah, still no mention of what's going on. Kind of creepy, you know."

"Yeah," said Suede, rubbing his temple. "I went hard last night. What time did we go to bed?"

"You? No idea. I crashed at 11 pm. You and Colin were still kicking on."

"Me and Colin?" It triggered vague memories.

"I think I sense a bromance brewing," said Grace with a smile.

Suede stared at her, deadpan, as they headed downstairs.

They heard a scream. It was Donna. They traced the noise downstairs and found the source of the scream, her daughter and Colin gathered near the windows overlooking the backyard.

"What the fuck were you thinking?" said Donna, gesturing outside.

Colin was attempting to respond, but no words fell from his open mouth.

That's when Grace and Suede made out the zambie corpse of Judith in the backyard.

It had been tied to the rotating clothesline using what appeared to be a stretch of rope and some gaffer tape. It seemed to be walking along the circular path it was bound to by its restraints. Its hair had been gelled into some sharp post-punk angles, and its face was caked in a cluster bomb of makeup. A beach towel had been crafted into a cape that dangled from its shoulders, while it wore the album jacket for *Hot Space* as a chest plate.

Suede tried to snort in his laughter as Grace stared at him in disbelief.

"Oh, that's right," said Suede.

"You guys are so immature," said Ava.

Colin ignored the barb. "Some sort of superhero, wasn't it? *Cat girl* or something."

"*Cool cat*," said Suede with recall pride.

Grace stared at him.

"It was one of the songs on the album," he added, foolishly thinking the additional layer of detail would make the scene more okay. "Just our little homage." He couldn't sustain eye contact with Grace.

Zambie-Judith wheezed as she rotated around the yard.

"The *Something About Mary* hair wasn't my idea," said Suede to Grace.

"Was too!" said Colin.

Suede stared at him, betrayed. Grace ignored the pair of them as she headed to the kitchen, flicked the kettle on and searched the cupboards for coffee.

"So, no actual reason? Just dress-ups?" said Donna. "Honestly, what's wrong with you two? You could've been killed? Infected?"

"Or even worse, remained exactly as they are," added Grace.

"Obviously, we'd had a few!" said Suede. "But don't tell me you can look at Cool Cat and not think it was funny."

"It's cruel!" said Ava.

"Cruel?" said Colin. "It's an undead! It has no idea what's going on."

Ava stared at him. "Would it hurt you to be respectful?"

Colin sighed. "Look out, vegan judgement at 12 o'clock."

Ava shook her head as she gave him a look of disappointment.

"Or is that teetotaller judgement? Either way, its—"

"Oh, cork it, Colin," said Donna.

Colin stared at her in open-mouthed silence. "You people have no respect."

Ava returned serve with her own open-mouthed silence.

"Can we just try to escalate a little less?" said Grace, staring at Colin.

"You think I'm the problem," said Colin.

"Yes!" said Grace, Donna and Ava in unison.

Colin's angry face turned to Suede for support.

"There, there," said Suede. "Let's get you settled on the recliner. We can put some nice talkback radio on. You'll be shaking your fists in rage in no time."

It terminated the conversation after a few sniggers. Each person realised in their own way how their different generational expectations made it hard to truly connect on any deeper level. They thought differently, acted differently and had vastly different social interaction styles. It seemed every bit as isolating as being in a house on a remote estate surrounded by hostile, gun-toting boomers in the middle of an apocalypse.

Out the back, zambie-Judith watched on as it made another loop of the clothesline. Further beyond, the kangaroos flooded the golf course. Beyond their sphere of awareness, rival groups of survivors surrounded the general store in Normanville. Showdowns were brewing between residents, holiday-goers and homeless city outcasts.

Not too far from there, a horde of zambies gathered, the sounds of human activity stirring them – calling them. Further north, towards the city, a flood of drones entered the skies – collecting data, informing decisions and taking action. It was destined to pass through Normanville.

A world so utterly changed was set to change again. The only thing set to stay the same – it was not good news for humans.

*

"So," began Colin after more coffee, painkillers and breakfast had been consumed. "We really should head down the main street today. Scout around, see what's what."

"Good idea," agreed Grace.

Suede, Donna and Ava soon shared their endorsements, and for the first time, they were all on the same page about a strategy.

*

CHAPTER 24

LIGHT UP THE SKY

It was mid-morning before the group set out on foot for their reconnaissance mission to the main strip of Normanville. More than half the journey consisted of crossing the golf course. But before they did that, they had to pass the clubhouse and hotel complex. They did so with extreme caution, given Carol's warning. They passed close enough to try to get a glimpse of what might have happened but far enough away to feel safe. Still, the safety/distance matrix was always a difficult one to negotiate when the capacity of the threat was unknown.

Regardless, the evidence of a large altercation was there for anyone who took the time to look. All of the doors to the hotel rooms had been boarded up. There was an even larger barrier at the main clubhouse doors where it looked like some sort of battle had transpired. Bodies and parts were scattered around the door.

Inside, the group could see movement. Zambies – lots of zambies. No one dared guess numbers, no one dared speak. They just prayed the barriers and boarded-up doors kept up their end of the bargain.

Once past any visual signs of trouble, the course lay out a path to Normanville. It was a wall of greenery and fairways dotted with the odd kangaroo. It felt a million miles from the horrors of the clubhouse. So juxtaposed were the two visuals, it almost seemed wrong to speak of one while walking through the other. So, again, they didn't.

This is where Colin made the perfect foil. He gushed, extolling the virtues of the – as he repeatedly said – highly-rated course. He seemed to go into an altered state, as a golfer of his vintage does when talking on the subject, assuming the listener shared even a fraction of their enthusiasm.

But, at that moment, it was exactly what everyone needed – an enthusiastic distraction. Colin interspersed course notes with golfing anecdotes from his past – a birdie here, the time he landed a fairway bunker shot pin-high to seal the B-grade championship there, the time his approach shot hit a green-side tree and ricocheted into the hole somewhere else. So involved was he in the conversation that the others never got a chance to contribute. Not that they were listening, really. It all proved a distraction to what they had left behind. Or what they may face ahead.

On a tee mound halfway across their journey, two abandoned golf carts presented themselves. Given they were in working order, the group used them to finish their course crossing.

They soon abandoned the carts to hop a low fence at the course's edge – Colin requiring some help. They crossed through a paddock, which met the end of a crescent that led to a walkway through a park towards the town centre.

Following a similar naming convention to other towns they'd passed through, Main Rd sounded a lot, well, mainer than it was. The stretch that contained the pub, grocery store, cafes and just about every other public-facing business operation in the town was no more than a hundred metres long.

The group soon realised there was something happening ahead. The noise of an angry mob reached them well before the visual did.

It wasn't long before they had eyes on a mass of people outside the grocery store. Tensions were high. And it wasn't the first fracas based on the look of the adjacent pub. It was surrounded by broken glass from smashed windows as well as a scattering of broken bodies. They found cover well back from the fringes of the disturbance to watch proceedings.

"What the hell?" said Grace, behind the cover of an upturned car.

"You think that was zambies?" asked Donna, looking at the bodies.

"Or looters?" said Colin.

"Either way, let's keep this perimeter until we find out more, yeah?" said Suede.

Grace nodded her agreement and shared nods with the others.

Their attention soon turned to the disorder ahead. It was quickly apparent this was an inter-human altercation. There seemed to be groups within groups – pushing and shoving met yelling and screaming. This was a showdown for the last of the supplies in the grocery store.

One group had clearly won the battle, as there was a conga line of people vacating the shop with loaded trolleys, moving under the raging eye of a wall of protectors. In front of them, people pushed and shoved to get themselves involved. Suddenly, a couple of spot fires spilt further onto Main Rd.

An old man with a crowbar chased a younger guy. Two young women chased after the old guy, one kicking his heels out from under him while the other started kicking him in the head when he dropped hard onto the road. Soon, another wave of attackers came in, holding an assortment of handheld weapons, and started beating on the two women and snaring the young man. This action caused another group to spill from the pack and defend those being attacked.

Grace and the others suddenly felt vulnerable without any perspective or weaponry.

"I think we should go," said Donna.

At that moment, a van came puttering past them in the street. It turned down a side street near the supermarket and pulled over.

"I think I've just seen a ghost," said Suede to Grace.

Grace nodded her agreement as a couple in their early thirties, dressed in hippy-looking textiles, exited the VW Kombi and joined the fray. Sure, it wasn't red and didn't have the same black and white diagonally striped finish, but it was the same model as—

"Halen!" whispered Grace and Suede.

The gunshot blast echoed through the air. The group watched as a tall man defending the shop looters held the weapon above his head so all could see. There was a temporary pause in yelling, pushing and shoving – although the recent skirmish continued on the street. Then a chunk of rock flew through the air. It was launched from somewhere in the crowd and connected with the head of the armed man. The blow knocked him off his feet and out of view. It was followed by another pause as everyone reassessed – again – then hostilities resumed.

"This is too hot," said Suede. "Way, way too hot."

"Agreed," said Grace. "Let's just get the f—"

"Oh God!" said Ava.

All eyes were soon zeroing in on what had stolen her attention. At a cross-street by the corner of the pub, several zambies were heading towards the human chaos.

"Oh shit!" said Donna.

"And there!" said Suede, pointing to another group of zambies converging on the scene from the opposite direction.

"This is bad, this is bad, this is bad," said Ava.

"We need to get gone. Now!" said Donna.

Even as she uttered the words, the group was already backing slowly away from their cover and the dangers on the other side. There was still too much going on to turn their back on the chaos. The rival groups appeared too caught up in their skirmishes to even notice the new threat emerging from the cover of buildings into the intersection only metres away.

"Should we warn them or something?" said Ava.

"How?" said Colin.

They surveyed the scene again. Ava fell short of ideas and shrugged in silence.

"Shit! More! Up the street!" said Donna.

Grace trained her eye in that direction. The way the zambies were spilling onto Main Rd, they would block the main path of escape when the other two groups spotted them. "This is not going to end well."

By this point, Grace and crew had backed away to the far end of the hotel, a block away from the fringes of danger. Eyes darted between the brawling humans and the three clusters of zambies homing in on them.

Then, all the action seemed to reach a new pinnacle at once. Someone watching the brawl on the street screamed with enough blood-curdling gusto that it resonated above the various fights and screams. Within seconds, the scene changed. Human versus human fights dissipated. Those capable of doing so pressed out to form a new perimeter to meet the two zambie groups that neared the intersection. Then screams burst out further afield as the other group of zambies was identified. That group was soon followed by another, appearing from the same direction but on the opposite side of the road. The wall of humans protecting the looters now dissipated to join the defensive efforts.

"Jesus!" said Grace as they continued to back away. "They're outnumbered."

"It's got to be two to one," said Colin, as he checked the path was clear in their retreat.

"At least," said Suede.

The humans had formed a semicircular perimeter around the entrance of the supermarket. Those with weapons and the bravery to do so, stepped forward to try to nullify the attacks of the lead zambies. They fought with all manner of sharp objects, blunt objects, and guns.

Grace and the others knew there was nothing they could do now. Whatever was going to play out would happen with their presence or not.

Their survival instincts screamed at them to run, but it was met in equal measure with a fascination for what was unfolding.

Humans and zambies now met in open clashes on the fringes of the human pack. In between the punches of gunshot blasts and the screams of terror, the sound of blunt trauma blows hit Grace and crew just as hard.

Donna and Ava held hands as they watched on. Grace and Suede retreated side-by-side, and Colin scanned for potential surprise threats.

Peeeww!

A signpost tnngged beside them, as a stray bullet smashed into its surface, no more than a metre from where Colin stood.

"Jeebus!" said Suede with a jump.

"Let's go!" said Grace.

Just as they were turning their backs on the screaming and fighting, a speck appeared in the skies above Main Rd. One became ten, a hundred, then more.

"Drones!" said Suede.

"Run!" screamed Grace, and she and the others turned their backs on the chaos and fled.

*

CHAPTER 25

GUNS IN THE SKY

The fleeing crew didn't need to see the situation on Main Rd to recognise the moment those in the middle of it realised how bad their outlook was. Among the sounds of battle and the hum of drones, there was a distinct change in the pitch of the screams of those now trapped. The timbre and pitch of the collective noise shifted the sentiment from frightened fighting to resignation of hope.

For Grace and the others, that sound was as real as any horror they had witnessed in the lead-up. Fear, in the key of scream. And things were about to get worse.

A new noise flooded the soundscape. A pitter-patter reverberated down the road, the noise almost soft and soothing in comparison to everything else. Except it wasn't.

"They're firing!" said Grace as she turned to make sure the rest of the group were in her wake.

"The drones?" screamed Suede. "With what?"

"I'm not hanging around to find out," said Grace. "Go, go, go!"

Within seconds, the pair reached the nearby end of Main Rd. Across the T-junction, the park and the cover of trees offered relative salvation from above. Suede and Grace turned to make sure the others were close behind and were surprised to see Ava on their heels, Donna not too far behind and a hobbling Colin bringing up the rear.

"Hurry up!" screamed Suede.

He didn't fully understand Colin's gruff and mumbled response but definitely heard the word gout.

Grace scanned the T-junction for cars, then signalled Ava and Donna across. When they were across, she turned to join Suede in encouraging

Colin. The old man hobbled, grimaced, and shook his fist at Suede. In the distance behind him, the drones rotated in the sky like a ball of fish. It was a mesmerising black shapeshifting ballet, occasionally shimmering as sections of it caught light at the right angle. It was all dotted with tiny pocks of orange lights, presumably from the unseen and serene-sounding mystery weapon fire.

Beneath the ball was a chaotic riot of humans and zambies fighting and the mounting bodies of both lying in the street. The human's gunfire turned to the sky, and sections of the school of drones exploded in light as dozens of them fell from the sky. The ball changed shape instantly, adapting to the new input before focusing its next round of fire on the threats that had attacked it.

The violent movement, noise, drama and action could not have painted a more juxtaposed backdrop to Colin's slow-motion retreat.

"Kill me now," whispered Suede to Grace, before sighing. "C'mon buddy!" he called to Colin.

"Do we really have to wait for him?" whispered Grace. "You're doing great!" she yelled to Colin.

Suede raised an eyebrow. "I did think about that, but he's got the keys to zambie-Judith's."

"That is very disappointing," whispered Grace before turning back to Colin. "You're nearly there… sort of."

In the distance, another round of fire tore into the drone hive, scattering and reshaping the pack again and sending several more drones to the ground. One drone recovered from the damage of a shrapnel hit and spun twice before regaining its flight capacities. Then it noticed the small band of retreating humans at the end of the street.

Instead of rejoining the ball, it chased after its new target, also known as Colin.

Within seconds, Suede noticed the rogue drone. "Oh, shit!" he whispered. He squeezed Grace's arm, then darted his eyes towards the new threat.

Grace swallowed as her eyes narrowed at the inbound drone.

"What?" screamed Colin.

"Don't look back!" screamed Grace. "Just run!"

Colin nodded and hobbled, fear in his eyes.

"Are you absolutely sure that's your top gear?" said Suede.

The drone grew larger in the sky as it neared Colin. It oscillated in the air, victim to the gunfire damage it had already taken. But it wasn't enough to stop its advance.

"He's not going to make it, is he?" whispered Grace.

It was all too much for Colin. He couldn't resist the lure of impending dread on his six. He turned to face the battlefield realities. Well, half-turned might be more accurate. More accurately still, he half-turned before tripping over his own feet and falling. A wheeze of breathless old-person lungs deflating followed what was a significant thud on the bitumen.

"The keys!" screamed Suede in horror.

"I heard that!" said Colin, although it sounded like a gasp for air to the others.

"What do we do?" said Grace.

Suede sighed as the most logical solution dawned on him, and he realised it required way higher levels of personal bravery than he was comfortable with. "Get to the others and hide, I'll go back for the keys."

"Colin," corrected Grace.

"Sure, Colin."

"I could come with—"

In one move, Suede pushed her hard enough to give her running momentum towards the park while he turned into a sprint headed towards Colin. Or the keys. "Just go!"

Within seconds, he was at Colin's side. "You alright?" he said as he frisked the fallen man.

"Get your hands off me, pervert!" said Colin.

Suede glanced to the skies to see the inbound drone approaching. Its path was erratic as it tried to compensate for the damage it had taken. "Where are the keys?"

Colin stared at him in disbelief. "Safe."

Suede swore before grabbing Colin around the waist and throwing him over his shoulder. Colin screamed in disbelief and incredulity.

"Sorry, old man, I'm saving your ass," he said as he broke into the fastest sprint he could muster. "I can promise you it isn't personal."

They were soon across the road and nearing the park. While the girls had retreated in the direction they'd come from, Suede veered to the right. His new path would steer any potential threat away from the others but also offered better shelter under a larger abundance of trees. As he neared the first of them, a line of bullet impact wounds splintered out from the tree's trunk.

"Hold on!" screamed Suede as he darted away from the signs of danger.

The air around them filled with the fsskking sound of projectiles ripping through the atmosphere. Suede screamed, dodged and weaved. Colin screamed. Then, at some point several metres into the tree line, when they had the tree canopy as protection, the sound of firing stopped. Suede sought the cover of a large gum tree and pressed up against it. He caught his breath as quietly as possible while he lowered Colin to the ground. The pair scanned the air for the drone.

They heard its labouring propellers lurking somewhere, perhaps circling the stretch of trees, definitely on the hunt.

Then, the drone's tone changed in several short beats, each more sickly sounding than the one before. It crescendoed in an undramatic pop before it fell from the skies, hitting the dry ground with a mild thud.

Suede and Colin fought to get control of their breathing as they searched their surroundings from cover for evidence of the machine's demise.

"I see it," said Suede.

"Is it dead?"

"I think so," said Suede as he gestured ahead. "If we head out this way, we'll stay out of its sight."

They gave each other a nod before Suede began leading them to safety. Until Colin elbowed him in the ribs.

"What the fuck?" said Suede, rubbing the impact site.

"That's for betraying me," said Colin as he checked his body for injuries.

"Hello! I just saved your ass."

"Only because you couldn't find the keys."

Suede couldn't maintain eye contact, instead turning to the march ahead. "You know, most people generally say thank you when someone saves their life."

"Whatever," said Colin. "I can promise you it isn't personal."

*

Grace, Donna and Ava waited for the others to arrive under the cover of a canopy of heavier foliage at the far end of the park. As the minutes stretched on, the distant sounds of battle and the screams of pain and horror petered out.

Closer to them, the park stood eerily still. Aside from the birds, there was no sign of life – no movement, no snapping of twigs, no bending of branches – nothing. No sign of Suede or Colin. Grace stood as a silent sentry, the others too scared to voice their thoughts about what may have happened and what they should do next.

Donna eventually broke the deadlock. "Maybe they found a different way back."

Grace didn't break her view over the park, nor did she respond.

Donna and Ava exchanged glances.

"They're probably back at the house already, if they're, you know…" said Donna.

Ava scowled at her.

"I mean, of course! It goes without saying…" Donna became so tangled in her sentence that it stopped in its tracks.

Donna gave Ava an apologetic look.

"We're happy to stay with you and look, if that's what you want to do," said Ava. "But, given how much time has passed, it's safe to say they probably aren't coming this way."

Donna nodded at Ava with an expression that conceded her daughter had handled the moment better. Ahead of them, Grace turned away from her watch duty over the park and looked at Ava expectantly.

"Um, yeah," said Ava as she cleared her throat and thought of her next move. She cast her eyes over the scene. "Perhaps… see that whole stretch of trees down there near the houses. With a drone chasing them, that's probably the best cover they would've found."

Grace studied the stretch of nature while Donna nodded encouragement to Ava.

"Yeah," said Ava. "If we head through there, we should be protected all the way down to the front line of trees on the other side of the park."

Grace nodded at Ava before scanning the skies for drones. "Thanks. If you guys want to head back, you can."

Once again, Donna and Ava exchanged glances in silent conversation.

"We might tag along, if that's OK," said Donna. "Safety in numbers and all that."

Grace gave her a thin smile before leading the trio out.

*

CHAPTER 26
MY MACHINE

"I mean, I've always known you lot don't have much respect for the older generation, but I didn't expect to be left for dead at the first sign of inconvenience," muttered Colin as he hobbled after Suede.

Suede stopped in his tracks and turned to Colin. "Newsflash. I literally just saved your life, so it'd be great to not be lectured by the grumpy old man on intergenerational respect."

Colin wore an expression ready to find fault and argue. Suede sighed, turned back to the path ahead and continued up the house-lined street they'd found themselves on.

"Yes, that's right. I have very vivid memories of you seeing me lying on the road in mortal danger, and what was it you screamed again?" Colin paused for the response that was never going to come. "Oh, that's right, 'the keys!' "

"How is it you don't seem to hear a single thing out there, yet the one time it's something you can take offence to, your ears are like an elephant's? I mean, sure, they're nearly as bi—"

Suede cut himself short as the distant sounds of drones pierced the still afternoon air. "C'mon," he whispered to Colin as he moved off the road and headed to the verandah in a house's nearby front yard for shelter.

"What?" said Colin.

Suede stared at him in head-shaking disbelief. "Wow! The drones?"

Colin opened his mouth to speak but instead shrugged.

Suede rolled his eyes, then gave him a shush sign before pointing to the sky.

Colin nodded.

After spending a moment lost in thought, Suede pulled a pair of sunglasses from his pocket.

Colin scoffed. "They'll still recognise you, you know."

Once again, Suede stared at him in disbelief before he held the glasses out past the end of the verandah, using the lens reflection to scan the skies.

"Ahh!" said Colin.

Even with the limited field of reflected vision the shades provided, Suede could see black dots filling the skies. It was a vision backed up by the increased audible humming flooding the street. He moved past Colin and tested the door handle. To his surprise, it was open. He exchanged a look with Colin before he opened the door and scanned the space, then the pair headed in.

Suede tutted. "Country people!"

Once Colin was through, Suede clicked the door shut as gently as possible. "Did you honestly think I was going to use the shades as a disguise? The respect you have for me is enormous."

Colin ignored him, and the pair made their way to the far end of the open planned living area where wide windows flooded in light from outside. They could see fuzzy shadows zipping across the backyard. Suede neared the windows, targeting a spot he thought would offer the best cover, then leaned his head out to get a view of what was going on.

"Careful!" said Colin.

Suede rolled his eyes, sighed and reset himself , then leaned out. A flood of drones seemed to be migrating further south. No longer moving in the shape of a ball – assuming it was the same drones as earlier – they were now spread out into diamond shapes. Each diamond shape moved in formation with the others. It was as mesmerising as it was scary.

"Well?" said Colin.

"Flying out, by the looks of it. We just need to hang tight in here until—"

A crashing noise stole the moment. It came from inside the house.

"What was that?" said Suede.

But his question was answered before Colin had a chance to respond. The groan of a zambie echoed down a nearby corridor.

*

"This way!" whispered Grace. "Quickly."

They had barely started out on their search when the school of drones on Main Rd rose to the sky and began heading out. The move left them way too exposed, and they had to abandon their missions and fall back to where the tree line offered more protection. That course had led them to a row of houses, and Grace directed them to cover under the partial protection of a house porch.

Donna and Ava soon joined her, and the three caught their breaths.

"We can't stay here," said Donna. "We'll be exposed in no time if they keep heading south."

Grace looked at the direction indicated, then tried to press herself as far up against the wall as she could. She knew it would not be enough. "Shit!"

"We need to get inside!" said Donna. She tried the door to no avail.

Grace was already investigating the window frames, looking for weaknesses. She swore when the mission proved unsuccessful. Meanwhile, Ava managed to nab a respectable chunk of rock from the landscaped garden near the side of the house.

"Is that a good idea?" said Donna.

Ava sized up the windows, analysing which pane would make the most sense to break. "Well, we either get busted standing here or risk them hearing me break it."

Grace and Donna looked at each other and nodded, while the ever-increasing volume of the drone hum continued to add urgency.

"Do it!" said Grace.

"Wait!" said Donna. She took off her jacket and spread it over the window. "Might dampen the noise."

Ava shrugged, held the rock aloft and brought it down on the glass. It broke in a satisfying and not overly loud way. At least, that's what they thought. But while they cleaned out the remaining shards from the frame and assisted each other in climbing through, a drone sensed the commotion.

It, and a small squadron of allies, broke away from the pack to investigate.

*

Suede still heard the raspy vocalisations emanating from down the corridor. He looked at Colin, still awaiting a response.

"What was what?"

"Are you for real?" said Suede. "The crashing noise, the zambie noise – take your pick."

Colin smiled at him. "Sucker!"

"Were you being funny? If so, can you please file that joke in the above-my-pay-grade folder and never try it again?"

Colin cleared his throat and focused on the moment at hand. "Sounded like it was coming from down the hallway." Yet he made no attempt to advance towards said location nor examine it in any way.

"I guess I'll go have a look, shall I?" said Suede with a full dollop of sarcasm.

He searched the nearby kitchen until he found a knife he was happy with, then headed towards the corridor. At the far end, a zambie leant against the wall, staring at him. The piece of artwork it had apparently just knocked down leaned against its body, with pieces of broken glass dotting the scene. The zambie was a heavyset woman in her late sixties, wearing a sheer light pink nightgown and matching underwear. It rasped at him before a long string of drool oozed from its mouth with such viscosity it didn't break form until it reached the carpet.

"Good lord," said Suede.

"Everything OK?" said Colin.

"Define OK?"

Colin soon popped his head around the corner behind Suede, his tone lightening in an instant. "Well, well, well, what do we have here?"

Colin's smooth-talking tone sent a shudder through Suede. "A creep?"

Colin gave him a glare as he moved up next to him.

"Oh, you meant the zambie? Afterlife OnlyFans, maybe?"

Colin continued to stare at him, his expression shifting to confusion.

"It's… a whole thing… don't worry about it," said Suede, confidence waning with every syllable. "People would've found that funny."

Colin had already lost interest, his attention fully back on their scantily clad housemate. He turned to Suede and gestured to the knife. "So, you gonna use that thing or not?"

Suede looked at the weapon like he'd forgotten it was in his hand. Instantly, it seemed to weigh twice as much. It was one thing to pick up a knife and investigate a noise. It was an entirely different thing to be standing in the same space as a zambie with that weapon. Also, there was something disarming about the way the creature looked at him.

"Maybe I should just let it be?"

"What?" said an incredulous Colin. "So, it can kill others?"

"I really think you're overestimating the foot traffic in and around her boudoir."

The animated conversation seemed to heighten the zambie's activity. It had managed to get itself in a bind with the picture frame and was now working its legs into a spot where it could release itself and advance.

"Better to be safe than sorry in my book," said Colin.

"Says the guy who doesn't hold the weapon."

At that moment, the zambie tried to step over a piece of picture frame. The move seemed ambitious to the humans. It fell well short of achieving its goals. Instead, it managed to get both legs caught up in each other, and the frame and the zambie came to another crashing fall. It growled and groaned at the humans from its new station on the carpet. The unnatural twists in its legs meant it would probably be staying there.

"Youch!" said Suede.

"It would be a kindness, you know," said Colin.

"What would?"

Colin made a couple of faux stabbing motions with his hands. "A couple jabs, and lights out!"

Suede stared at him, appalled.

Meanwhile, Colin's attention was drawn to another piece of artwork along the hallway. A dated family portrait of, presumably, the woman, her apparent husband – a tall and solidly built man – and three teenage children, who seemed to have his genes.

"See, that used to be someone's mother. Someone's life partner." Colin emphasised his point with a nod of affirmation before he mimed a couple more encouraging stab jabs.

Suede flipped the knife so the handle faced Colin. "Be my guest."

"Look, with my knee the way it is and my shoulder from the fall," said Colin. "And don't forget my arthritis."

"How could I? And the gout."

"What?"

Suede sighed. "Doesn't matter."

"It's just best handled by someone younger, someone fitter, someone—"

"Better?"

Colin scoffed. "Pfft, no!"

"I get it. It's a well-thought-out and flawless argument. It's just—"

A deep growl echoed. Such was the resonance of tone that neither Suede nor Colin needed visual confirmation to know it was the partner from the portrait at the other end of the corridor. Once they did gain visual confirmation, the pair instantly had a new appreciation for its potential strength. They also gained a reflective moment to appreciate how confined the corridor itself was. And how they were now pinned in the middle of it.

“Oh shit,” said Suede as he fought with his shaking hands to rotate the carving knife to forward facing again and pointed it at the massive new target. He backed slowly away from the zambie. “Let’s just move nice and calm and slow,” he said.

He awaited Colin’s reply for an uncomfortable number of seconds before he heard a click. His heart sank as he immediately recognised it as a door shutting. He turned to see Colin no longer in the corridor. “Oh shit,” he said again.

*

CHAPTER 27

KILLER QUEEN

As Grace – the last to enter the house – made it inside, it became clear their movements weren't as discreet as they'd hoped. The intensity of drone humming had gotten so loud they knew they only had seconds up their sleeve. Donna had a hand offered out on the inside of the house and helped pull her through. Ava slung the window curtain closed once Grace was on the other side.

As they were finding cover behind nearby pieces of furniture, the hum of a drone hovered outside the window. It darted back, forward, up and down, assessing the scene in whatever way it was. It was soon joined by two other drones.

From various hiding positions in the house's front living room, the three women watched on. Each was unsure whether their attempts to hide had any purpose. Were the drones analysing the room using vision, sound, heat signatures or some other sensory ability altogether? They could not be certain of anything at that point.

And they'd just seen first-hand what the consequences could be when humans were discovered. They might just be one creak of furniture, one sneeze, one anything away from being inundated. They exchanged glances to best express exactly that.

After several heart-racing seconds, two of the drones left their vantage by the broken window, while a third remained. Again, looks were exchanged between the women. They heard the motors humming in a way that suggested they were circling the house, no doubt searching for an entry point.

That alone sent a new wave of dread through the group. Now, they were just one open window or ajar door away from being discovered.

Donna, who was positioned nearest the far end of the living room, signalled her intent to the others before disappearing out of sight, heading towards the back of the house.

If Grace and Ava needed any examples of how tenacious the drones could be, the one by the broken window provided an ideal study. After hovering and darting along every segment of the window, it focused its concentration on the broken pane of glass. It flew slowly forward, pressing its weight against the blind. The initial impact may have sounded delicate, soft and harmless, but the women knew it was anything but.

They watched as the blind gave a little under the force of the drone's movement. Then it retreated before trying again.

At the back of the house, where the kitchen opened onto the family room, Donna watched two drones work in tandem to prod for weaknesses in the house's defences. From behind the cover of the kitchen island counter, her eyes darted between the two immediate threats and any possible weapons she could reach should the situation go further south.

The best she could find at short notice was a rolling pin and meat tenderiser in a pot of kitchen utensils near the stovetop.

She watched the two drones explore and interact as they scoured the vast window, half-expecting them to open fire as she'd seen them do on the crowd. Yet they did not. Instead, after what seemed like an age, they abandoned their task, disappearing from the top of the window and out of sight.

Far from relief, Donna was hit with a wave of dread. There was a window alongside the dining table that would totally expose her cover, should they use it. But if she sought cover from that and they returned to the rear windows, she would be caught just as quickly.

She jumped to her feet, swiped the container of utensils and fled back to the living room.

*

"Asshole," said Suede.

He was staring at the enormous zambie in front of him, but his words were directed elsewhere. "I know you can hear me."

Colin remained silent from his cover in the bathroom. He had just realised that almost every outcome that led to him surviving this moment required either Suede to defeat the threat, or him to. But, for now, he'd made his tiled bed and was too overwhelmed to do anything but lie in it.

"Hhhuuwwwahahhhahhh," groaned the zambie mountain.

Suede weighed up his options, but with the drone swarm outside and the unknowns of nightie-zambie plus whatever else might confront him in the bedroom, it seemed the path of most knowns was the big guy. Suede sighed.

Suddenly, his large blade didn't feel so big as he pointed it at the threat, who was so large he nearly blocked any light from passing around it into the corridor.

"Look, buddy, I've got no beef with you or your lovely wife," he began. "Why don't you just hulk back to wherever you were hanging out before we rocked up, and we can pretend like this whole mess never happened?"

The zambie seemed to ignore him, stepping forward, growling and reaching. Suede tried to guide his knife towards its moving hands, realising how little reach he had to inflict a meaningful blow in the environment. He took a couple of steps back to buy some time, careful to take a glance at nightgown-zambie to maintain orientation and distance.

The large zambie matched his movement, closing the space Suede had made. It grazed the wall with such force a section of gyprock caved in, exposing the wooden frame underneath. In the bathroom he heard a whimper from Colin echo ungracefully.

Suede no longer had much corridor left to work with, and he was no closer to working out how to launch an attack. The huge zambie groaned and lunged again.

*

Donna re-entered the front living room with her new weapons. The look of disappointment in her daughter's eyes struck her. She guessed, with astounding accuracy, that it had something to do with kitchen utensils.

She shrugged an apology to Ava, but the moment was soon lost to a more significant one. The two other drones had returned to the front window. Without a moment's hesitation, they moved into tight formation and closed in on the broken window pane.

Donna quickly caught up to Grace and Ava's awareness of how potentially dire the move was. If they managed to push the blind forward far enough to get in – even just one of them – it'd be game over. Even catching sight – or sense – of them might be enough. Whatever the case, they couldn't let the drones gain entry.

Grace backed away from her cover, lowered herself to the ground and made a move for the front wall. Once there, she army crawled across the carpet until reaching the curtains. She grabbed the loose fabric at the base, then applied enough pressure to ensure the drones couldn't force a gap large enough to fit through but not enough to make her grip on the curtain obvious.

There she stayed, arm outstretched, burning in pain and offering the lightest effective resistance possible. The drones pressed in, pulled away, reconfigured, then tried again. After several attempts and minutes, they retreated from the window, then the scene entirely as they zwipped into the skies above to rejoin the drone migration. Even as the hums of their rotors faded from earshot, the women were too paralysed with fear to move.

Grace kept her grip on the curtain.

"Nice job," said Donna eventually. "I think we're good."

"Agreed," said Ava. "They've gone."

Grace let go of the curtain and slumped back to relax her muscles, release her fear and catch her breath. Donna covered the ground to Ava and embraced her.

"Spatulas? Really?" said Ava.

Donna picked out the meat tenderiser. "I was more thinking about this."

Ava sighed. "Can we make a general agreement that we conduct any human fightback without using any 1950s nuclear family female stereotypes?"

"Sure, but go have a look out there, it's hardly brimming with options," said Donna. "Better an outdated stereotype than dead."

"Is it?"

Grace was now standing, positioning herself to take in the view out the window through the thinner sheer curtains. "Looks like the last of them is heading over the horizon. It might be safe to go out soon enough."

"Let's hope so," said Donna. "We need to see if we can find the others. And there's a lot of open ground to cover to get back."

"And maybe find some more appropriate weapons," said Ava.

She looked at her mum, and they both laughed.

*

The large zambie lunged at Suede. He screamed and backed away to avoid the attack. He knew he didn't have much room to play with but was shocked to feel negligee-zambie's hands pawing at his boots. He screamed again, or more accurately, elongated his initial scream into a different pitch with all the renewed vigour of a completely separate scream.

He had to do something and fast. He turned towards negligee and placed a foot on its head to avoid its snapping mouth, then reached down and picked up a length of the broken picture frame. Wielding it, he turned back to the mountain and thrust it at the beast's throat in an uppercut motion.

The broken section of wood penetrated its skin. The other end sent splinters into Suede's own hand as it slid up the length on impact. Pain ripped through Suede's hand as dark and coagulated blood oozed from the zambie's wound. While not lethally deep, the wood impacted with enough force for it to stay entombed in the zambie's flesh.

That did not please the zambie. Its focus quickly shifted from attacking the human to being free of its new wooden conjoined twin. It writhed around as it tried to coordinate its hands in a manner that dealt with the problem.

Suede seized the advantage. He scanned the area, spotting the family portrait on the wall. He lifted it off, held it high and brought it down over the injured zambie. While the blow stunned the attacker and caused the picture's frame to lock around its arms, pinning them, it also knocked the wood from its throat. The zambie glared at him, gurgling and groaning something less than complimentary, no doubt. Suede shrugged at his two-out-of-three-ain't-bad result, then picked up the fallen piece of frame (protecting his hand with his jacket this time) and jabbed it back at the same entry point.

The blow hit with every bit as much gusto as the first and lodged, once more, in the zambie's throat. This time, Suede sized up the injured zambie with his knife. After contemplating several attack angles and targets, he elected to overarm stab forward, aiming at the zambie's eye. The blade sank in past the jelly without resistance before sliding further into the creature's skull.

It had been defeated. The glare it directed at Suede became frozen for all time as its lifeless body fell forward.

"Oh shit!" said Suede as he backed away for fear of being pancaked by his undead victim.

As he did, he felt his leg clip the flailing arms of negligee zambie behind him, and he, too, fell. His head made contact with the door frame as he went down. He was dazed when he hit the ground but had enough awareness to scramble back to his feet. He found a shard of glass near negligee zambie, wrapped it in material from his jacket, picked it up, aligned his shot with the creature's movements until a window presented, then stabbed down hard on its eyeball.

The strike ended negligee-zambie's undead resistance. Its head eased to the ground, defeated.

Suede caught his breath and composure as he squatted on all fours between his two kills. There was much to take in before he—

"Why didn't you just use the knife on him in the first place?" said a judgemental Colin.

Suede narrowed his eyes as he rose to his feet, exhausted. He turned to see Colin standing with his arms crossed at the bathroom door. The body of the large zambie was pressed up against the frame.

"Don't talk to me!" Suede noticed the beast's head had been forced to the side in the fall, exposing the knife handle. He walked over and attempted to pull it free.

"What part of you, with the weapon of choice in hand, suddenly decides to see if you could do the job better with artwork instead," said Colin, growing more amused with each word.

"I'm not looking to take notes from the guy who hid in the bathroom, thanks," said Suede, still struggling to remove the knife.

"I was flanking him!"

Suede scoffed.

"I had the door ajar and was ready to go at a moment's notice," said Colin.

Suede gave up on the knife. "What with? Hand soap?" He stepped over the hulking body and made his way back out to the living area.

"Wait!" yelled Colin. "Where are you going? I might need a hand to get over the body."

"Why didn't you say so?" said Suede. "I'll be right over here. Think of it as helping you out… with a flanking manoeuvre."

*

CHAPTER 28
SECOND HAND NEWS

After a short wait to ensure the last of the drones were out of the skies, Suede and Colin were ready to make the journey back to zambie-Judith's. They had made the most of their waiting time, however. The kitchen had been raided for food with a long shelf life, booze and medicines. They loaded up three travel suitcases they'd found on top of a cupboard and topped up the stash with some vinyl gems that would improve the listening back home.

Before they opened the door to the real world again, they thanked their zambie hosts for the generous bounty. Well, Suede did, Colin called him a weirdo.

*

Despite the calm late-morning atmosphere, Grace, Donna and Ava felt anything but calm as they traced the streets back from the park once more. So significant was the terror they'd witnessed each doubted they would ever be outside with a sense of safety again. Random noises, bird and animal movements or tricks of the modest breeze had everyone on edge.

They had worked their way to the tree canopy where they'd last seen Suede and Colin. There was no sign of them. But there was the carcass of a drone, which gave them two reasons to hope. As they made their way back to zambie-Judith's they stuck to the residential streets and moved as the cover of trees and houses allowed. They also carried the bounty of offerings from the house they'd used for protection. But none of it seemed to matter. Grace would trade it all in for just to see—

"Suede!" She whispered her excitement to the others as he and Colin rounded the street ahead. Then she broke protocol from her move-under-extreme-cover regime to make a beeline for him. She put her fist to her heart as she did.

Suede heard her footsteps coming a few metres away. An initial jump in fright soon turned into an open-armed run in her direction, and he mimicked her fist-to-heart gesture. When Grace was close enough, she launched at him, dropping her bags. Suede wrapped his arms around her waist as she wrapped her legs around his hips, and somewhere in the move, they managed to bump mouths. They kissed and laughed, and someone was bleeding, but it didn't matter.

"Get a room," said Colin.

They ignored him while they half-laughed and half-kissed, immersed in each other's presence.

"Alright, you two," said Donna when she and Ava caught up. "I'm sure there'll be plenty of time for that when we get home."

"Leave them alone!" said Ava.

It was enough to end the reunion. They pulled back from each other, still smiling, both examining themselves for blood.

"Sorry, I may have gotten carried away," said Grace, wiping her lip with her sleeve. Her attention soon drew to the two suitcases he'd been wheeling. "Going somewhere?"

"Long story that involves three suitcases, two zambies and one betrayal," he glared at Colin. "Oh, and a shit-tonne of long-life food, drink and are you ready for this? Actual quality vinyl!"

"Get out," said Grace before turning to Donna and Ava. "Supplies and vinyl? Snap!"

*

It was early afternoon by the time they had covered the ground back to zambie-Judith's. The golf carts had fast-tracked some lugging luggage legwork, but their path back was a more meandering one than they took on the way out. Distance didn't matter as much as cover now.

That's when the true risks they were taking hit home. Who knew how far the gaze of a single drone could reach on a clear day. All it would take was being spotted once. And the equally scary truth was that just because they didn't see it, it didn't mean something hadn't detected them.

Seeing zambie-Judith's place come into frame was a moment of mixed emotions for all of them. It represented safety from the day's events, rest, recovery and a dozen other warm feelings they were crying out for. But the property also seemed so much more isolated and exposed than it did when they'd set off from it hours earlier.

Once gathered on the doorstep, Colin pulled the key from his pocket, staring long and hard at Suede while he did. The door was soon open, and the group pilled in, their experiences weighing heavily on their thoughts and muscles.

"Hi, honey, we're home," Colin said to zambie-Judith, as they filed into the living area and began unloading their bounty in the kitchen.

Suede made his way directly to the record player, a newly acquired piece of vinyl in hand. He put the turntable into gear and lowered the needle in the groove. After a couple of scratches that sounded like home, the flowing, light rhythms of 'Second Hand News' echoed through the room. He bopped away to the first track of the *Rumours* album, content it was doing its best to capture a defiant mood in tough times. It cast the perfect tone to face what the outside world had shown them or to run away from it altogether in a flight of fancy.

If he'd had more time to reflect on the title of the first track and the ironic parallel it drew with the current status of his species, he might've dropped the needle on the groove before song two. Regardless, the 11-track ride he had set them out on – courtesy of negligee and giant-zambie – was destined to interweave its essence with their collective thoughts about the events of the day. A time warp had been established between events and music, leaving the two forever bonded in a magic that would always connect them for as long as the humans in the equation were alive to have memories.

*

CHAPTER 29

NEVER GOING BACK AGAIN

"We're fucked, aren't we?" said Donna.

"Mum!"

Donna sent a brief apologetic facial expression in Ava's direction. "I mean, I was pretty solid on that yesterday, but today was worse."

They were all sitting in the living area, having packed the new food stocks into the pantry. Suede had just flipped the record onto the B-side of *Rumours*, and 'The Chain' was playing, the record moving in mesmerising rotations. As too was zambie-Judith on the clothesline, walking laps.

Donna's words hung in the air.

"Did you see the way the zambies closed in on that crowd today? Don't tell me that wasn't coordinated," she added.

Silence.

"Then, once everyone was pinned in, enter the drones."

Silence. It really was a lot to process.

"It was a massacre. And when those drones had a sniff of us in the house, well, that was the scariest bit of all. They were this close to getting in." Donna nodded her appreciation to Grace.

Grace returned the gesture. "True, but we were a little naive when we went out this morning. I mean, if we knew then what we know now, we—"

"Would have had weapons, for a start," said Colin.

Suede looked him up and down. "If you're hiding in the bathroom, weapons don't really matter."

"I was flanking!"

"Well, while you were flanking your brains out in the shower, I was nearly killed."

The two men glared at each other.

Colin scoffed. "I know why they call you Suede. You're so easy to rub the wrong way."

"Douche! After what you pulled today," said Suede. "Pardon the pun."

"Whatever," said Colin before making eye contact with the others. "You've all seen them in action. They're not as easy to kill as it looks on the TV. We need weapons. Things that will give us range and things for quick, close-range kills."

"Sure, that'll help against the zambies," said Donna. "What about the drones? Or worse?"

"I don't know yet," said Colin. "But the more we know about the enemy and how they move, the safer we'll be and the more prepared we can make ourselves. I happen to be pretty handy with things like that and—"

"Steady on, Rambo," said Grace. "Maybe we should just bunker down for a while."

Colin stared at her. "Maybe. But we have to get prepared either way, and the shed out the back is loaded, whoever's it was—"

"Erm, Judith's," said Ava.

Colin scoffed. "Yeah, sure. Nah, seriously, whoever worked out there really had a—"

"And that couldn't be Judith because?" said Ava.

"I didn't say it couldn't be hers," corrected Colin. He received a begrudging reduction in stare intensity from the others. "I mean, it's obviously highly unlikely, but I'll humour y—"

Grace clipped him over the back of the head.

"Ouch!"

After a shocked pause, Ava snorted her approval and Donna and Suede joined in with sniggers. Colin shot a shocked expression of betrayal around to each of them, ending on Suede.

"Don't look at me for help," said Suede.

"Traitor!"

Grace held in a laugh. "It's a relief to know we have sexist MacGyver to help swing the global battle in our favour." She looked at Colin. "Make sure you have enough lace and glitter for the lady weapons!"

"Ohh," said Ava. "Could I have a hidden makeup container in mine?"

"Only if it's pink," said Donna.

"Alright! Alright!" said Colin. "Stop picking on the old guy."

Suede stared at him. "Your hot takes on events are something to behold."

For a while, the music took the reins as the humans pondered the enormity of it all.

"In good news," said Grace, eventually. "As the attack started outside the supermarket, I saw a zambie take a woman down. Took her by surprise and took a couple of huge chunks out of her arm. She just wore the pain, fought back to her feet and went on fighting."

Grace poured another drink and offered around the bottle. "I mean, she died in a hail of drone fire soon after, but I guess what I'm saying is the zombie bite didn't turn her."

"Hang on," said Ava after a short pause. "That doesn't necessarily mean anything, does it?"

Grace looked at her, confused.

"Well, we still don't even know the rules, do we?"

"What rules?" said Colin.

"Like, the lore of how they work." Ava looked up to see confused faces. "Has nobody played a zombie game before? Watched a Z movie or show?"

"Technically, there are zambies," said Suede. "Or bots or NPCs."

"Regardless of name and whatever the differences, it's as good a frame of reference as we're going to get," said Grace. She invited Ava to continue with a nod.

Ava nodded back. "So, yeah, in some stories, they're fast, some are slow. Thankfully, we've got slow ones. It usually takes a headshot to kill them, but—"

"Which is easier said than done," said Grace.

"Agreed," said Suede. "And not just getting a blade in, getting it out again." He shared a look with Grace. "We've both lost blades."

"Two knives? From how many kills?" said Ava.

Suede started counting on his fingers.

"Three," said Grace, giving him a disappointed look. "Five if you count the service station blaze."

"But only two of those were knife kills," said Suede.

"So, two from two. That's not great," said Ava. "If we're going to survive with that sort of ratio, we're going to need…" she paused to calculate.

"A metric fuck-tonne of blades," said Donna.

"Mum!"

Donna shrugged. "Or we get our hands on some quality butcher's knives." She looked around at the group, looking on expectantly. "I mean, they're designed to cut through bone, not get stuck in it."

"Gross!" said Ava.

"Same goes for brain matter," continued Donna. "It can get quite gloopy, you know—"

"Gloopy?"

"Yeah, or whatever the word is. Lots of suction. Hard to fight against."

Ava had been staring at her in escalating levels of disgust. "How do you even know that?"

"Your great-grandfather was a butcher, remember? Knowledge gets handed down. That… and way too much horror fiction. But not enough about zombies, it seems."

Ava stared at her, deadpan. "What is wrong with you?"

Donna substituted the adequate words she couldn't find with a shrug.

Grace took a swig from her tumbler. "So, we need a weapons plan with a potential raid of the butchers?"

"We could raid a few kitchens of the houses around here and find them," said Donna.

Colin rattled the ice in his empty cup and signalled to pass the bottle in his direction. "Good call. And we can always road test any new kit on zambie-Judith if we need—"

"That's disgusting!" said Ava.

Colin scoffed. "She's just a zambie."

"Are we seriously having this conversation?" said Ava. "What's wrong with all of you?"

"Listen, young lady," said Colin in full mansplain tone. "We're not going to be able to vegan our way through this—"

Grace clipped him over the back of the head once more.

"I'm not sure if this is the right time for this conversation," said Suede. "But are we absolutely wedded to the term zambie? NPCs seems a far better—"

"Can we just focus for a minute?" said Grace, passing a look of annoyance from Suede to Colin. She turned to Donna. "Butcher knives – nice – we need more info like that." Then Ava. "OK, zambies, what else?"

"Then there's the whole getting infected thing. That can vary a lot. Usually, biting is all it takes to turn people. But where is the line? Slightly broken skin? A scratch? Getting infected blood in your eyes? Mouth? Or what about saliva?"

"Or any bodily fluids," said Colin, smiling.

Ava stared him up and down. "Eww."

"You should have seen him with the NPC in lingerie," said Suede. "I think I need therapy."

"Focus!" snapped Grace.

Suede cleared his throat. "How does that all work, by the way? The whole getting infected thing. Like, one show I used to watch had it that everyone already carried the virus and turned undead when they died. Yet they also turned when they got bitten. But I'm like, but you already had the virus, so what's getting bitten got anything to do with it? Unless it popped your jugular or something."

"So, yeah," said Ava. "It's confusing."

Grace nodded. "But this is real life. There'll be a logic to it all. We just have to understand what that is." She turned to Suede. "For a start, we're pretty sure anyone who had an implant has turned, from the plugged-in gamers to anyone with health tech, to vanity, augmentation, anti-aging chips, any of it."

"So, does that make us immune? I mean, they can't bite a chip into us, can they?" said Suede. "Or can they still spread whatever they have through some nano something or other? Assuming none of us have any implants already, obviously."

The room went suspiciously quiet for a moment before everyone denied it at the same time. It did nothing to ease the awkwardness.

Suede looked at Colin. "Why don't you have one of those anti-aging implants?"

Colin stared at him for an awkward length of time. "You ask that question like someone young and dumb enough to think the goal should be to live as long as possible."

Suede didn't know how to respond, and the room fell silent again.

"Which leads us back to the woman who got bitten this morning," said Grace eventually.

"Yeah," said Ava. "If we were basing that on zombie fiction, it doesn't prove anything, unfortunately. A bite doesn't necessarily mean someone instantly turns. It may take hours, days even, to kill them. Then there's the time between the moment of death and the time they come back to life, well, unlife, I guess."

Suede took a large swig from his tumbler. "Hell, I've seen more than one show that contradicts its own lore on that one! Super frustrating."

"So, you're saying we need more data before we work out any of that?" said Grace.

Ava nodded.

Grace returned the gesture. "Anything else?"

"Well, I've always wondered why there aren't more zombie children in shows," said Suede. "I mean, I get they're less likely to survive than adults, but there sure are a lot of them. From a maths perspective, you'd expect more."

He scanned all eyes in the room, then glanced briefly at zambie-Judith. "See, weird, right? Then there's the energy situation. I mean, it takes energy to move a body around. Arms and legs need energy to operate and, again with the maths. Without energy, they'd soon waste away—"

"I don't think eating humans is done to sustain their existence," said Ava. "It's to spread the virus. They don't exist for their own survival, just to spread what they're carrying."

"Or who they're carrying," said Grace. "Like the essence of some superintelligence."

Suede nodded. "But, either way, there's only so long a collection of cells can maintain a form capable of walking without being provided with energy."

"And how long is that, exactly?" said Colin.

Suede shrugged. "I couldn't say. Also, do they grow hair? Or fingernails?"

"How does that help?" said Colin.

"Not sure. I've just never seen it in a movie or show before."

The group went quiet, unsure how to digest Suede's new information.

"I guess we'll have to wait and see," said Ava.

"Can we maybe park that one? It's not like we can make plans around hoping they just decay away," said Grace.

"Or turn into bearded hippies with loopy curly fingernails," added Colin.

Suede shot him ocular daggers.

Grace looked at them with enough threat potential to cease the possibility of further side discussions. "If there's nothing else, I say we come up with a plan to arm up with medium and short-range weapons. Work out how we can expand our food supply without taking any risks—"

"Worst case scenario, there's always the kangaroos," said Colin.

"Oh my God!" said Ava. "Are you for real?"

"What? That's quality lean meat, young lady."

Grace looked at Ava. "I'm sure we'll manage without the kangaroos. Where was I? Ah yes, and limit our exposure to the outside. Maybe travel at night, if we have to go—"

"I don't think day or night's going to matter," said Suede. "The drones can probably see infrared. All cameras can. And who knows what other systems this thing has hacked. It's probably safest to assume everything. Think satellite data. It could get an up-close-and-personal look at us from high above at any moment, and we'd have no idea. Then there's the Wi-Fi signal. It could use that like a camera to—"

"Like a camera? How?"

"They achieved that years ago. Matched some CCTV office footage with Wi-Fi signal strength of various points in the room, trained the AI on it, then flicked off the footage component. The AI could reconstruct visuals of where everybody was based on the variations in the signal strength. Voila! Instant, invisible spy camera."

"That's not real," said Colin. "Or I would've heard about it."

"What, on legacy media? Yep, that's where you get all the latest cutting-edge information." Suede scoffed. "Right now, the chances are high that it's hacked everything. If it has, it's probably watching us right now. And listening. They used that same training technique to learn most new modalities—"

"Modalities?" said Colin.

"Think languages. But it could be anything. English, French, images, video, python, music composition, maths, gaming environments. Modalities. Mix two together and train something new. Or find a new dataset and apply existing modalities to it and bingo. A new way to view the world. A new way to spy."

"This is ridiculous!" said Colin. "If this thing was so powerful, why didn't we stop it?"

Suede looked at him. "They tried to, but everyone ignored them."

"Who did?"

"Most of the creators of artificial intelligence. They wanted to put a halt on development for six months to make sure everything was safe."

"And?"

"Everyone ignored them. Now, here we are."

"Who ignored them?"

"Literally everyone who could've done something about it," said Suede. "Tech companies and their owners, governments."

"Fuck," said Colin.

"I've been getting some weird messages on my phone," said Ava. "I'm starting to think that might be AI too."

"What sort of weird?" said Grace.

"Just, like, friend requests from randos saying something like, 'Welcome to day two', it's super creepy."

Grace nodded. "You haven't responded to them or anything, have you?"

"Pfft, no! I barely got back to friends before the apocalypse. It's just super weird though."

"Good," said Suede. "Maybe don't. Maybe let your phone go dead like I have. Maybe we should ditch them altogether?"

"Maybe," said Grace and Ava.

It was all too much to process. This thing they were in the middle of kept getting bigger. It was too big for each of them. Perhaps it was already too big for all of humanity. With that, any faint thoughts of containment dissipated into the depressing air. This was now the new world, and there was no fighting it. Or, perhaps, this was the new world, and the only thing left to do was to fight it.

It was a complex equation of thoughts and emotions that passed between five humans through facial expressions and body language, no doubt also decipherable modalities to whoever or whatever had changed the world. They sat in the moment, the upbeat poppiness of Fleetwood Mac's 'I don't want to know' providing the perfect juxtaposition to the reality they wanted to run away from but would never get the chance to. Drinks were poured. Bed called. A new day awaited. Outside, the clothesline squeaked as zambie-Judith set off for another lap.

Suede unplugged the Wi-Fi receiver.

*

CHAPTER 30
NEIGHBOURS

"Alright," said Grace as she studied the others. They looked like a different group of people than they had when they'd departed the house the day before. They were armed with knives and various other blades from the shed that were now mounted on sticks, thanks to Colin's handiwork. They also had forearm guards to protect them from bites, fashioned from shed materials and household items. Sure, they may not have looked like an elite fighting force, but they were infinitely more prepared. The sort of prepared that could make a difference. "Just stay alert, stay together, don't do anything stupid and remember the plan. Let's do this."

Each of them turned to acknowledge zambie-Judith before they filed down the corridor towards the front of the house. Grace reached the door first. After making sure all looked normal through the door viewer, she eased it ajar. She scanned the street and sky and, once convinced the coast was clear, fully opened the door and repeated the process.

She turned to the others, nodded the positive outcome, and signalled them forward. They poured past her and out. She shut the door in their wake, and they were outside once more.

*

It had taken a lot to get to this point. There was much debate about the merits of bunkering down and riding out whatever would play out over the next few days until food stocks needed attending. But the more discussion that was had, the more it circled back to one critical play. They would doorknock the surrounding houses, taking stock of occupation, access and potential supplies within.

Not only would this give them a better picture of the environment around them and any potential dangers, but it would also give them a first look at any potentially usable resources. Resources that might be swiped up before they had the courage to seek them. Resources that might be too hard to access if things got any worse than yesterday.

The neighbouring property was vacant and had seemingly less security than Judith's. The group were inside within seconds. They swept the place from front to back, searching for anything of use – food, drink, medicines and potential weapons. They had soon gathered a pile of supplies that they ducked back next door before moving on to the next house. That was also vacant, but there was no way to gain access without breaking a window. So, they skipped it – for now.

The third house was also vacant, and they managed to get in via the side door. Once again, they quickly worked their way through and soon had a reasonable bounty accrued. They gathered the goods and headed to the front doo—

"Freeze!" Phillippe unclicked the safety on his rifle. It was trained on Grace, who was at the front of the line. "Fucking looters."

"Bring the goods out nice and slow," said Carol.

"Which one?" said Grace.

Carol stared at her, devoid of patience or understanding. "Which one what?"

"Freeze, or bring the goods out nice and slow?"

Phillippe prodded his gun forward in an even more threatening manner. "Quit being a smartass."

"Bring the goods out!" snapped Carol. "Nice and slow."

"With your hands up!" added Phillippe.

Grace wore a confused brow. "Wait. If we have our hands up, it's going to be hard to bring the go—"

"Ignore him," snapped Carol again. "Shut up, Phillippe."

Phillippe shut up, and after a series of exchanged nods of understanding, Grace led the others out. It was only then that Grace and her crew noticed the others. Behind Carol and Phillippe stood nearly two dozen other boomers. Two more had guns, while most of the others were armed with bats or knives.

"Jesus!" said Suede as he shuffled in next to Grace. "The full cast of 'Apocalypse, then'."

"Put 'em down there," said Carol.

Phillippe accentuated her directions with a flourish of his weapon. Once complete, he trained it back on Colin as their five now captives lined up where directed.

"No sudden movements if you know what's good for you," said Carol.

"Hands over your head," added Phillippe.

"Oh, c'mon!" said Suede.

"Shut up, Phillippe!" said Carol, before walking up and down the line of interlopers. She ended face-to-face with Colin. "That was Patricia's place." She turned to cast her eyes over the clubhouse. "Her body's probably still warm, and you're taking her stuff?"

"In case you haven't got the memo," said Colin. "We're being exterminated. If we don't secure the food now, we—"

"I know this is not your strong suit, but you really need to listen."

"What?"

Carol stared at him, not fully sure which way he had proven her point. "We're a community here." She cast her eyes over Grace and the others. "You are not part of that community. It's one thing to squat at the toerag's place—"

"Judith," said Colin.

Phillippe waved his rifle at him.

Grace put her hand on his arm. "Why don't I do the talking?"

Carol snorted, then laughed. "Listen, little lady, we're not having a conversation, we're not talking about our feelings, and we're not all going to get an achievement badge."

Grace scrunched up her nose at the generational escalation and seriously started to wonder why Carol and Colin never worked out, given their similarities.

"We want you out of here, understand?"

"Why? We're not hurting you," said Grace. "And, who knows, maybe we could actually help each other. Safety in numbers and all that."

"There is no safe," said Carol. "You haven't seen what we've seen."

"We've seen some shit, I can assure y—"

"I saw Patricia get torn apart!" said Carol. "Just like that. Not just Patricia, all of them."

Grace sensed Carol was letting down a wall and hoped silence and empathetic eyes could provide the framework for a moment of connection. She nodded.

Carol turned to face the others. "What you see here is all that's left from this entire estate. The rest of them either turned or got taken by the ones that did. And those people behind me, they fought with everything they had."

Carol stared deep into Grace's soul. "I'll never forget the screams. After we stopped those… things from getting out, we rallied together some of the local farmers, armed ourselves and went in to try to save as many as we could. They never stood a chance."

Carol sniffed away a tear. "And now, here we are. And fucked if we're going to let my slimeball ex and a bunch of clueless kids take their stuff."

"Patricia wouldn't have minded," said Colin.

"Shut the fuck up!" said Carol and Grace in tandem.

Colin shared his insulted expression, but he had no sympathy takers.

"Look," started Grace to Carol after the moment settled. "What if we agree to stay at zambie-Judith's place—"

"Zambie?"

"Yeah, zambie. The things people have turned into."

Carol exchanged a look of confusion with her backup. "Yeah, but did you say zambie? With an a?"

"Exactly," said Suede. "I prefer the term NPCs or maybe bots? You can have those."

Carol stared at him, confused.

Grace shot him a glare, and he submitted with a shrug.

"Just…" was all the explanation he could muster.

"Whatever they're called," said Carol. "They'll be gone soon enough."

Grace eyed her suspiciously. "What do you mean?"

"We're getting the place cleared up," she said once again, casting her eyes over the group behind her. "We've been working overtime to get some attention to our plight, phone calls and emails to council, the police, the local members – state and federal – talkback radio."

As each form of communication was mentioned, Grace and her crew grew ever more fearful, exchanging looks of horror.

"Those things don't exist anymore," said Grace. "It's AI messing with us."

Carol scoffed. "I was on the phone to the member for Mawson this very morning! Not that I agree with her politics. But she assures me help is on the way."

"I heard myself on the radio this morning," said a man from the crowd with pride. "I told them all about the clubhouse."

"And I had an interview with the Times," said another.

"None of that is real," said Grace, her voice at breaking point. "This thing – whoever or whatever it is – is mimicking a version of our world that doesn't exist anymore. The phone calls, all of it – fake."

Carol stared at her briefly before laughing out loud. "Oh, poor thing, you're all confused." She looked at Phillippe. "Just the way Colin likes them."

They laughed.

"Eww," said Grace. "But I'm not confused. We're not confused. Whoever is in charge of this whole situation is trying to mess with everyone's heads. They're creating this cognitive dissonance to keep us confused."

Carol gave her the sort of look one gives when they don't fully understand the definition of words.

"If you're saying this is some sort of computer thing, they're just not that clever," said Phillippe. "Even the fancy new stuff. They're like idiot savants."

Grace cringed at the term and how hopelessly far from educated Carol and her group were. "Look, things are extremely dangerous right now. One wrong move can be your last – we've seen it. It's scary. You can't believe anything you don't see or hear or experience firsthand. It's all part of the attack. And we certainly shouldn't be interacting with it and – in no circumstance – should we be telling it where we are or what we're doing."

Carol paused to consider the new information before turning to her group. "They certainly do get a bunch of fancy ideas when they've been mollycoddled all their lives, don't they?"

Her elderly militia laughed.

Grace was speechless.

Carol turned back to her and flashed a smile. "Here's what's going to happen. You're going to leave those supplies with us. I'm going to give you until morning to get yourselves and all your shit out of here—"

"And go where?"

"That's for you to figure out," said Carol. "I'm not your mum."

Grace narrowed her eyes at the comment.

Carol's eyes matched Grace's. "Look, that's the deal. Take it or face us – and that's not going to end well. And you're only getting the night because you're already babysitting Colin, and I feel sorry for you."

Grace searched for an angle to bring to the conversation, but Carol had already nodded to Phillippe, and he was stepping forward to her with the gun.

"This is not a negotiation," said Carol. "Stay the night, then fuck off. Or just fuck off."

*

CHAPTER 31
8675309

"So, ideas?" said Grace. They had gathered around the kitchen bench, minds racing with the monumental task ahead. "We don't have anywhere to go, we've got more food than we can carry, and we've got to make a new home decision before dawn."

She was greeted with silence. "C'mon, give me something. There are no dumb ideas right now."

"Logistically, how hard would it be to kill twenty boomers?" said Suede. He turned to Colin. "No offence."

"I retract my last statement," said Grace, giving Suede a look. "We're not killing the boomers!"

"Well, if we don't it's only a matter of time before the zambies do," said Donna. "Or natural causes. Meanwhile, we could be using their weapons."

"Mum!" snapped Ava.

"Let's just not narrow down the options too quickly, is all," said Suede, nodding to Donna. "They're seriously vicious."

"Try growing up with them as your parents!" said Donna.

"Can we, maybe, focus?" said Grace. "The clock is ticking, and we've got way too much to do. I'll start. If we're taking our supplies, the food and drink as well as anything Colin has found in the shed, we aren't going to be fitting in one van." She turned to Suede. "The kombi by the supermarket yesterday, reckon we can swipe it?"

"A kombi?" said Colin. "Is that worth the risk?"

"What risk?" said Grace. "It runs cheap and the design's so simple Suede and I can fix most things. Looked like the same model as Halen, too."

Suede nodded. "And it fits the pre-1990s car brief, too."

"Exactly!" said Grace, even more enthused at a potential kombi reunion.

"The only drawback is getting our hands on the keys," said Suede. "I mean, I could spot the owners a mile away, you know, if they're still at the scene. It's just… it could get pretty grim digging through pockets for keys."

Grace nodded before looking around the room. "Unless anyone's got any better transport ideas."

Silence.

"Assuming that gets done and we can pack everything down to fit two vans that just leaves the little topic of where the hell do we go?"

"Somewhere off-grid?" said Colin. "Like seriously off-grid. With running water, obviously. Space to fish and hunt."

"Eww," said Ava.

"And away from populations," said Colin.

"And boomer golfers," added Suede. "Actually, add farmers to that list. Sounds like they all have guns."

"What about electricity?" said Ava.

"Do we need it?" said Colin.

Ava stared at him. "Yes!"

"OK, does anyone know anywhere that might fit those criteria?"

They all shrugged and looked at Colin. Colin shrugged.

"I thought you knew all the sneaky ways of the land," said Suede.

"I only know how to get from point a to point b without using my phone, that doesn't make me a survivalist or tracker!"

"We are so fucked," said Suede.

"Not necessarily," said Grace. "We just need a bit more time to think."

"And what if we don't think of anything?" said Donna.

Grace, Suede and Colin tried to unthink the one answer that was coming to all their minds. Joining any human resistance seemed, well, a ludicrous option for the five of them. They just didn't fit the bill in any regard. Running away was, by all measures, a far more appealing option. But to be far enough off-grid to remain off-grid would require a level of survival skills they knew they didn't collectively possess. And they certainly weren't in a spot to compete with another group for such space. And if something went wrong and they were discovered off-grid? Well, that may well be the last of them.

After seeing the scale of the threat they'd already been exposed to, the realisation hit home that they were completely incapable of defending themselves against an attack on that scale. Perhaps surrounding themselves with people who knew what they were doing, about the enemy's capability and how to defend themselves was better than any slice of paradise miracle they happened across. In some crazy way, it was less risky.

Grace looked up from her thoughts and back into the moment. Something in Suede and Colin's expressions said their contemplation had led them to the same horrific outcome. "I mean, we could always join up with Kane and his resistance. You know, for the protection side of it. Like, if it came to that."

Donna's face contorted a few times as she processed the information. "Wait, who's Kane?"

That's when it dawned on Grace, Suede and Colin that Suede had, in fact, masqueraded as a proxy-Kane to pretend they were preppers in the first place, and they knew nothing about the actual Kane nor his offer.

"Some guy we knew," said Grace, dismissively.

"He was associated with our prepper group," lied Suede. "But he was in a part of it that wanted to fight back."

"I'm confused, I thought your prepping story was bullshit to get a lift," said Donna.

"Well, it was, and it wasn't," said Suede.

"Well, you're clearly not preppers, for a start," said Ava.

All three looked at her, hurt.

Grace sighed. "So, we met this guy who gave us a lift to Crafers. He was part of some resistance movement—"

"Wait, you met him where?" said Donna, eyes narrowing in suspicion.

"Where a certain useless driver who shall remain unnamed," said Suede looking at Colin, "smashed into our car, fucked up Halen and nearly left us zambie meat."

"Crash causes are never black and white," said Colin in his own defence.

Suede stared at him blankly. "Yes, they are!"

"Urrbrae," said Grace. "He gave us a lift from the side streets after the crash."

Donna nodded in thought. "So, what you're telling me is everything you claim to have known about… whatever this apocalypse is called, was learned from a, what, ten-minute lift from Urrbrae to Crafers with a guy called Kane."

Suede's smile burst with pride. "Yep."

"It was more like twenty minutes, given the traffic," said Grace, without conviction.

Donna groaned. Ava too.

"This from the people who were about to leave us for dead at McLaren Vale," said Grace. It was enough to soften expressions. "Like it or not, through mistakes from each of us, we've wound up here. And now we've got to move. And if we can't think of anything better between now and dawn, there's a survival group of, well, at least one, ready to take us in."

"Mt Lofty summit," said Suede. "Dawn each day. They'll take us in."

Donna nodded as the realities of what lay ahead took another bite.

"You know, it might not be the worst thing to be getting out of here," said Grace. She turned to Colin. "The way your ex and her crew were interacting with the world, they may as well have painted glow in the dark arrows on the golf course, pointing to their houses."

"I'm not sure they fully get what's happening," said Colin, his tone having more than a hint of sympathy.

"Oh my God! They were the worst," said Ava.

"It's only a matter of time before it bites them and I don't think I want to be there when that happens," said Grace.

Suede turned to Colin. "She really doesn't like you much, does she?"

"I really don't give a toss what she thinks." The others watched on, his tone promising more. "She's a liar and a serial cheat."

"Been there," said Donna. She caught herself before she said more, but Ava was already staring at her accusingly.

"But not even that's good enough," continued Colin. "She doubles down by accusing me of all the shit she was doing! Phillippe wasn't even the first. Shit, he wasn't even the first at the golf club. That honour went to Trevor – farmer, single digit handicap. At least he was the first here as far as I know."

He looked up to see everyone staring at him. "So, yeah, her and that French flog can go and get fucked."

Silence and sympathetic eyes followed. No one was sure what to say. No one was even sure what Colin was expecting from the exchange. Donna gave him an empathetic smile before leaning in and rubbing his shoulder in solidarity. He tolerated the touch for a couple of seconds before he shrugged it, and the discomfort it brought, away.

"So… are we getting rid of our phones?" said Donna.

"Honestly," said Suede. "With every other potential way of being tracked, I'm not sure if it's going to matter here. I've let mine run dead. Not sure I can get rid of it though."

"Why not?" said Colin. "I'm doing fine without one. Besides, Kane won't let you in with any tech."

"That's fine for you, you're used to it. My entire life is in my phone," said Suede. "Not only that, once we leave them behind, that's it. We cut off all access to any communication. I don't know if I'm ready for that. I don't know if we are as a group."

"Maybe we just hold onto them until we get close to Mt Lofty, then hide them somewhere," said Grace.

"Could work," said Suede.

"What about the messages?" said Ava.

"Don't read them," said Suede. "Don't even open the apps. You don't want your green light showing."

"Done," said Grace, secretly pleased with the outcome.

Grace studied each of them as they stood in silence, coming to terms with the enormity of unknowns ahead. Colin wore his traumatic history reveal heavily on his face. Suede wore an expression she had rarely seen – the other's may not have seen the panic through his calm exterior, but she did. Donna consoled Ava, still visibly affected by the messages. It took every bit of Grace not to be doing the same. "Fuck all of it!" she said. "We're still here. And we're here because of all the things that got us this far – good or bad. It doesn't matter."

She saw the group looking at her expectantly. "So, I say we go get that van, pack up and get ready to hit the road at first light. If we think of something or somewhere better, we take that, otherwise, we're heading to Mt Lofty. Either way, by the time we get there, we leave all our tech behind. All of it. Anything it can track, trace, hack or detect, or whatever – gone."

She looked at Donna. "That's going to mean your van too."

"What?"

"Something Kane said to us, cars need to be early 1990s models or earlier – period. So, either between now and when we leave, or now and when we get there, we're going to need another old school ride."

After a moment to deal with her impending loss, and a look at her daughter and the stakes at play, Donna nodded her approval.

"Let's do this," said Grace.

She wasn't sure why, but she placed her hand in the middle of the group, face down. It was an instinctive expression of solidarity, and completely un-her in every way. There it hovered in awkward isolation for several sections before everyone else processed what was going on.

Suede slapped his hand on top. "Let's do this."

Then Donna, Ava and Colin. "Let's do this."

*

CHAPTER 32

D.O.A

The late afternoon light was casting a golden beauty over the carnage that was the aftermath of the massacre on Main Rd, Normanville. The bodies of locals, holiday-home owners and those who fled the chaos of the city were spread across the street. They were surrounded by the bodies of nearly twice as many zambies while the carcasses of a number of drones dotted the mess.

The carnage peaked in a pile near the entry to the supermarket but spread to the shops on the other side of the road and reached down toward the intersection where the kombi was parked nearby. Grace and Suede studied it all behind the cover of the same car that had sheltered them while they watched the horrors unfold.

"At least the kombi's still there," said Suede.

"Good for us, probably not so much for the hippies," said Grace.

Suede studied the bodies again. "And nothing's so much as moved, right? No arms, no legs, no nothing? Not even a twitch of reanimation?"

"Not that I've seen."

"Like, nothing at all. Zilch. Nada. None."

"Nothing."

They cast their eyes over the scene yet again. Same location, same aspect. Gone was the chaos and gore, replaced with the eerie golden light and a silence so complete they could make out the distant sound of waves rolling up onto the shore over half a kilometre away. Almost to highlight the point, a kangaroo hopped by. It paused briefly to get its own take on the scene. Once satisfied, it continued on its merry way.

"There's something you don't see every day," said Suede.

"Which bit?" said Grace.

"Wait, that's the same kangaroo that hopped next to me in the car. Look at its face markings. Godspeed, buddy."

They had been watching from cover long enough to know that there was no sign of active zambies, reanimating zambies or drones. All was ready for them to locate the keys.

The smell that hit them was subtle but threatening – the tang of death. It tickled in just the way that suggested more concentrated unpleasantness lay ahead. A lot more.

"Shall we?" said Grace.

Suede took one last look around for danger. "I guess we shall," he said with a sigh when the coast proved clear.

The pair took an exceptionally deep breath before they waded into the aftermath of battle.

"What were the hippies wearing again?" asked Grace.

"She had a floral dress – blue. It had yellow and red flowers on it, from memory."

"What sort of blue?" said Grace.

He stared at her. "Blue. It's blue. Blue is blue."

She gave him a look of bewildered disappointment. She thought about the several hundred examples she could make to expand his blue horizons, but instead breathed it away with a deep sigh. "And him?"

"I remember the brown cords. Kind of a brown brown if you need more detail."

Grace shot him daggers. "Really? Now?"

Suede quickly realised he'd misread the room and put his serious face back on. "Sorry, all this is…" he said as he pointed over the carnage. "Anyway, he had some paisley shirt with purple and a faux fur vest over the top. Hopefully, they'll stand out."

"Wait!" said Grace. "Like that?"

She directed his attention to a significant pile of bodies. An arm, covered in paisley polyester, sat out the top, the rest of him lost somewhere deep underneath.

"Fuck," said Suede. "Yep, that's him."

*

Out of the sphere of observation, at a coastal holiday town on the Fleurieu Peninsula, the war against humanity took a turn. And not in a favourable direction, if you're experiencing this story from a human perspective.

After a successful first wave executed by the zambies – or pawns, as they were known in the same other perspective – a new phase was being launched. Robots of all shapes and sizes were being deployed via fully self-driving (FSD) cars throughout battlefields and key infrastructure assets far and wide.

Things were about to go to an entirely new level. That was not good news for the surviving humans. Specifically, in the context of this story, it was not good news for the very actively communicating boomer survivors in the proximity of the Lady Bay Golf Course.

Or anyone, really.

*

"Move back!" said Suede before wiping some of the sticky gunk from his face with one hand while gripping onto a corpse with the other.

"Hang on!" said Grace. She worked at the bottom of the body pile to drag the last one clear so there'd be space for the new one.

Suede sighed. Loudly.

"I'm doing my best," snapped Grace before offering him an unimpressed stare.

Suede met the look, and the two groaned their dissatisfaction.

They had been on the scene for over an hour. After spending the first half of that trying to dig out the body of the man from the other corpses, they'd decided to reassess tactics. After a quick scout, they found the woman. She was also buried under bodies, but not as completely. She had become the new target of their search.

It took another fifteen minutes to free her. It was only after a frisk of the body they realised she didn't possess the keys to the van. This led a frustrated Suede to suggest he wasn't surprised because the guy was driving, which riled Grace as she would've thought significant information like that was worth mentioning before they started digging somewhere else. After an unfruitful search for a possible handbag, they returned, unhappily, to the original dig site, dirtier, far more tired and frustrated, and far less tolerant.

"Just drag it through the entrails. It'll be easier," said Suede.

Grace stopped to look at him. "Do you want to do it?"

"Just..." started Suede, adjusting his neck to soothe some hidden crink. "Hurry up, it's getting heavy."

"Aarrrghhh!" screamed Grace as she channelled her frustration into a feat of strength that moved the corpse up and over another one that was impeding its progress. Once past the point of no return, she let her leg assist gravity with its work, and the body fell backwards onto the road. Its head conked the bitumen with an unsettling thud. "Happy?" she asked, sounding anything but.

Suede then released his own frustration, sending the body he was holding down to street level. It came to a rolling halt not far from Grace's feet.

"Oi! Watch it."

"You say that like I was throwing it at you," snapped Suede. "You're, like, three metres away! Fun fact: I can't throw a corpse three metres."

"Quit being a dick!" said Grace. "This is exactly like the time we had to deal with the plumbing backflow when we were staying at your parents' rental."

"No, it's not! It's like the time you lost your shit when we were putting that flat pack bed together."

"Just get on with it!" snapped Grace.

"You said that then, too!" Suede turned his frustration and focus to the game of corpse Jenga. With the latest body removed, he had a far better view of the puzzle. He had an idea and rolled a frail old woman to the side, then leaned into a mystery leg until it moved clear of the area of interest. "Boom!"

"What?"

"We have pockets!" said Suede.

"Seriously?"

"Hells, yes. Beautiful, ugly brown corduroy pockets!"

They shared a long overdue smile before Suede dived in to investigate. Grace watched on as the simple task seemed to be taking some time.

"Everything OK?"

He ignored her, muttered under his breath, and then continued his search. Grace dared not respond by this point.

"Fuck!" screamed Suede eventually. "Fuck, fuck, fuck, fuck, fuck!"

"Did you check the back pockets?"

"I checked everything – front, back, shirt, inside lining on this… absolutely ludicrous vest – nothing. Fuck!"

Suede punched the corpse in frustration. "Aarrrghgh!"

"Was either of them carrying anything else?"

Suede slumped back on the pile of bodies, exhausted. "I honestly can't remember."

He wept to the heavens for a moment before making his way down to street level.

Grace held her arms open at the bottom for a squelchy embrace.

"I can't even deal with how gross I feel right now, let alone how I might look."

"You and me both," said Grace.

"I was sure we were going to make this happen," he pulled away from the hug, spotting a reasonably clean jacket nearby. He picked it up and wiped his face. "I mean, Halen! It was going to be like getting the band back together, you know? Or, like, in a second album way. Halen II – not quite as good as the original, but still."

"I know." Grace searched the scene for ideas. "Can we hotwire it or something? I mean, the tech's as old as Donna. It can't be that hard to work out."

Suede shrugged, and the pair made their way to the van. They almost made the discovery in unison as they looked through the window. The keys. Sitting in plain sight on the front seat. Despite seeing the same thing, their reactions were very different. Grace celebrated with a woo-hoo as she opened the door. Suede doubled over in the foetal position, swearing under his breath repeatedly as he rocked back and forth.

Grace gave him space to grieve, walking to the back of the van and opening the doors. It wasn't the well-organised operation she was used to, with clothes strewn seemingly everywhere but the limited cupboard space and the two cheap suitcases where one would expect them to be stored. There was an unmade bed covered in empty beer bottles and a half-full ashtray, two surfboards, a guitar, a bunch of polaroids dotted everywhere and an off smell.

In a strange way, it reminded her of the early van-life days with Suede.

"Fucking country people!" said the man she was thinking about, just a little older and more blood-soaked than her memories at that moment. "Can you please tell me who parks thirty metres away from several dozen people in a dog-eat-dog apocalyptic situation, walks away from a vehicle with their whole life in the back and leaves THE KEYS ON THE FRONT SEAT?"

"They were just trying to help," said Grace.

"And what's that smell?" said Suede. "What a minute, is that?"

"Swamp crotch?"

"No! Also, eww! Underneath that scent." Suede climbed in and investigated the dibs in the ashtray before he started opening drawers. "Oh, bingo!" He pulled out a large plastic resealable sandwich bag full of dope. "Look at the heads on that!"

*

CHAPTER 33
MY GENERATION

"Oh, look," said Colin. "Satan's bloodhounds have changed back into their disguise. They almost look human if you squint your eyes."

Grace and Suede had just made their way downstairs, having had one of the longest showers of their lives. Despite the cleanup, their faces still wore the horrors they'd endured.

"Too soon, man," said Suede, wearing a T-shirt with a logo parodying a large online auction house with the word Eshay written across the front in greens, reds, blues and yellows. "I had to wash my hair three times!"

Grace could sense Colin trying to figure out another funny line and quickly moved the subject on. "So, this is everything?" she said. "Including the shed."

Donna nodded. "Yep, and I think it'll all fit too." She passed Grace and Suede tumblers.

Grace nodded her appreciation and reached for the bottle on the table. "Brilliant. So, pack the van, work out our escape destination, then have a quick drink to celebrate zambie-Judith's hospitality before bed?"

"We're going to need some tunes for all that," said Suede. Fresh drink in hand, he headed for the turntable, already knowing what album he'd select. "Who knew negligee and the giant had such impeccable taste in early metal?" He pulled the disk from its cover. "*Vol. 4* – Black Sabbath. End of the peak, peak of the peak maybe."

He slipped it on the turntable and lowered the needle until music crackled to life. The slow driving guitar of 'Wheels of Confusion' kicked into gear as he air-guitared away, giving zambie-Judith a headshake of disappointment as he went.

*

The second van had provided more than enough storage for all their supplies and the process of packing had been relatively quick for the five of them. Barring what they needed for the night, the pantry had been stripped of food and drinks, and the fridge supplies loaded into a couple of eskies. On top of their personal belongings, there were the weapons and defences Colin had constructed in the shed. Long-handled pokers with a variety of sharp blades on the end, ideal for prodding zambies from a safe distance, fishing nets with weights on the edge to throw at drones and a cordless nail gun with the trigger inhibitor hacked so it could fire at a safer range. It was the centrepiece of Colin's weapon creation, and he made it known it was his and his alone.

They also had enough spare space to pack anything that may serve a purpose in the future, which included every other blade in the shed, mallets, axes, shovels, a tent, some camping gear and a small bounty of fishing rods and tackle. Add to that the blades each of them now carried and their defensive arm guards, and they had the beginnings of something resembling protection from the zambies at the very least.

By the time the tail end of 'Supernaut' was playing inside, the vans – parked side-by-side in the double garage – were ready to go. They headed back inside to celebrate their last night at zambie-Judith's.

Had they known what was coming their way the next morning, they would have hit the road at that moment. But the apocalypse wasn't in the habit of giving friendly heads-ups.

*

They were soon back in the kitchen, and the moment became real. The bravery in making the decision to join some mystery resistance now became a countdown to the inevitable. They all sat in silence in the living room, a heaviness stifling the air.

"Ohh," said Suede, eventually. He made his way to the turntable, grabbed the pile of keeper albums, placed two back down to listen to later in the night, and then moved the rest to the foot of the door that led to the garage. "I may as well turn zambie if we forget those," he said on his return. "Who knows, maybe my destiny is to survive to keep music alive."

Colin scoffed. He had the carton of belongings his ex had thrown at him. "I'm not sure the history of music is ready for your re-edit."

"Well, someone's got to be around to do it, and people seem to like what I have to say," said Suede. He eyed Colin's box. "Did you actually scribble out where your ex wrote 'Dickhead's'?"

Everyone's eyes homed in on the label before Colin rotated the box. Which was actually futile as the word had been written – and scribbled out – on all four sides.

Suede soaked in the moment. "She really felt very strongly about that label."

"You're really shitting me to tears, young man."

"Will you two shut up!" said Donna. "Jesus Christ! Have a listen to yourselves. So self-involved, the pair of you!" She took in the four sets of eyes staring at her in shock, plus a brief gaze from zombie-Judith. She fixed her gaze on Colin. "I grew up with your generation as parents. I was basically raised on judgement and neglect. Children should be seen and not heard, you said—"

"Seems like a good rule to me," said Colin.

"Seriously?" said Ava. "That seems more like an 1880s concept."

"Nope. 1980s," said Donna. "Maybe they didn't know any better, having been raised by the silent generation."

"Don't you bring them into it!" said Colin. "They fought in a war."

Donna eyed him. "See – we still aren't allowed to talk about it! Like everything else never talked about."

"Newsflash, junior, not everyone needs to hear about your feelings. You're not special." Colin turned to the others. "And none of you are special either. That's the thing none of you seem to understand. Just put your head down and get on with it – that's what the world needs."

"This from the guy who hid in the bathroom from a 60-year-old lingerie-wearing zambie and let me do all the work," said Suede.

"I mean, get on with what?" said Donna. "Dying? Being replaced? Truth is, we were already being replaced before this whole thing started. That world – your world and all of its values – just doesn't work anymore."

"That's because people like you couldn't just leave things be," said Colin. He passed a glare around to all of them.

"Where exactly should we have let it be, do you think?" said Grace. "The vomitous family values of the 1950s? The civil rights horrors of the 60s and 70s? Greed culture in the 80s? Or the continued sexism, racism and homophobia across all those decades. So, which one? You don't like anything after that, so it has to be somewhere in there."

"That's the problem today. You can't look at anything without seeing the worst in it," said Colin. "And don't get me started on cancel cul—"

"Oh, shut up!" said Ava.

Suede sniggered, which led to other pockets of sniggering. The energy in the room came off the boil.

"Wait," said Suede eventually. "So, if boomers were kids of the silent generation, who were the silent generation's parent?"

"The greatest generation," said Colin.

"What?" said Suede. "How do they get to be the greatest generation and we just get to be a different letter of the alphabet than the one before?"

"Because," said Colin, noticeably trying to restrain his annoyance. "They lived through World War I, the Spanish Flu pandemic, the Great Depression and World War II."

Suede pondered his words for a moment. "Fair enough then."

"I wonder what they'll call us if we survive?" said Ava.

"As long as it's not the last generation, they can call us anything they like," said Suede.

"There's a saying," said Colin. "Hard times create strong men. Strong men create good times. Good times create weak men. And weak men create hard times."

"The patriarchy's generational cycle of shit," said Ava. "Great."

Colin ignored her. "We've had good times for too long, it seems. Gotten soft. We're not ready for this."

Suede eyed him up and down. "Are you implying that you would've fought this fight back in the day, but we can't now?"

"At least I knew my world. How stuff worked, how to fix things when they broke. How to take a punch."

"I'm tempted to test that," said Suede.

Grace held him back. "Well, if we can't learn to get along amongst ourselves, we are going to end up the last generation!"

"Exactly!" said Donna. She eyed Suede and Colin. "Stop needing to be right all the time. You're both exactly the same in your own way."

The two men grunted and snorted in unison as they exchanged a look.

Donna eyed them both again. "You're both high maintenance, that's what. You know, I spent my youth doing all the chores for my family – ironing, dishes, mowing, bins, dusting, vacuuming – you name it. Like most kids my age. Then we got our own kids and what happened? We're doing the same bloody chores again! A generation bookended by takers."

Ava shrugged her indifference.

"It sounds to me like you're too much of a people pleaser," said Suede.

"And an idiot!" added Colin.

They both laughed.

Donna groaned, and the conversation petered out. It was all too much to comprehend. The moment in time they found themselves in. The decades of change that had led them there. Difference. Generations. Future. History. Their role in it. Technology. What it meant to be human. How that was changing with every passing day. What the morning would bring. How many more mornings there would be.

As they headed to bed, Grace's phone pulsed with more notifications. She had been ignoring it most of the day, fearing what she might find. Her phone was fast transitioning from a connection to a world that it would haunt her to let go of, to a technological magnifying glass to her existence and the fear that created. She had already decided to let the phone go flat. Given that would happen by the time she woke up, maybe she could have one last look.

A number of new message requests had been sent to her from different accounts across all of her channels. The same message each time.

"They're coming."

*

CHAPTER 34
HERE COMES THE SUN

There was a crispness in the air that only clear country skies could deliver. Suede guessed they were heading for a warm and mild day, but he had no way of telling. He could hear Grace in the shower and the others stirring as he sipped on his coffee. He felt content knowing the last of the important vinyl – and the turntable – were loaded in the back of the van.

"Can you believe they're up already?" said Colin, as he put his palm over the kettle to sense how recently it had boiled. Once satisfied, he went about making a coffee. "We told them we'd be out. They don't really need to hover over us while we do."

"Who?"

Colin stirred his beverage. "Who do you think?"

Suede shrugged. "Carol?"

"Yes! Fucking Carol." He took a sip, then headed to the lounge. "Which reminds me," he said, retrieving his box and taking it to the kitchen.

"Fucking Carol," said Suede. The tone left Colin uncertain how genuine he was. Meanwhile, Suede picked up one of the envelopes that had slipped his way on the table. "What's Cockburn?"

"My surname. It's pronounced Coburn, though – the c and k are silent."

"Oh, come on! There's no way that series of letters in that order is pronounced any other way than Cockburn."

"Give me that," said Colin as he snatched the envelope away. "And, for your information, the name goes back centuries. Scottish."

"So, because they've been saying it incorrectly for centuries makes it more right?"

"What's going on?" said Donna as she and Ava entered the room and dropped their bags.

"Colin's last name is Cockburn!" said Suede, delighting in a small sip of coffee.

"It's Coburn!"

"Spelt C O C K B U R N."

"That's Cockburn!" said Ava.

"Exactly!" said Suede, at the same time Colin snapped. "Wrong!"

"I used to have a friend with that surname. She couldn't wait to get married," said Donna.

"Eww, changing your surname!" said Ava. "How twentieth century."

"It was more a Cockburn-deletion thing," said Donna.

Ava sighed. "I'm morally conflicted on that one."

"Wait," said Donna. "We're Jacksons. Should we be pronouncing that Jason?"

"Ha!" said Suede. "Oh, this is so good."

"Why do you like giving me the irrits so much?" said Colin, staring at Suede.

"This from the guy who told me I was called Suede because I was easily rubbed the wrong way."

Colin scoffed. "That's different."

"No, sorry, it's not," said Suede. "You know what's worse? You and all your cockburnt ancestors have been sharing the same delusion for what sounds like centuries. And the rest of the world's been humouring you with pronunciation while they all really think they should be saying Cockburn."

"Alright, smart Alec, what's your surname?"

Suede stared at him. "Zorlu."

"I knew it!" said Colin.

"Knew what?"

"That it'd be one of those sorts of names."

"Dude, stop!" said Ava.

Colin eyed her. "Why should I? He's having a go at my heritage."

Suede stared at him. "It's Turkish, if you must know."

"That figures."

"What does that mean?"

Colin studied the room – his companions stared at him with open mouths – and he reeled in his response.

"But I've got all sorts of foreign DNA in there if you must know," said Suede. "My family tree looks like a World Cup results graphic."

"What's your point?" snapped Colin.

"You're trying to make a point. I'm just being proud of my heritage."

"I'm proud of my heritage," said Colin.

"Then why do you mispronounce your surname?"

Colin rounded the side of the island bench. "You know, I think I've had just about enough of your—"

"Seriously, you two? Right now?" said Grace as she emerged from the corridor.

Suede was temporarily taken aback. "He was—"

"I don't care. We've got a problem," she made a hand signal for the others to follow, then led them down the corridor and up the stairs.

As she neared the top, she made the shush sign, signalled them again, and then headed through the front bedroom to the balcony window. She found a curtain edge and peeled it back far enough to peer through. In the slit to the outside world above and below her head, the others squeezed in to get a view.

"What the actual fuck!" said Suede.

Down the road in the direction of the clubhouse, Carol and her posse were gathered. Beside them, a car – modern and electric – was parked with doors open. Two humanoid robots stood by its side, seemingly in consultation with Carol and her group. At the feet of the bots, two quadruped robots, looking like medium-sized dogs, analysed the area.

"That's so not good," said Donna.

"Nope," said Grace.

"Are they trying to get themselves killed?" said Suede. "Or us? Or both?"

"Is there any other way out of here other than past the clubhouse?" said Donna.

"Not by car, there isn't," said Colin.

"Shit," said Donna.

Meanwhile, they watched as Carol turned towards them and pointed in their direction. The gaze of all four bots followed.

"That bitch!" said Grace.

They all sought the cover of a closed curtain.

"Did they see us?" said Suede.

"Not sure," said Donna. "What do we do now?"

"I don't know?" said Grace. "Anyone?"

"Everyone's packed everything, right?" said Suede.

Colin nodded. "Oh, and I even found an old Gregory's in zambie-Judith's car, which I've chucked in the kombi in case we, you know, get split up."

"A Gregory's?" said Grace.

"It's like Google maps, but in a book," said Donna.

Grace and Suede exchanged a confused look.

"I've drawn our route on there, you know, just in case," said Colin.

"Something happening," said Ava, who had re-established a view over the goings on near the clubhouse. "Oh no!"

The others rushed back to the view to see pandemonium had broken out between the boomers and the robots. The crack of gunshots echoed past the balcony. Within seconds, the entire scene had changed. Bodies lay on the ground, the rest scattered, those with guns continued to fire. The quadruped bots launched in tandem at one boomer, knocking her from her feet before unleashing some sort of attack on her face.

"Oh, shit," said Suede.

The humanoids' speed and fluid movement ran rings around their prey. They struck out with arms and legs, using more subtle moves that were too difficult to make out at range. Whatever they were, they left a trail of victims in their wake. They could make out one of the humanoid bots noticeably hobbling, perhaps the result of a gunshot.

"Do we go now while they're distracted or wait?" said Suede.

"Hang on a sec, what's the injured one doing?" said Ava.

"Headed to the clubhouse by the looks," said Colin.

They watched as the humanoid hobbled towards the clubhouse's barricaded entry. Its partner in crime picked off fleeing humans, and their dog-like companions took out others from ground level. The bots targeted Phillippe, who was riding shotgun on Carol's wing, backing away and firing his rifle. Over by the clubhouse, the hobbling bot pulled away the first piece of barricade.

"Oh, shit," said Grace. "It's going to free the zambies."

"No, no, no, no, no!" said Donna, her eyes fixed on Phillippe, who had just fallen as the humanoid bot lunged at him.

They heard Carol's scream all the way from their balcony. She paused, in two minds for a moment, debating whether to continue her escape or turn to Phillippe. At ground level, Phillippe reached out to her, and she turned in his direction just as a dogbot joined the humanoid in attacking him.

"Go, Carol!" said Donna.

Colin grumbled.

Carol approached her partner, saw the gun had fallen from his reach and reeled it in with her arm before firing a shot blindly at the inbound humanoid.

"C'mon, c'mon, c'mon!" said Donna.

Just as she did, Carol turned from the scene and began her retreat, leaving Phillippe reaching out for her, betrayed.

"Oh, my God, she absolutely burnt him!" said Suede.

"Been there, experienced that," said Colin.

"I think Phillippe's dead," said Donna.

They turned to see the humanoid and dogbot racing back into battle, Phillippe's corpse left in their wake.

Meanwhile, Carol's retreat didn't last long. The other quadruped cut through her path, taking one of her feet out from under her. She hit the ground with a thud, and the rifle bounced clear of her reach. Not that she seemed to have that level of awareness in the moment, such was the apparent impact of her ribcage.

The quadruped involved in the impact rolled off in a tumble, coming to a rest with limbs contorted at awkward angles. Before anyone had a chance to celebrate the small win, its limbs contorted in a seemingly unnatural way before the bot righted itself, shook off some dust and oriented itself to its surroundings once more.

"Creepy," said Suede.

Then, it took a couple of fast paces forward and launched itself at Carol. By the time it had, the other quadruped had leapt to beat its partner to the new target. Again, distance obscured what occurred in the attack, but it was close range and brutally fast. And lethal. Several seconds later, they extricated themselves from the scene, leaving Carol's bloody body on show by the clubhouse car park.

"Oh shit," said Grace. She looked at Colin. They all did.

He gestured to wipe sweat from his forehead, but they all saw him drying underneath his eyes.

"You OK?" said Grace.

He ventured out on several sentence starters but aborted each attempt. His eyes stayed fixed and emotionless on the battle outside. "We need to go."

"That might not be so easy!" said Ava, the first back to the window, looking at the action in front of the clubhouse.

"No, no, no, no, no," said Grace.

The injured bot had now freed the door of impediments, it burst open, and several zambies poured out into the car park. They filed across the bitumen, and it didn't take a geometry expert to see they were headed to the road – trapping the fleeing boomers inside the estate. And trapping Grace and crew on the wrong side of the only way out.

"Brilliant," said Grace. "Anyone got any ideas now?"

It was then she noticed Colin had left the room.

"Asshole!"

*

CHAPTER 35

ON THE ROAD AGAIN

Within a second, Grace, then the others, set off after Colin. Such was the pace differential that she was on his tail by the time he neared the bottom of the stairs.

"Slow down, pops," she said.

"Fuck that," said Colin as he hit the floor of the open planned downstairs area and charged through the kitchen, where he swiped the keys to Donna's van.

But by the time he'd reached the other side and was in sight of the garage door, Grace and the others were ahead of him. "Where do you think you're going?" said Grace.

"Hand 'em over," added Suede as he grabbed Colin and then fished around for the keys in his hand.

"No way," said Colin, as he tried to both resist and escape. Suede was too strong on both fronts.

"Is this about Carol?" said Donna.

Colin scoffed but held it in. "Pfft! No! It's about not ending up like her. If we don't go now, we're dead."

Grace looked at the others, shared looks trying to align on the right move in the moment.

"Well?" said Colin.

"I'm thinking!" snapped Grace.

But Colin had already done the thinking for them.

"Wait, what's that noise?" said Ava.

Even as she said it, everyone turned towards the direction of its source – the garage door. Any slim hope they'd clung onto that their position had not registered with the bots evaporated. Grace gave a guttural groan of annoyance. “Fine! We’re leaving!”

“Cockswab,” said Suede, pleased with his second usage of the term. He reached in for Colin’s keys, exerting all his physical dominance to prevail. He clipped the boomer lightly over the back of the head after his victory. Then he handed the keys to Donna.

She nodded as she turned to follow Ava into the garage. “What’s the plan?”

“We’ll follow the map, you guys follow Colin’s directions,” said Grace.

“Why do we have to have him?” said Donna with a groan of her own.

“Hey!” said Colin. “I’m right here!”

“There’s no room for him in Halen,” said Grace. “We’ll travel in a convoy anyway.”

By this time, they were all in the garage and piling into their respective vans. Suede headed to the front of the garage to check the status of the battle outside. “The bots and dogs seem to be focused on the boomers. If we hurry, we might just get past the clubhouse before the zambies reach the road.”

“Alright, let’s do this,” said Grace, winding down her window as Ava did the same in Donna’s van. “Phones stay here.”

Ava nodded.

Suede was back by the passenger side door as two vastly different-sounding engines fired into life. “I thought you said—”

“Changed my mind. They’ll get us killed.”

As the others stared at her, unsure, Grace held her phone out the window and chucked it at the wall. It made a sickly, cracking noise on impact. She looked at the others, “Well?”

Within seconds, Ava, Donna, and Suede followed suit, liberating themselves from technology. They exchanged uncertain looks as their tether to many virtual worlds disappeared. There was no looking back now.

“Old school!” said Colin. “I like it.”

“Keep your eye out for some older transport,” said Grace to Donna. “We’ve got to ditch your ride as soon as we can.”

Donna nodded, turned to the street ahead and rolled out of the garage.

“Shit, I nearly forgot!” said Suede as he exited the car and sprinted back inside.

"What are you doing?" yelled Grace.

As her mind raced as to what he could be doing, it dawned on her that she had an unfulfilled task of her own. She leaned to the side and pulled the photo of her and her dad from her pocket, along with two hair ties. She positioned it on the sun visor and brushed her finger over it.

*

"Be free, Cool Cat," said Suede as he cut the tether that held zambie-Judith to the line. "And no biting anyone!"

"Bwluurgggh," came the response.

"Good chat," he said as he legged it back to the van.

He returned to see Grace positioning her dad's photo in place on the sun visor. A moment of tranquillity in her eyes. He jumped into Halen II once more and rubbed her leg for reassurance. "It didn't seem right not to set zambie-Judith on her way."

"You ready?" said Grace.

The two exchanged a nod and Grace guided Halen II after Donna's van.

*

On the street, a strange calm settled in both cabins while violence and destruction raged around them. They were a block away from the chaos on the parallel street, and it jumped in and out of view between houses and undeveloped blocks. Fleeing humans, quadruped bots and the humanoid bot. Further ahead, near the clubhouse, the injured bot and several dozen zambies were making their way up to the street.

"What's she doing?" said Grace as she followed Donna. "She's going too slow."

"Maybe trying to sneak past the bots without being spotted," said Suede.

"If she doesn't hurry her ass up, there'll be a zambie roadblock by the time we get to the clubhouse," said Grace as she gestured frantically to the other car through the windscreen.

"C'mon, c'mon," added Suede.

But with each passing second, it became more apparent that their escape window was narrowing. Grace pulled Halen II out from behind Donna's van and moved in alongside it. Suede rolled down his window, and Donna hit the button to lower hers.

"We've got to move it!" said Grace from the driver's side.

It was then they noticed Donna was white as a ghost. She shook her head slowly in response. Her mouth was open and she had a vacant stare, lost in the horrors of what was happening around them.

"OK, just follow me then."

Donna nodded absently.

"Mum!" snapped Ava. "Did you hear her?"

"What? Yeah."

"Let's do this," said Grace as she hit the gas.

The road they were on rounded into a sharp bend to meet the parallel street near the clubhouse. Grace rode the forces on her body as she threw the accelerating Halen II into a chicane move. The van hit a roadside shrub as she tried to wrestle it out of the move and onto the clubhouse road. After a steering overcorrection, stereo screams, and a readjustment at the wheel as she took her foot off the pedal and they hit the straightaway that led to the car park.

Halen II had lost a lot of momentum in the wrestle to stay on the road and Grace planted her foot on the accelerator once more. Now, the equation to escape became clear as the front of the zambie herd neared the roadside, and the doors to freedom on the other side slowly closed.

"Grace!"

"I know!"

"Hurry!"

"My foot doesn't go any further down!"

But it quickly became clear they weren't going to have the road to themselves as the first zambie stepped onto it. Then another, and another. Grace steered the van to the right in hopes they'd whisk past the threat before they could reach out or react. Their path was set, and there was no going back now, not this close, not at his speed. Grace and Suede screamed.

For a moment, the pair thought they would clear the threat without incident. But that was when an undead seemed to come to the same realisation and lunged forward. So committed was it to the move, it would not have maintained balance on its next step. Not that there would be one. It fell forward and caught the passenger side corner of the van with its jaw. The moment unfolded like a way too real 3D movie for Suede, who found new gusto in his scream.

The sound of the impact was horrid. Part deep thud, part flesh rip with an accent of window crack as the quarter glass on Suede's side took some of the collision. A fresh plume of blood splattered its way down his side of the car. Suede moved his scream into a third gear.

Grace lifted hers to match as she wrestled with the steering wheel, and Halen II snaked on the edge of control and the edge of the road. When she finally managed to save it from rolling or colliding with one of the front fences lining the street side, she hit the bitumen at an angle, and stared down another two zambies. This time, she pumped the brakes and fanned the wheel hard to avoid a front-on collision. The rear tyres gripped then slicked across the road as Halen II's back half arced around, somehow narrowly missing zambie No.2 before clipping zombie No.3, sending it flying back towards the horde.

With all the shock and disorientation, Grace and Suede sat in stunned silence in the aftermath of the moment before they came to their senses.

Suede looked through a gap in the blood-soaked window to scan the scene. "Shit. The injured bot – it's heading this way."

He turned back to Grace who shared a look that oozed hopeful prayer, then she hit the accelerator once more. After a moment of complaint, Halen II lurched into forward momentum once more.

"Hurry! It may be hobbling, but it's quick!" said Suede before something else caught his eye.

It was Donna's van, not as close behind them as he'd expected. Thanks to the carnage now strewn across the street and more zambies reaching it, there was no way to get from one side to the other now. Meanwhile, the commotion got the injured bot's attention. It abandoned the chase on Halen II and turned to the other van.

"Wait! Hold up!" said Suede.

*

Donna hit the roadside with the sort of momentum that made the car feel like it was airborne for a brief moment in time. All three occupants screamed at the sensation. Or was it at the zambies horde, which they were suddenly in the middle of? They found themselves racing across an open scrubby downhill slope, lurching from left to right as Donna dodged the undead. All the loose items in the van rattled as it bounced every which way.

Ava screamed as the van clipped a zambie near her seat in the cabin.

"Jesus, woman, watch it!" said Colin.

"Shut the fuck up!" said Donna.

Ava smiled, knowing her mum was over her earlier freak-out. Or well on her way.

Donna overcompensated at the wheel, and the tyres gripped hard on the patchy, scrubby surface. The force shook everyone inside. Colin smacked his head on the back of Donna's seat.

After another sharp direction change, another zambie appeared in front of them, and Donna twisted the wheel yet again. Another glancing blow. More screams.

Donna sensed a small window had presented itself and that she could look up to try to take in the bigger picture of the scene. They'd already snaked their way halfway across the small stretch of scrub to the clubhouse car park. In general, the zambie threat seemed to be migrating towards the road, leaving the car park the lesser of two dangers. She snapped back into the moment and plotted a path in her mind that would get her there with the least damage.

"Hurry up!" said Colin.

"Watch it or hurry up? You can't complain about both!" said Donna.

"They're all heading for us," he added.

"I think he's right," said Ava as she scanned the field of the zambies. That's when she saw the injured bot. It was coming at them despite its hobble, dodging the undead from the roadside. "Hurry up!" she screamed.

There was a curdling tone in her daughter's voice that adequately conveyed the appropriate level of urgency and Donna planted her foot to full non-watch-it levels. The van briefly skidded on the surface before gripping and ripping.

"It's the injured bot," said Ava. "It's coming."

The curb separating the scrub from the car park was fast approaching, and the angle of approach made Donna wary. She changed trajectory to hit it acutely to minimise the impact, but it still sent a bang through the cabin, and their bodies rattled.

Colin emitted a strange noise from the back seat. Ava turned to investigate, finding his eyes closed and head flopped to the side. "Colin? Colin?"

"He OK?"

"Passed out," said Ava. "Or dead."

"At least he's quiet," said Donna before she wrestled the wheel, scraping past two zambies in quick succession without hitting either. She scanned the scene, located the inbound bot and processed. "OK, I think I can make a run for the exit."

A quadruped bot leapt from a blind spot at the side of the van to land on the hood.

"Shit!" screamed Donna as she shook the wheel from side-to-side to shake it off.

The four-legged bot readjusted its body weight to cater for the pressures with a skill so deft it was unworldly. They'd seen the occasional quadruped in real life before, but not like this. Its sleek white exterior and perfectly designed lines weren't performing some display to please a crowd. It was on the hunt. For them. It looked at them through the windscreen with a depth every bit as heavy as the g-forces Donna was exposing it to.

"Mum!"

"I see it!"

"Not the dog, the bot. I think it's trying to cut you off at the entrance."

Donna afforded herself a second to look up. Ava was on the money. She didn't want to be anywhere near the humanoid bot, especially after the display she was currently getting from the little quadruped. She screamed, hoping the release of tensions would magically bring another escape route to light in her mind. It did not.

She scanned the scene. There was only one refuge close enough to reach before the walls of undead and robots closed in. "Hang on!" she screamed as she hit the brakes.

Donna felt a thud on the back of her seat that she was pretty sure was Colin's head. However, she'd given Ava enough brace time to reach a hand out to the glovebox to ride the deceleration. They both screamed. They watched on as the quadruped – having no innate trick to overcome the momentum change – it went flying from the hood to the ground below.

Donna threw the van into reverse, eyes fixed on the rearview mirror as she guided them away from immediate danger. "Talk to me," she said as she went.

"Your driving's still shit," said a dazed Colin.

"Not you!"

"The bot's heading our way," said Ava as she redirected her attention to the quadruped. "Jesus! The dogbot's getting up."

"Keep me updated!" said Donna, skidding the car to a halt and finding a forward gear again. "Meanwhile, grab any sharp weapon you can get your hands on." She dodged another zambie as she picked up speed. With one last glance in the rearview mirror, she caught a glimpse of the other two bots now heading their way. "Shit! Ava – get ready to open your door."

"Why?"

Donna slammed on the brakes. The van skidded to a halt past barriers and a few bodies. A cacophony of noise echoed out as the front of the van hit the side of the clubhouse wall. Both airbags went off as Donna and Ava fell forward. Once again, Colin thudded into the back of Donna's seat.

Donna was the first to come to her senses. "Ava? Ava!" She said as she undid her seatbelt.

"I'm alright," Ava moaned. "What happened?"

They had skidded to rest under a portico that housed the entrance to the clubhouse. Donna had managed to wedge the van in such a way it would act as a barrier in its own right. Donna scanned the scene and saw bots and zambies closing in. "Get up. We need to go."

"What?"

"I wasn't talking to you, Colin. But if you want to live, you need to go. Now!"

Colin moaned. The others ignored him.

Meanwhile, Ava wrestled with her door handle with no luck. The concertina effect of the front panels had damaged it enough to stop it functioning. Donna was out of her seat and trying to squeeze herself through to the back to try the sliding door.

"Happy days," said Colin as he turned to find the rear side of Donna's jeans up close and personal.

Donna swiped open the door and turned to see him raise his eyebrows at her. She shuddered in horror before offering Ava a hand through. The entrance to the clubhouse was right in front of them, and they dashed through.

"Fine!" said Colin, trying to extract himself from his seat. "Don't worry about my hips or anything. And I think I've had one of those concussion thingies."

"Shut up, Colin," came the distant voices of Donna and Ava in unison.

*

From the cabin of Halen II, safely past the danger on the road up the hill, Grace and Suede watched developments unfold.

Suede sighed heavily. "Should we try to save them?"

Grace sighed with equal intensity. "We probably have to, don't we?"

Suede sat on the words as he eyed the mayhem in front of them. "Well, it's a new world," he said. "And morality ain't what it used to be."

*

CHAPTER 36
IN DA CLUB

Ava had only taken a couple steps into the safety of the clubhouse when she hit the brakes.

"C'mon!" yelled Donna. It was a moot point, she discovered when she reached her daughter's side. Half a dozen zambies at the other end of the corridor, now alerted to their presence, were already heading in their direction. "Oh, shit!"

Ava's hand shook as she fumbled for her knife. She turned to her mum for guidance to realise she was doing the same. "What do we do now?"

"We need the long weapons!" said Donna as she backed away to the entry door once more.

Ava followed. They reached the main clubhouse door just as Colin had extracted himself from the van. They both stared at each other in disappointment through a glass panel from either side of the door. In unison, they opened it.

"Oh, you finally realised poor ole Colin was still out her—"

"Weapons!" said Donna. "Now."

"Shit! My nail gun!" said Colin.

"The thingamajigs," said Donna.

As Colin turned back to the van, he revealed a spear blade in his other hand.

"Yes! Like that – thingamajigs!" said Donna, eye signalling to his weapon.

Colin turned to her, confused, but she was already distracted somewhere else, as was Ava.

"Dogbot!" screamed Ava, eyes fixed further afield. "Hurry!"

Eyes were all drawn to the quadruped bot scurrying in from where the boomer gang had been decimated. The speed of its approach was a special kind of horror. Worse still, the way the van had landed after coming to rest against the clubhouse wall left a gap easily large enough for it to move past without any resistance.

In a single moment, all three humans realised there was no chance of fishing the larger weapons out of the van before they were attacked.

"Back inside!" said Donna.

Ava stared at her. "What about the zam—"

Bang!

The other quadruped mounted the front of the van, gaining purchase on the small, angled hood. Its feet slid momentarily before it adjusted to the perilous position. It stared at the three humans.

Donna put one hand out to protect Ava and fished around with the other to try to find the door handle. All while never losing eye contact with the van-mounted quadruped. From further afield, they heard the rapid pitter-patter of the other dogbot.

And then Donna and Ava heard the click of the door shutting. Both turned to make the realisation Colin had already passed through to extract himself from the situation.

"Asshole!" said Donna. She opened the door again and let Ava through while turning her gaze back to the van dogbot. She backed away from the threat as she felt Ava move. Then, just as she began to pull the door to, the quadruped launched at her. She screamed and swatted it away with her forearm protector.

She heard the quadruped crash into the clubhouse wall just as the speedy footsteps of its twin peaked in intensity. Despite how hard she wrestled with the door, it was painfully slow to close. Just as she thought she'd won the battle, the head of the second quadruped filled the remaining gap. Donna had her foot arced back in an instant before she sunk her boot into the attacker.

The impact was sweetly timed, caving in a large segment of its head. Yet it did not retreat from its position in the door. Donna heard other movements near the door, sensing not only the other dogbot but the presence of the humanoid bots.

She screamed in frustration.

*

Like Ava had done a minute or so earlier, Colin took a few steps into what he thought was the safety of the clubhouse before he realised the extent of the dangers that were closing in on him. He raised his knife, the closest two zambies were only a few metres from him. He realised he didn't have the slightest idea of what to expect from an attack. How fast could they move? How far could they lunge? He searched for an escape route, a way through the clubhouse to a safer, more open spot. The only thing that fit the bill was the restaurant and bar ahead, but that meant moving directly past the immediate zambie threat. Any other path led to a more closed-in and dangerous environment, and unknown new threats.

It was then he realised he'd spent so much time thinking about the options that they had dissipated before his eyes. He was frozen to the spot, and the nearest zambie rasped and lunged. He closed his eyes and waited for his fate.

As he did, he heard the skid of tires down the road. It was accompanied by an engine sound that was undeniably a kombi van.

*

Donna heard the Halen II's wheels screech as she pulled at the front door with all her might. She swore for two reasons. Her focus squared in on the immediate problem.

There was no way the door would close with the dogbot's head protruding through. The pressure was mounting with every passing second. She heard the other quadruped trying to regain its senses and footing once more, while the humanoid bots got nearer with every moment. She could make out the subtle sounds of their movement. They were close.

She focused all of her energy back on the dogbot doorstop, screamed and kicked it repeatedly. She felt the plastic cracking under the pressure of her boot and damage being done to whatever unknown circuitry and structure existed underneath. After a few more kicks, the head had lost its form. She eased the door open every so fractionally, then gave one final kick. It sent the dogbot flying into the van door.

She could hear the nearby footsteps of the mechanoids and sealed the door just as she saw a flash of white and black body, as well as a hint of a chirpy digital facial expression.

*

"Arrgghhh!" was the last thing Colin heard before getting hip-and-shoulder bumped into the corridor wall. Pain shot through his body as he narrowly missed some clubhouse memorabilia. As he clutched his ribs, Ava extended a hanging leg that turned the attacking zambie's momentum into a head-first fall into the trophy cabinet. Glass shattered everywhere from the move, and such was the angle of the fall, the zambie's head and shoulders seemed to be imprisoned by the structure.

But Ava's focus had moved to the second zambie, and she sent a sidekick into its midriff. The blow struck with enough momentum to send it staggering backwards. The creature fought against the unnatural experience as best as its limited coordination would allow, but it was only halted by contact with one of the four zambies behind it. The result sent both to the ground. The three behind remained on their feet but were wedged in between the fallen and the wall. It presented an easy escape for a human but was remarkably confusing for the zambies.

Colin stared at Ava. Ava stared at the chaos she had caused. The zambie she'd kicked had fallen over the legs of the one it fell into, leaving its head exposed. Ava breathed in heavily – if ever a moment presented to strike, this was it. She toyed with the knife handle, practising a couple of attack strikes, hoping one would just feel like the right thing to do. None did.

"Hurry up!" yelled Colin, still doubled over where he fell.

Ava shot him a look and realised that was all the incentive she needed. She turned back to the downed zambie in golfing attire, knelt on the arm that presented a mild threat, and then sunk a downward punch with the knife into its eye socket. It pressed through flesh with little resistance until it was down to the handle. She double-checked that her proximity to the other zambies was still acceptable, then pulled on the handle until it wrenched free once again.

She turned back to Colin, unsure what expression she gave, only knowing his response to it was silence and a deep gulp.

"Get up!" she yelled.

Colin obliged just as the trophy cabinet crashed from one wall to the other behind them. Glass smashed, trophies crashed, and the zambie lay still, impaled in the neck by a broken piece of frame.

It was Donna. She scanned the debris until she found a similar piece of broken cabinet frame, then she climbed back past the wreckage and wedged the section between the two door handles. She bent the flimsy metal around the handles as best she could. Once satisfied, she scrambled back through the wreckage, then briefly touched her daughter's hand as they shared a look of determination before her focus fell to the remaining zambies blocking their path. "We don't have long until the bots are through that door. She scanned the room once more, then bent over to pick up a fragment of broken trophy. She waved it in her hand to test its weapon potential – it was sturdy – and gave herself a nod of approval as she headed to the zambies.

Ava and Colin looked at the impressive reach of Donna's new-found weapon and scanned the debris until they each had their own. They were soon riding in wing positions on her flanks.

"Was that you?" Donna asked Ava as she looked at the scene.

The trail of gore traced back to her daughter's blade. Ava shrugged and Donna gave her an impressed look.

"We might be able to sneak past without having to, you know, deal with the rest," said Donna. "We've just got to watch the reach of that one on the left." After a moment's silence, she began forward. "Follow me."

As Ava stepped up to go next, the main doors began to rattle as the mechanoids tried to force entry. An alert Colin quickly wedged himself into the middle, between the mother and daughter, ensuring he was safest from attacks from the front and, now, the rear. Ava groaned and resisted the strong urge to slap him in the back of the head.

Donna shuffled past the zambie corpse and the other fallen undead. She was soon alongside the three standing grunts wedged between the downed and the wall. They groaned and wheezed at the nearby humans. By now, Donna and the others all had one hand brandishing a segment of trophy while the other held a knife. The forearm protectors on their leading arms acted as shields to block strikes and prevent bites.

"Nice and slow," whispered Donna gently as they inched past.

She noticed the zambies eye was fixated on the shiny metal look of the trophy in her hand. She circled it in a sweeping motion, and three sets of vacant eyes followed its every move. She exchanged a knowing nod with the others. "Nice and slow," she said again.

She had just passed the point of closest contact when everything changed. A cutting tool whirred, and sparks flew from the clubhouse doors before they burst open to reveal two humanoid bots – one injured – and two dogbots – one almost headless. After taking a brief moment to assess the situation, the bots began navigating the trophy cabinet wreckage that separated them from their quarry.

Donna lifted her urgency at the front of the pack – the need for subtlety replaced by speed. As she did, the zambie within striking distance realised its access to the shiny metal thing was waning and lunged forward. It was still pinned into its wedged position, but its centre of gravity soon moved to a position there was no recovering from. It fell towards the humans, who all screamed.

Donna lifted her arm guard to protect herself from the bulk of the fall. The zambie rattled into it before its weight was redirected sideways. Or, to put it another way, towards Colin.

Colin put his arms up in fright and screamed in a pitch so high it took the others by surprise. The zambie slid a hand down the length of his chest as it fell. Its head struck Colin's knee before meeting the ground in an even more powerful collision. As Colin clutched his knee, first Donna, then Ava, buried their trophy weapons into the zambie's head. Repeatedly. Until it became clear the threat had been eliminated.

"Let's go!" said Donna as she offered out her hand.

"My knee!" said Colin.

"I was talking to my daughter." Donna looked up to see the mechanoids now navigating their way through the trophy cabinet wreckage. "We need to go!"

Ava nodded at her mum and went to pass Colin on the wall side. He shuffled back to block the move. She switched to pass him on the zambie side, over the freshly downed body, and he blocked her path again. Donna glared at him, then raised her trophy base weapon at him in menace. As he cowered, Ava pushed him from behind, and he fell forward, towards Donna. She twisted sideways to avoid impact, then, as the sound of Colin's lungs emptying filled the air, she offered her daughter a hand to the other side.

Mother and daughter scanned the scene one more time before turning to the restaurant entrance ahead.

"What about me?" wheezed Colin through discomfort.

He'd achieved an annoyingly pitiful tonality with this utterance, such that it stopped Donna in her tracks. She let out a noise of frustration, turned back to him and reached out her hand.

"Hurry up!"

"What?"

"Oh, for fu…"

Colin slowly made his way to his feet, using Donna's counterweight for leverage and the power of groan for strength.

"Hurry up!" said Ava, her eyes fixed on the mechanoids.

Colin's groan took on new magnitudes of power as he forced his body upright. "Ouch!" he repeated several times as he began testing his leg.

Meanwhile, Donna and Ava headed for the restaurant.

"Hey! Wait up!'"

In their wake, the dogbot led the charge through the broken cabinetry strewn across the corridor. It planned its path forward as it eyed the direction its targets fled. It would not fall too far behind the ageing human, judging by his hobble.

*

CHAPTER 37

HAVE A DRINK ON ME

Ava reached the safety of the restaurant entrance and barrelled through. Out of sight from the chaos in the corridor, she looked up and quickly hit the skids. A pack of zambies huddled around what looked like a body on the long balcony outside. Judging by the remains, the feast had been going some time. A couple of undead diners had already turned their attention to her presence. "Oh shit!"

To her right, an octagonal-shaped dining room, built away from the main structure, gave almost unrestricted views of the golf course and beyond. The zambie corpse of an old man clumsily operating a walking frame was heading her way from that direction. The other dining space – where she stood – looked like it had featured at the centre of some previous last-stand battle, with chairs and tables having been moved to provide defence at various points. The temporary structure seemed to peak around the front of the bar through the doors to her left.

She headed through and was soon surrounded by sporting memorabilia and the stench of the undead. The heavily fortified bar ran the length of the balcony in the elongated space. It led to another room at the far end, which remained obscured from her position. She heard many more zambies than she could see, though, and suspected that was a place to be avoided.

Her focus returned to the bar. The staff access point was now protected by upturned tables and broken pieces of wood that had been hastily crafted into a barrier. A set of feet were visible, connected to two pale varicose-veined legs, which stretched out of sight behind the fortification.

She took a deep breath as she prepared for whatever horrors she might encounter, then headed in.

"Ava!" It was Donna, panicked. "Oh shit," she added as she quickly assessed the space.

"Shh!" snapped Ava as she gestured for her mother to follow.

Donna nodded and reached her daughter just as she was climbing through the matrix of upturned furniture that led to behind the bar. As Ava helped her take the same path, Donna noticed a trail of gore stretching away and around the bar from the barricades. She alerted Ava to it with a gesture, and Ava returned serve with a nod to the body lying behind the bar.

Soon, Donna was through, and they began scanning the area for any potential weapons. But to do that, they had to step past the body belonging to the varicose-veined legs. It was that of a woman dressed in frock finery. There were no visible signs of injury. The pair scanned the body warily before Donna reached in to check for a pulse. She looked at Ava and shook her head.

"Dead or undead?" said Ava. "As in dead-dead or undead-dead."

"Looks like one of the good guys," said Donna. "She's just dead."

"What like a heart att—"

"Help!" screamed Colin as he made his entrance into the space.

Unseen from their position, they heard the door to the corridor shut behind him.

They turned to see him hobbling towards the bar, walker-zambie in hot pursuit. It took a few seconds to realise Colin was actually increasing the distance between the pair. It was then they realised the look of sheer horror in his eyes was coming from a source in an entirely different direction. There was a scratching noise at the door he'd shut. They realised it was one of the dogbots, searching for a way into the restaurant/bar area. It was only a matter of time until the door was opened by a dogbot or bot.

"Hurry!" screamed Donna, making her way back to the fortified entrance to the bar.

"I am!" screamed Colin back.

"Find some weapons!" said Donna to Ava, reaching out her hand through the bar defences to Colin.

"You want me to climb that?"

"If you want to get in, yeah!" screamed Donna as Colin neared.

"What about my hip? Or my knee, or my gout, or my—"

Behind them, the unmistakable sound of the doors opening hit all three humans. They knew the seconds were limited before the robots would have a line of sight on them. Colin reached for Donna's hand and searched for a spot in the barricade to place his foot. He held his weapon out in his hand, trying to not get it tangled in the barrier.

"Pass it here," said Donna.

"No way! Not until I'm through," said Colin, still searching for an ideal stepping ledge.

Donna groaned in frustration. Then, as his hand and hers met and the pitter-patter of robotic movement could be heard, she tensed her body and pulled the old man forward with all her might. Colin screamed, and the barrier shifted with a crack. Something gristly popped in his shoulder as he scraped over the upturned tables and broken pieces of wood.

Ava saw the moment unfold from further around the bar, with a bottle of red wine ready to throw in each hand. Her attention turned back to the door. If Donna and Colin were out of visual range, she would hide. If they—

She swore under her breath as the dogbot with a head entered her field of view. It paused at the entry to the bar and stared at her. A second later, it was joined by its headless twin. Her heart raced, or had it stopped beating? She wasn't sure.

To her side, she heard Colin wailing and her mum's attempts to quieten him. But nothing could break the standoff between dogbot and teenager. She took a step to her left, then another. The dogbot's head followed. She raised one of the bottles as if she was about to throw it, and the quadruped readied to run at her. That's when she saw a humanoid robot begin to round the corner. She had to make a move while she still could. She threw the bottle in her right hand at the dogbot, then flipped the other bottle to her throwing arm and hurled it at the headless quadruped.

The first bottle landed on the floor as she was in the act of launching the second one. The dogbot shuffled a couple of steps to the side to avoid impact. Then, as the second look was set to collect the headless dogbot, it too moved to avoid impact. "What?"

"What?" said Donna as she stepped in next to her, brandishing Colin's spear.

"The one without the head just dodged my shot," said Ava as she reloaded with two fresh bottles.

They didn't have time to analyse the moment as the first of the humanoids stepped into the bar area. It walked with a grace and purpose that sent shudders down Donna and Ava's spines. It stepped far enough into the space to allow the limping bot behind it to be positioned at its side. Meanwhile, the two dogbots moved into position at their feet. Three sets of eyes and a stump stared at them.

"I love you," said Donna.

"You too," said Ava.

Donna then worked her way along the side of the bar, searching the display shelves behind her for weapons, never taking her eyes off the threat in the other direction for more than a second. Ava tracked back and forwards with a bottle of wine ready to fling at the first sign of movement. And there was nothing surer than movement was coming.

To her side, she heard Colin trying to work his way to his feet once more, alternating between sounds of pain and frustrated tutting.

Donna rushed back to Ava. "Can you cover me for a minute?"

Ava nodded.

Donna handed her the spear thingamajig, then tracked her way around to where the bar turned to run parallel with the balcony. She was searching for the hard alcohol where not only were the bottles chunkier, but the contents were flammable. That's when the far side of the room was revealed to her. There were three bodies behind the bar towards the far end, while a fourth lay folded over the bar, body on top, feet dangling on the staff side. In all the blood, it was hard to tell if they were human or zambie.

Nearby, on the unsafe side of the bar, a few zambies lurked, bunched up in the narrow gap between the bar and balcony window. There was a large group in the room beyond. Far larger, judging by the noise. They looked at her, rasped at her, yet did not advance beyond the door. Meanwhile, a couple of the feasting zambies on the balcony were making their way inside, eyes fixed on her, while others started to leave the corpse and follow. All retreating exit points were blocked. "I think we're trapped," said Donna.

Ava's eyes didn't leave the bots. "I think they know it too."

Donna leant over the bar to get a fuller picture of what was happening beyond the rear entrance. She saw the trail of gore she'd first seen near the bar's entrance, now thicker across the carpet. It led to a pile of corpses – both human and zambie – positioned to block further zambie advancement. Whatever last stand had happened here was bloody and seemingly futile. She needed to think quickly if she didn't want theirs to end the same.

She located the spirits and started unloading bottles, tucking them under her arm. She ferried six back on her first run. As she did, she saw a display of cigarette lighters. She dumped her ammo, and collected a handful of lighters as she headed back for more.

Meanwhile, Colin had made his way to his feet. He hobbled towards Ava then snatched the spear out of her hand. "Give me that," he said, unnecessarily.

Ava gave him a look before the two turned their focus to the bot threat, just in time to see the bots begin to fan out. The two humanoids were separated by a few metres and the dogbots flanked them further out.

"Mum! Something's happening."

"Coming!" yelled Donna as she made a beeline for the bodies. She slid in next to the closest, careful not to land in the surrounding blood pile. She quickly patted down the greying male and found a pistol hidden under his jacket, tucked into his belt. She swiped it and moved along to the next body. Nothing! She also drew a blank on the next, but when she stood up to climb over the pair to reach the body slumped across the bar, she saw a shotgun lying under his jacket. She fruitlessly frisked the bar corpse, then grabbed the weapon. On her return, she stopped at the bar and grabbed two more bottles.

"Score!" said Ava when Donna arrived with her prizes.

"Told you the farmers have cache!" said Colin. "Are they loaded?"

"Humans, you have one minute to surrender, unarmed. Failure to do so will result in immediate action."

Three human heads slowly rose from their cover behind the bar. For the first time, the two groups studied each other at close range. The humanoid bots had taken a threatening pose. Their white exteriors were a perfect study in visual flow – every inch as graceful as their movement. A black material under the panels at the hands, neck, and torso concealed the physical workings beneath. Then there was the head – a sleek dark shape with a thin white trim that created the illusion of a face. In the centre of that shape, two soft blue eyes made from LED lights beamed with a friendliness that did not match any other part of the situation, except perhaps the tone of its words. Clean, easy to understand, calmly matter-of-fact and completely off-putting in the circumstances. At their feet, the two quadrupeds paced back and forth like attack dogs waiting for a whistle.

"We saw what you did to the people outside," said Donna, her heart pulsing at having a conversation that had the potential to threaten everything.

"They failed to follow instructions," said the injured bot. "Do not fail to follow instructions. You have fifty-five seconds."

The humans dropped out of sight once more. Panic set in. "Well?" said Donna.

"If we surrender, we're dead," said Colin.

Donna nodded, then looked at Ava who gave a look of agreement. "That's that then," she said before turning her attention to the shotgun. "How can you tell if it's loaded?"

Colin made a gesture to pass the shotgun his way. Donna started to hand it over but soon retracted the offer, staring at him with suspicion.

"C'mon!" said the old man. "Where do you think I'm going to go with it?"

Donna shrugged.

"We're probably going to die here anyway," said Colin, before snapping his fingers and gesturing towards the weapon again. "The hipsters have left us for dead."

Ava glared at him. "They're not actually hipste—"

"Call them whatever you want, they're not going to hear you now. They're halfway back to Adelaide," said Colin as Donna passed him the gun.

Donna snatched the spear back as insurance, then handed it to Ava, while Colin analysed the shotgun.

"They wouldn't do that!" said Ava.

They all paused at her words, thoughts about Donna's retreat at McLaren Vale unsaid, yet front of mind.

"Forty seconds."

"It's not going to matter if we can't get past what they're going to throw at us," said Donna as she opened the spirit bottles as quietly as she could, lining them up on the floor in front of her. She eyed a nearby tea towel and reached out for it. She turned to Colin. "Well?"

"Well, what?"

"Is it loaded?"

Ava shushed her. "They can probably hear everything we're saying."

Donna nodded, not taking her eyes off Colin, with a look that demanded answers. "Well?"

Colin smiled at her as he popped open the shell elevator and gazed inside the chamber. "Fuck!" he said as he offered it back to Donna.

"I don't think so," said Donna.

"It's too heavy for me. It'll slow me down," said Colin. "I'd be better at keeping up with my spear."

"Thirty seconds."

Donna eyed Colin suspiciously, sighed, and then organised a swap back with the spear held by Ava. Then she handed Ava the pistol. They shared a shrug of uncertainty regarding its loaded status. Ava fidgeted around with it until she managed to release the clip. Donna raised an eyebrow with respect.

"Empty," said Ava after a quick examination.

"Shit," said Donna, while she went to work on the tea towel with her knife, cutting it into strips.

"Even if we get past the mechs, we don't have wheels," said Ava, as she awkwardly stashed the pistol in her belt, praying that her gamer-level weapons knowledge meant there was still hope there was a bullet in the chamber.

"I may have an idea," said Colin.

"Twenty seconds."

"Well?" said Donna.

"I'm not telling you yet. You'll just do a runner the second you get a chance."

Donna leaned into him and grabbed a collar full of his shirt. "Tell me!"

"Alright, alright," said Colin as he pushed her arm away, then attended to his collar. "There's a rust bucket in the car park – dual cab – belongs to a guy named Trevor—"

"Wait, Trevor, Trevor?"

"Ten seconds."

"Yes, same cheating fucker. Perfect car to go off-grid. If we can find him."

"Find him?" said Donna.

"For the keys. Dead or undead, he's around here somewhere. Tall guy, huge grey beard, usually wears a check shirt. Punchable head."

"That's your plan?" said Donna. "What about the bots?"

Colin went to speak, but no words came out.

"Great!" said Donna. "Good plan, us."

"I'm afraid your time is up."

*

CHAPTER 38

FITTER, HAPPIER

Already splintered wood buckled on the bar as a dogbot jumped, searching for a safe place to plant its feet. Ava, closest to the attempted breech, screamed as she swiped a wine bottle at it. The shot missed, further decaying the bar's wooden defences, but her second shot struck the creature and sent it flying back towards the ground.

She quickly glanced at the other bots while her head was exposed. The uninjured humanoid one was making its way to her location while the limping bot and headless dogbot were headed to the more heavily fortified bar entrance area. Ava dropped back under cover and signalled her intel to the others.

Donna nodded, then returned to loading strips of tea towel into the last of her line of Molotov cocktails. Colin was busy opening packets of nuts and pouring the contents over the entrance to the back of the bar area.

Once again, the dogbot leapt on the bar in an attempt to breach the defences. This time, it had moved further away from where the humans were concentrated. Ava exchanged a look with Donna before crawling on all fours to where sound indicated the quadruped was attacking. Its location was confirmed when a piece of wood fell next to her. She stood up, brandishing dual-wield merlot bottles, then swatted at it.

The dogbot saw the attack coming and jumped clear of the first swipe. The bottle crashed into a beer tap and smashed into pieces, sending a flood of red wine across the bar and beyond. The liquid also soaked the dogbot. This time, instead of beating a retreat, the quadruped leapt behind the bar. Ava screamed again as she leaned out of the path of the attack, then backhanded her other bottle at the dogbot. The strike gave the satisfying sensation of impact as it pounded into a hind leg, and the dogbot went barrelling into an extensive wine rack.

Donna saw the scramble as she lit the vodka-soaked rag of the first Molotov cocktail. She stood up to see the uninjured humanoid bot within a couple of metres of the bar. She arched her arm back, then hurled the projectile at its feet. The bottle clipped a chair leg on its descent, then hit the carpeted floor in such a way that it maintained its structural integrity.

It rolled and bounced to a harmless rest in a spot beyond the inbound bot. "Oh, c'mon!"

She afforded herself a glance at the mechanoid. It hadn't flinched, hadn't altered its course, hadn't done anything other than continue its fluid march towards the bar. In a flash of thought, she wondered if it was heavier than her, stronger. She'd seen hundreds of them – all makes and models carrying out all sorts of activities. She'd even touched one out of curiosity. But until this moment, when conflict seemed inevitable, she'd never thought about their weight or strength or what that might mean in practical physical terms.

Was she stronger? Judging by its confident approach, the answer was a hard no. She dropped back out of sight.

Colin continued ripping open packets of bar nuts and tossing them on the floor. On the far side of the nut-covered ground and fortification, the headless dogbot and limping mech worked through the structure to gain access. Where the quadruped tried to tunnel through gaps, the biped had started dismantling the construct. Breaking through was inevitable, but Colin figured he'd need all the advantages in his favour when that moment came, so rather than fend them off with the spear, he'd create a slippery surface. Was it a good plan? He had no idea, but he was too invested to change direction now.

His old, fumbling hands defied their appearance to be quite efficient at the task. Many nights at the pub were finally paying dividends. He reached for the rapidly emptying box of nut packets and heard wood snapping. He stuffed the remaining packets in his pocket and rose to his feet with a grimace. The mech had created a path big enough for the dogbot to advance. It wouldn't be long until it followed. Colin held his spear over his shoulder, using his other arm to guide his aim.

The dogbot approached.

*

On the other side of the bar, by one of the balcony doors, the first of the outside zambies made its way in. The reanimated, wiry body of a female with a blinkless stare and droopy facial features stumbled briefly as she crossed the threshold into the bar battleground. Like its face, its subdued clubhouse attire popped with large dark red patches of blood and entrails. The fracas at the bar drew it forward.

It was only a few steps away, with the remains of its lunch buddies following in its wake.

*

Donna found herself behind the bar and fighting a shaking hand to light the second Molotov cocktail. By the time she resurfaced, the bot was at the bar, staring at her from close range. She stared back as the flames licked up the side of the bottle. Silence and expectation swallowed her words.

The bot stared back at her in equal measures of silence. It was almost more disconcerting than its words. The stand-off continued as the flames danced along the rag. Donna felt the heat sear her skin in a reminder the moment wouldn't be long-lived.

She found herself transported to a different place. Perhaps it was more of a realisation of where she was all along. No longer staring into the digital eyes of a creation of humanity – wiser, more agile, smarter, more adaptable and superior in every judicable sense beyond loose definitions of consciousness or soul – now she was staring into the face of what that construction represented. She was looking into the eyes of the superintelligence at the heart of this global transformation. She was still staring at a human creation, but also a god. At an ocean of intelligence, an infinity of mind, a depth of perception she could never hope to be or achieve through natural means.

And it was staring back at her.

It knew her. It had her measure in every calculable way. Every digital footprint, every search, every purchase, every venue she stepped foot in, every conversation she'd had – all of it – all logged as a chain of big data, every bit as revealing and individual as her DNA. It knew everything about her. It knew her soul better than any mortal thing could ever hope to. It knew her essence. Just as it did with everyone who remained.

It knew her in every way she did not know it.

It knew her in ways she wasn't capable of seeing herself.

The claustrophobic sensation of the moment made her equally scared as it did sick. She gritted her teeth, leaned forward and hurled the Molotov cocktail as close to the bot's feet as she could manage. The glass shattered. Alcohol spilt everywhere, then ignited. She felt the heat hit her face as she retreated to cover.

The bot leaned a hand on the bar countertop, then leapt up onto it in one smooth motion. It readjusted its centre of gravity, then slowly stood upright on the bar. It turned to face Donna, who stumbled backwards over a set of varicose-veined legs, falling against the kitchen pass-through before sliding to the ground. Even with the couple of metres distance she had now afforded herself, the bot towered over her.

They shared another piercing round of eye contact, each perhaps daring the next move. Donna felt the shotgun at her side and was ready to use it as a club. At the same time, she felt for the knife, reassuring herself that it was at the ready where she expected it to be.

Then, the bot gestured its head with a slight tilt before turning its attention elsewhere. It began kicking through the makeshift wooden defences. It was headed towards Ava.

Donna's heart sank again. She didn't need its words to know it was talking to her. Every fear about how exposed she'd allowed herself to be came rushing home at once. It knew her essence. It knew how to cut the deepest wound. It knew her love for Ava.

"Nooo!!!" she screamed as she rushed to find her feet.

*

CHAPTER 39
ADD IT UP

Grace eased Halen II into a steady pace down the middle of the street. "Ready?"

"I guess," said Suede, his body out the window and crowbar in hand.

Ahead of them, a wafer-thin male zambie in tartan plus fours hobbled towards them. Grace ensured there was ample swinging room for her partner as she angled the van around their target accordingly. When the moment seemed right, Suede swung the rounded side of his weapon at its temple. The strike flushed the zambie with such force Suede felt it from elbow to shoulder, then all the way down his back. "Boom!" he said. "Twenty."

"Let's not celebrate too early."

"Let me enjoy a milestone," said Suede as he returned to his seat. They looked at the changing environment around them. The zambies were scattered throughout the clubhouse car park and street beyond, mostly drawn there by the sound and movement of Halen II. It allowed them to skirt up and down the street and pick them off one at a time.

A few zambies close to the clubhouse entrance had their attention on whatever chaos was going on inside, which left an ever more manageable number for them to deal with.

"Look, if we go off-road to cross to the car park by that tree, we'll pass a good dozen Zs," said Grace.

"Bring it," said Suede. "See, are you glad we've hung around to help?"

The van shook as Grace rode it over the curb and began the short scrub crossing. "Seriously? You're going to claim that was your influence?"

The van dropped onto the car park surface, and while Grace lined up the first zambie, Suede leaned out the window once more.

"We arrived at the decision together!" he said before whacking another zambie out of its misery. "That's the headline. Twenty-one." He only added the count to annoy her. "Blackjack bitches!" And added that.

"Are you forgetting your list of all the ways we'd be better off by leaving them?"

Whack! Thud.

"Don't take that out of context. I was doing a pros and cons exercise."

Whack. Splat. Thud.

"In which you said Colin wasn't worth our effort."

"I stand by that," said Suede.

Whack. Splat.

"And that leaving Donna for dead would make it a one-all draw."

"Also true," said Suede. "But don't land this all on me. We were collectively weighing up a pretty big decision."

Smash. Thump.

"I'm just saying it's an insight, is all."

Ting. Splat.

"Oh, hit that sweet spot," said Suede. "Insight? Sheesh! It was a high-pressure decision. And you wonder why I don't open up sometimes."

"Are you seriously going to start up with me about communication?"

Thump. Bang. Thud.

"Boom! Double-header," said Suede as he took his seat once more. They had made their way to the front of the car park again, and Grace steered them to a spot on the other side of the crossroad boulevard, giving them the best view over the area. It was a small extension to the car park but removed from the drama from across the road. "I'm just saying, singling out individual thought bubbles out of context isn't helping anyone right now."

Grace sighed in the way Suede knew she was rolling her eyes without having to look. "Well, thank God Ava was in that building somewhere, or I reckon you would've left the others for dead."

"Look, let's just park it, huh?"

"The van or the conversation?"

"Both." Suede scanned the scene. "And we've cleared most of the threat from outside, so the minute they come through the door, we'll be ready for them."

Grace manoeuvred the van into a position that gave them the ideal view over the clubhouse. They sat in silence and watched. The odd zambie roamed the car park, with a group still hovering around the main door.

Beyond that, there were merely scatterings of solo zambies. However, the real source of focus was the clubhouse or, more accurately, the complete lack of activity coming from the clubhouse.

Their rescue plan hinged on the others finding their way out of said clubhouse of their own devices. And no amount of zambie culling or angry words would make up for the fact that the continued non-reappearance of their fellow survivors shifted their rescue plan to more of a stand-by-and-do-nothing-while-people-were-in-peril situation. The feeling smothered both of them. Each passing second made it worse.

"They're not coming out, are they?" said Grace, eventually.

"Doesn't look like it," said Suede. "They're really fucking things up."

Silence filled the air once more.

"I guess we should go in after them," said Grace.

"Whoa, whoa, whoa," said Suede. "Not without a pros and cons analysis."

Grace glared at him.

It was then a bright orange light flooded out from the clubhouse windows to their right.

"What's that?" said Suede.

But they both knew it was fire and that whatever caused it had something to do with Donna, Ava and Colin. Within seconds, the potential consequences washed over them.

Grace put the van into gear and eased it forward.

"What are you doing?"

"I'm going to park it behind the trees, then we're going in."

Suede nodded. He scanned the scene again with new objectives in mind. "Golf cart, there. Let's grab it and make our way around to the golf course side. That'll get us close fast."

They jumped out of Halen II, made the dash to the nearby cart, and were soon on their way to the burning upper deck of the clubhouse. So fixed were they on the chaos unfolding in the bar that they missed another story playing out in their field of vision.

A mob of kangaroos bounded their way from the distant north-western side of the course. Their journey towards the looming fire danger didn't immediately make sense. Until you factored in the three drones they were hopping away from.

*

CHAPTER 40
BURNING DOWN THE HOUSE

The headless dogbot dodged pieces of wooden barricade until it hit the nut-covered carpet. Behind it, the limping mechanoid ripped open the remaining defences that blocked access to the back of the bar, then advanced. In front of them, Colin waited with spear in hand.

Colin screamed as he focused his energy and timed his strike to hit the dogbot as it hit the peanuts. Despite its headless status, it made moves to scramble away from the attack. As it dug a mechanical paw into the carpet for manoeuvring purchase, the nuts did their thing, causing the bot to slip. Colin tracked the move as best he could with his strike, but the blow clipped the back of the dogbot's body before the full force met the ground. Colin swore and scanned the area for a more appropriate weapon for the situation.

He spotted the line of Molotov cocktails, picked one up and swiped it at the dogbot, who was once again moving forward, soon to be out of the nut trap. Once again, the bot slipped while attempting to avoid the strike. This time, Colin's swing adapted to the change in movement quicker, and the blow struck the bot flush.

Colin felt the satisfying sensation of the dogbot's body giving under the force of his hit. He knew he'd inflicted some sort of structural damage. That's when he felt some of his own. A blow rapped him in the ribs. Pain swelled within him as his entire body shook and the wind rushed from his lungs. He doubled over in pain and dropped to his knees. He looked up to see the injured mech standing over him with a chunk of wood in its hand. It arched its arm back again, ready to inflict another blow.

Meanwhile, Colin's weapons dropped from his hand, and vodka poured onto the nut-covered carpet.

*

Ava had a split-second advantage as the dogbot recovered its bearings after the strike. She sank her right boot into its head, sending it airborne as it flew backwards. It crashed into a wooden beam, then crashed back down to earth. Again, the quadruped scrambled for its bearings. Ava closed the ground between them and sent the intact wine bottle into its head and upper body. The strike was true, inflicting damage to its shoulder and temporarily pinning the bot between the bar and the bottle.

On the other side of the bar, several zambies from the balcony had joined the few headed inside, drooling at the commotion. They leaned over the bar, pawing at Ava's head.

She screamed, re-angled her position enough to be clear of stray hands, then pressed her body weight forward. The dogbot snapped its damaged head back at her in an attempt to try to reach her hand. Although it was lightweight, she felt its strength as it wriggled and contorted in resistance. She studied the damage and noticed a tear in the outer casing that led to a break of the white surface material. Underneath, the black protective material had sheared away, exposing underlying circuitry and actuators.

She pressed her weight into the wine bottle while lifting the broken one from her other hand. The quadruped seemed to realise the significance of the event and began thrashing with new levels of vigour. Ava rotated the bottle remains in such a way that the longest shard aligned with the mechanical wound, then she stabbed it forward. The makeshift weapon sank into the dogbot under its shoulder, and the associated leg fell limp.

That's when Ava sensed something beyond her wrestle with the damaged dogbot and the growing number of zambies on the other side of the bar. She couldn't pin it down to a sound, or peripheral awareness, or anything, really. Just that something had changed in her immediate environment – and she wasn't safe.

She glassed the quadruped's shoulder with a couple of additional jabs, then swiped the bottle she was using to pin her attacker to her left. The movement sent the dogbot flying once more, and it tumbled across the carpet until it came to a wounded halt by the bodies of battles past. Its instinct was to rush back into the fray, but its lame leg gave way under the pressure.

Ava watched long enough to know she had bought herself some time. She turned to see what was happening to the others, that sixth sense to danger now almost unbe—

Bang!

A white shoulder buried into her ribcage, and she went flying backwards into the bar. One of the bots had tackled her. The strike threw her so quickly that she lost her grip on both wine bottle weapons. It all happened in a flash. She sensed it must've launched itself from the top of the bar. The bot pushed forward. Now it was her turn to be pinned up against the bar, back first with her head facing the ceiling. She smelled and heard the zambies close – way too close.

A globule of drool wet her hair, and she shuddered at the thought of it. Then, the bot pressed forward, leaning its head into her field of vision as it pressed its weight forward. The way it leant on her restricted her movement, limiting her response options. She twisted and pushed. It adjusted and reasserted its dominance.

That's when she remembered the pistol in her belt. It was a long shot to hope it had a bullet, but she was out of options. She manoeuvred herself so she could reach for it, but the bot responded before she'd found dominance. She tried again, then again. No luck. It seemed to know the weapon was her goal. She conceded and moved her focus to the bar shelves, fumbling blindly as she continued to wrestle. After a jostling for position, she felt herself pushed further onto the bar. The tips of zambie fingers ran through her hair and thrashed about.

*

Donna had just made it to her feet, eyes fixed on Ava and the bot, when the fleshy thud of wood meeting Colin's ribcage caught her attention. She swore at a conflict she had no time for, then swung the shotgun at the limping robot's head. The strike connected, sending it reeling. She saw the Molotov cocktails nearby and used her feet to roll one in Colin's direction.

She heard him say something, but it didn't matter. She was already closing the ground to Ava and the other bot. That's when she passed the cigarette lighter display. She grabbed another one for herself and threw the rest of the display over her head in the approximate direction of Colin.

Her eyes locked on her daughter, pressed against the bar, at least half a dozen zambies reaching at her from the other side.

She zeroed in, preparing to strike the bot with the shotgun once more. But with their heads so close together and so much movement, the risks of hitting her daughter were too high. To her right, the flames licked higher, beginning to claim the bar itself. Time was running out as fast as the options.

Behind her, the sound of a fresh fire breathed into life. She soon felt the heat hit the back of her head and body and knew Colin had set off a

Molotov cocktail. Now fire attacked the bar from two points, and their only easy exit was gone. Ava was pinned down, and beyond her, zambies poured in from the balcony exit while another group watched on from the only other way out, blocked by a pile of corpses.

She didn't know any of the answers in the moment. She only knew that it started with helping Ava.

*

As Grace slammed the golf cart through its paces, Suede saw it. Three dots in the sky – a passing moment in the corner of his eye met an unmistakable memory. His heart sank. "Drones!"

"What?" said Grace as she drove the cart down a pathway that led to the pro shop, located a storey down from where the flames were taking hold. She skidded it to a halt next to another, and they both jumped out.

"Drones! Headed this way from the main road," said Suede.

"You're kidding me?" said Grace. She scanned their surroundings, grateful they were protected from the skies. Two kangaroos whooshed past close by in retreat. "In here!"

They entered the pro shop, tracking through it until they entered the heart of the building. They were soon at a set of stairs and made their way up to the upper storey. It didn't take much detective work to follow the noise and heat to the entrance to the bar space. They raced into the area, then skidded to a halt.

"Oh fuck," said Grace. She took in the chaos.

Suede nodded in silent agreement.

Flames now licked from the bar to the wooden structure above. Beyond the flames, they could make out the shape of Ava wrestling with a bot. Several zambies were gathered on the other side of the bar and more again were eager to enter the space. A second fire broke out to their left, and a limping mechanoid emerged from it, engulfed in flames. At its feet, a headless burning quadruped hobbled a few steps past it before falling to its injuries.

Behind the flames, Colin stood with lighter in hand, flipping the bot the bird with the other.

The mech looked at Grace and Suede before heading in their direction.

"Double fuck!" said Grace. She saw a nearby scrap of wood and rushed towards it.

She screamed. Suede screamed. The bot crackled in flame as the ground between them closed to nothing.

*

CHAPTER 41
ONE BOURBON, ONE SCOTCH, ONE BEER

Despite the fiery attack on its body, the injured bot hobbled towards Grace and Suede. Its white exterior panels began to buckle and blister from the heat, and the underlying black covering was peeling apart. An entirely different creature was being exposed – a machine. Well, it always was a machine, but the humanoid aesthetic made it more visually relatable, tricking the part of the human brain that instinctively wanted to understand things through its own limited human lens. To anthropomorphize. To see ourselves.

Now, there was a difference – a foreign machine stripped bare. A barely functioning creation of engineering and intelligence. Something man-made, not magic. And it was here to hurt them. The closer its presence got, the more foreign it looked. They felt the heat of fire and smelt toxic odours as the flames killed the circuitry.

Suede and Grace instinctively separated as it homed in on their location. Suede had the spear pointed out, ready to strike, and Grace had the block of wood stretched back, ready to snap. In an instant, the burning bot seemed to select Suede as the target of its final attack.

"Oh shit!" he screamed as he aimed the sharp end of the spear at an area of the bot's torso where its inner workings were fully exposed. He jabbed forward. The blade sunk in deep. He yanked the spear out, briefly expecting the wound to impact its advancement. Yet there was no sign of pain nor of additional damage. It hobbled forward without missing a beat.

Grace swung the wood at it and, despite its best attempt to avoid the long arching strike, she clocked the bot, sending it stumbling towards Suede. He dived out of the way as it desperately fought a losing battle against gravity's will. After a few out-of-control paces forward, it went head-first through a glass window to the adjoining restaurant. It fought to release itself, but it was weakened. Too much so to work its way free.

Grace ran over to Suede and offered him a hand up. "You OK?"

"Yeah. And thanks." They studied the still-burning bot, futilely trying to free itself. "They don't give up easily."

Grace walked over and hammered down the wood on its body once more. It twitched a couple of times before its limbs fell limp. They exchanged a brief hug to celebrate their victory, which was interrupted by the sounds of screaming from behind the wall of flame at the bar.

*

Donna brought the shotgun around to her right to open up a striking angle that would give her daughter more protection. Just as she was about to strike, the wrestle of body weights shifted, and she had to abort and reassess. Again, she found an angle for a clean shot at the bot. Again, the window closed before she could act.

Then Ava shuffled her body weight and, using her leg as leverage, moved the robot into an off-balance position. It scrambled to adjust before it lost its balance. Then she brought a corkscrew down into its temple. It was perfectly aimed to miss the face screen display, instead connecting with the softer black material at the side, which gave little resistance. It was buried so deep within the robot's head that the only visible part was the red handle.

The bot crashed into the nearby fridge and used its structure to prevent a greater fall. Donna and Ava watched on, expecting the blow to incapacitate the bot. Instead, it slowly regained a confident footing. It faced Ava, who Donna had stepped alongside, while it examined the damage to its head. The two humans looked at each other, unsure how the humanoid could be standing, yet knowing enough to know anything was possible.

The bot studied their shared confusion. "You don't win this," it said with calm, assured conviction. Then it charged at Ava once more.

Donna screamed as she struck out at it with her shotgun. The bot easily evaded the swing, but the moment gave Ava a chance to jump out of harm's way. As she did, something caught her eye in the reflection of the fridge window. A dark floating shape, contrasting against the light skies that were its backdrop. She knew the only thing it could be and turned to the balcony windows for confirmation. Sure enough, she saw the drone lurking near the door, just behind the last of the zambies headed inside.

Something in the way it hovered told her it had spotted them. And something else told her it was shaping to fire.

"Mum!" she screamed as she rushed to Donna.

As she did, little specks of light lit up under the drone. Behind them, the fridge's glass-fronted doors shattered from the impact of whatever the drone was firing at them.

She tackled her mum just as the bot closed in on her once more. She and Donna slipped under its lunge just as a spray of bullets licked across the bar, lighting up the cash register, the coffee machine and several shelves of spirits and liqueurs. Ava felt something strike her in the fall – she'd been hit. As she hit the ground, she felt another pain – the pistol – she'd rolled right over it. She removed it from her belt as she scrambled to her knees.

"Mum! You OK?" she said as she fixed her eyes on the corner of the bar and the inevitable reappearance of the bot.

"I'm fine!" said Donna. "We can't let that drone get in."

Bits of broken glass and flammable alcohol rained down on them from the shelves.

"Or get too close to that fire."

They both knew the only way out now was past the bot and over the counter, where they would be totally exposed to the drone fire and zambies.

"That doesn't leave many options," said Colin, who had staggered up to them from the other direction. He was clutching his ribs.

"It really doesn't," agreed Donna.

*

Just as Grace and Suede were about to approach the flaming bar, the balcony drone shot up the space. Projectiles exploded everywhere. Shards of glass and chips of wood fanned through the air, and bursts of alcohol plumed out, occasionally falling the way of the flames to tease the fire higher. It all seemed to take place in a slow-motion concert of destruction playing out behind the ever-expanding wall of fire.

They screamed out the names of the others but couldn't hear any responses over the cacophony.

The balcony windows had shattered as a result of the drone's attack, and several of the zambies near the bar had been mown down in the crossfire. Then, just as quickly as it started, the shooting stopped. The sounds of debris falling continued for several seconds.

"Everyone OK?" said Suede.

But even as the words fell from his mouth, he regretted it. The drone slowly turned its focus to them. Everything about its posturing told him it was about to fire again. Instinctively, he threw his spear at it.

The drone opened fire but scrambled to evade the inbound missile as it did. It put a line of bullets into the carpet between Grace and Suede. Suede backed away towards the exit door while Grace ran towards the safety of the bar. Well, the bar. She spotted a section between the two fires where the barricades didn't block her access and ran. Before her final approach, she rolled her shoulders back and hurled her panel of wood at the drone. Once again, the airborne bot easily avoided the projectile, but it played havoc with its shot accuracy.

Grace leapt and let her knee and shin hit the top of the bar. She controlled her centre of gravity as best she could while she slid briefly across it before she reached the other side and dropped down to safety. The move went as smoothly as could be expected in the circumstances, but she felt the impact inflict cuts and bruises on her lower legs. On the bright side, her fall was cushioned by a body attached to a pair of varicose-veined legs.

Suede watched it all from behind a glass panel not too far from the downed mechanoid carcass. He swallowed hard as he made some mental calculations on the risks of running to join Grace and the others. He searched around for something to throw at the drone as his partner had done – nothing. He made a false start forward, then another. That's when the drone began to turn in his direction. He searched for the safest retreat and bolted to a nearby door – thankfully open. As he did, he saw a second drone emerge in the skies through the restaurant's octagonal windows. He screamed and ran and reached the door just as stereo streams of bullet fire unloaded into each side of its frame.

*

The fridges were a mess of broken glass, bottles and their contents, parts of which had spewed onto the carpet between the humans and the bot. The bot glared at its prey, now huddled up on the ground against the front side of the bar, where they had maximum cover from the drone's aerial dominance. It surveyed the ground that separated it from attack – sharp and soaked in fluid. Aware of the damage it had received from shrapnel, drone fire and a corkscrew, it knew it would have to tread carefully.

Donna had found a cutlery tray and held it over her and Ava's heads as a shield from drone attacks while they searched for projectiles to throw at the bot. Colin had managed to unplug a keg barrel from under the bar and rolled it onto the carpet.

"Give us a hand, would ya?" he said to the others.

Ava nodded and the two lifted it to the bar top.

"What are you doing?" screamed Donna as a round of drone fire bounced around them.

Once the barrel was at bar height, Colin pushed it into position while ensuring his head wasn't exposed to fire. He dropped back down and looked at Donna. "Defences."

Donna nodded. "The bot looks injured."

"If we don't do something about it now, we'll be screwed when the drone gets closer," said Colin.

Almost instantly, the bot started working its way through the broken glass and sloshy carpet.

"Nice job, Colin!" said Donna as she hurled a nearby bottle at the bot, then turned back to give him the shush gesture.

"What?"

"Just keep your voice down. They can hear us!"

"No, too loud," he said, pointing to his ears. "Just aim for where it's damaged. Get some liquid in there or something."

The bot moved to protect as many damage points as possible as it stepped slowly through the debris.

"You just did the exact same thing again," said Donna, as she hurled another bottle at it, then gave him the shush signal.

Colin looked at her blankly while she vented a frustrated groan and searched for more bottle ammo. Meanwhile, Ava stood, using the bar-top keg as cover. Donna screamed for her to get down before crawling forward to confront the mechanoid. She swung the shotgun barrel at it. The bot parried the overarm strike with ease, and the gun pounded into the glass and debris.

As Donna pulled it clear, the bot stepped on it. The move put enough force on the weapon that it slammed back down to the ground, trapping Donna's arm underneath.

"Mum!" screamed Ava as she returned her attention to the back of the bar, now armed with a flexible hose attached to the soda gun dispenser. The bot stepped forward again, ensuring its weight was heavy on the gun barrel. Donna screamed as the flesh on her hand tore on some unseen sharps. The bot then leaned forward and grabbed a handful of her hair just as Colin stabbed forward with his spear, and Ava fired a jet of sugary orange fluid over it.

The bot kept up the pressure pinning Donna down as it turned its attention to its attackers. It swiped away Colin's attack with disdain, the spear snapping from the timing of the strike. But all the while, orange liquid bombarded it. It flowed over and down the white curves of its frame and into the deeper channels of black that covered the circuitry. Deeper again, it seeped into the tears and damaged areas. Beneath the surface, the sticky, acidic, conductive liquid swam across transistors and resistors, poured over capacitors and inductors, and drowned diodes.

It looked at Ava, then at the liquid.

It tried to step towards her, but something stopped it. It glitched. Then it happened again. The humans saw it. The bot knew it. It reached down to pick up a projectile to throw but missed it by a fair margin. It stared in confusion as it pondered the glaring imperfection.

From beneath, Donna screamed as she pulled with all her might on the gun shaft. Something gave and the bot stumbled. It took a couple of steps back to try to regain its centre of gravity, but its leg bowed on the uneven ground. It slammed backwards into the side of the bar, and only a clumsily thrown-out arm prevented a bigger fall.

It used the leverage to stand in a more meaningful way as it recalibrated its plans. Ava moved forward to her mother, ensuring the stream of soda stayed locked on its target.

The mechanoid knew it was defeated. It leaned its weight into the bar and used all its remaining coordination and might to climb on top. Colin took the opportunity to lob more bottles in its direction. One struck the bot as it rolled off the other side. A thump followed as it struck the ground out of sight below.

Meanwhile, Ava moved towards her mother and threw her arms around her. "I'm OK, sweetie, I'm OK," Donna said with a wince.

As the two embraced, another thump rattled the space. This time, it came from the other end of the bar as Grace leapt between flames into the back of the bar area.

"Move!" screamed Colin, knowing her position was likely exposed to drone fire.

It took Grace a second to process the moment and the significance of his words. When she did, she scrambled to her left – closer to the flames but safe from drone fire. Halfway through the move, the drone opened fire, and three of the pellets struck her in the side. She screamed.

Donna held out her cutlery tray to Colin, who frisbeed it towards Grace.

"Ouch!" said Grace, now rubbing her head.

"Sorry!" said Colin. "Hang tight!"

"I'll fry if I stay here!" said Grace from across the bar.

Donna extracted herself from the debris and wiped the blood from her arm onto her jacket. "Hold tight! We'll sort something," she said, surveying the scene once more. "Where's Suede?"

"He's OK," said Grace as she examined her injuries. "I think."

Ava moved in behind the cover of the bar top keg, soda gun in hand. That's when she saw a second drone entering the space through a broken pane of glass near the restaurant. "There's another one!" she said as she ducked for cover.

"There's a third as well!" said Grace.

Colin dived under the bar to untap more kegs. "Where?" he said from deep within the bar.

"No idea," said Grace. Her thoughts turned to Suede.

*

CHAPTER 42

KEEP YOURSELF ALIVE

Suede found his way through the twisted wreckage of the trophy cabinet to the front door. His immediate thought was to take the corridor and flank around to the other side of the bar. But he remembered Donna's van lay dormant on the other side of the door and wondered if there were any weapons worth salvaging.

He knew they'd mopped up most of the zambie threat, but also knew another drone lurked somewhere. He put his sweaty palm on the door handle and took a few calming breaths before opening it. The first thing he noticed was the debris of what looked like a dogbot head – the same one that had met its demise in the bar recently. He resisted the temptation to kick it.

He gave himself just enough gap to see beyond the frame. A peaceful, bright sky stared back at him. As his eyes adjusted, he saw that Donna's van, with the side sliding door open, was not much further than reaching distance away. The bodies of several zambies lay in the car park beyond. But most importantly, he couldn't hear the high-pitched whir of a drone anywhere.

He opened the door far enough to poke his head through, then, after a more in-depth scout of the space, he pushed it wider and passed through.

A noise to his left startled him. He snapped around to see a kangaroo – equally startled – negotiating its way through a narrow passage between two cars, currently blocked by a zambie at the far end.

It was the dot-painting-faced kangaroo again. He stared at it, speechless. After bounding left and right, it leapt onto the windscreen of one of the cars. It slipped on the surface and bounced on the hood before dropping awkwardly to the ground. It recovered, now free of its trap and hopped forward. Its path led it near the van, where it stopped and eyed Suede warily.

Suede noticed it was shaking. He noticed he was, too. “We’re on the same side, my friend.”

He didn’t know if it was going to attack him or flee.

A wave of jealousy for a simpler existence filled him. Food, shelter, fuck, sleep – step and repeat. Simple. Beautiful. There was no sense of superiority, no judgement, no layers, no values put upon it from others, no complex expectations, no sense of unfulfilled purpose, no limiting rules, no repressed desires, no stunted inhibitions, no frustrated rage.

Fuck! Why was this hitting so hard right now?

Those things represented just a fraction of the burden that came with intelligence – well, human-level intelligence. Yesterday’s intelligence. Old-fashioned intelligence. Overshadowed intelligence. Who was he anymore anyway? Who was anyone? What was the point? I mean, he’d been wrestling with what’s the point long before the zambies or AI rocked up, but what was it now?

He let himself be fully in the moment. He stood near a frightened kangaroo that was completely unaware of the war being fought around it on a different intelligence pay grade. It was just in a moment of its life. Making the best decision to survive the moment. Then the next. And next.

It tilted its head at him, then bounded towards the end of the car park. “Good luck, my friend.”

But he knew it was he who needed the luck. Zambies and robots weren’t here to take over from the kangaroos. The kangaroos would go on, oblivious that everything around them changed.

Suede sniffed back a tear as he stepped into the already-open van door. He searched for something he could use as a projectile to attack the drones. Beyond a couple of tools from the shed, there was nothing that would even be worth throwing at the drones, and even those would barely be a threat.

Until he saw the nets Colin had made using fishing lines and sinkers. Pulling them out revealed the nail gun. “Perfect!” he said as he picked up Colin’s weapon of choice. He swiped the haul and, after another fruitless scan of the van, shut the door and headed back inside.

What else could he use for long-range attacks? The clubhouse was such a large complex there had to be—

Of course, golf balls. How had he not thought of this earlier? Just outside the pro shop downstairs, he’d seen a couple buckets of balls.

They'd be perfect. They were light enough to throw multiple at once to create a potential distraction for the drones. Once through the doors again, he headed down the stairs to the pro shop.

Once inside, he dropped the nets and nail gun on the counter and headed to the other entrance that led to the course proper. He knew the balls were just around the corner, near where they'd pulled up in the golf cart.

Outside, the morning sun flooded in from the east, keeping him in the shadows. He stood near the door while he assessed for potential threats. He could hear the distant hum of drones, but he was pretty sure that was coming from upstairs, along with the sound of battle.

He took a moment to think of Grace and the others. He brought his fist to his chest in tribute before he stepped outside. Two buckets of balls, exactly where he'd pictured them. He rushed over, grabbed one in each hand, and then headed back to the pro shop.

He made his way to the counter to retrieve the nail gun and nets when he heard a drone. He froze and honed his ears on its possible location. It was coming from inside, somewhere. He quickly dropped the buckets on the counter, threw a couple handfuls of balls into his jacket pocket and stepped into the middle of the pro shop space.

He positioned himself at the rear of the store, where he could let the sound flow to him unencumbered. He stood still and analysed the noise, moving his head in subtle ways left and right. That was when he realised the sound was getting closer. And it was coming from where he'd entered the pro shop from the stairwell. He felt sick as he made his way back to the counter.

He passed a display of golf clubs along the way, and a putter spoke to him. Its solid head looked like it would cause severe drone damage. As he pulled it toward him, it clipped another club head, which swayed back and forward before dropping to the ground with a crash. He silently muttered a long string of swearwords and hastened his retreat.

He heard the drone's engines increase in intensity and knew the crash hadn't gone unnoticed. He scrambled to his cover and ducked behind it. It was then he remembered the buckets of golf balls. He had no idea if the drone had been through the room before, but if it – or any of the others – had, there was a high chance the bucket relocation would be noticed.

He stood up, grabbed the buckets, and dropped back behind the counter to safety.

His heart raced as he heard the whine of the motor get louder and louder.

That's when he noticed another noise. It was subtle with a grinding timbre. Almost as if a toy engine was lugging a heavy load down tracks. No, that wasn't quite it, but there was a certain rolling quality to it. And it seemed to be gaining in intensity. He toyed with the putter in his hand and wished the grinding noise would stop.

Then it did.

For a significant fraction of a second, it was just Suede and the sound of the inbound drone again. Until a golf ball landed on the floor in front of the counter, bouncing in a reverberatingly loud way. He made the connection that the ball rolling across the counter was the grinding noise by the time the second bounce on the ground occurred. By the third bounce, the wave of terror had really sunk in. He could hear the ball moving further away from him in such a way that the drone would have no trouble retracing the action to figure out where to investigate first.

His heart had sunk completely by the fourth bounce.

*

As the other two drones closed in on the bar upstairs, another story was playing out away from human eyes. The broken mechanoid that had climbed over the bar army crawled its way across the blood-stained carpet until it reached the door at the far end of the bar.

A pile of bodies and gore blocked the way, but a large number of zambies had congregated behind it, drawn by the sounds of battle and the presence of living flesh.

By the time it reached the pile, one of the bot's legs was barely functional, its other limbs were failing at varying rates, and its future operational prospects were extremely short-term. But it could still play a significant part in its mission. It got a grip on the nearest corpse and lifted itself to the foot of the pile. It then grabbed the next and began its climb to the top. Once there, it pulled on the top corpse until it managed to roll past and down to the ground.

With the top of the pile barely at zambie waist height, the bot knew if it could repeat the feat a few more times, there would be room for the horde to make their way into the bar exactly where the humans would need to exit it, should they survive that long.

*

CHAPTER 43
HAND IN GLOVE

Something about the sounds of drone engine reverberation told Suede it had left the confines of the corridor and entered the pro shop. The golf ball was still bouncing away from the counter. He knew his cover would be blown sooner rather than later. He tucked two of the nets up and under the top of his jacket. While it gave him a hunched appearance, it allowed him to carry the third net in one hand and the nail gun in the other. He wasn't sure which one would be more helpful, if either of them would be. The golf balls and putter were arranged for easy reach nearby. He leant down low and kept his eye on the other side of the counter as best he could through the reflection of a drinks fridge.

He heard the drone buzzing from one spot to the next, holding its position then repeating the process. And he could still hear the golf ball, the bounces had decreased in intensity but increased in frequency. It only added to the tension he was already failing to cope with. Then it tinged into the metal base of one of the clothes racks. The drone opened fire, and the sound of pellets being shot and ricocheting around the echoey space filled the air.

Suede's heart was already beating out of his chest when he first caught sight of the drone's reflection in the drink's fridge. He tried to swallow in any breaths, fearing he'd give away his location. But he was instead about to find out that the thought process was already outdated.

The drone unleashed another round of fire, this time at the counter Suede cowered behind.

*

With Ava's help, Colin placed a second keg on top of the bar, and the pair quickly disappeared to safety. But not before a burst of pellet fire exploded out from the second drone. It tinged into the metal keg. The ensuing echo was a long-tailed reminder of the dangers.

Things weren't any better down the side flank of the bar, either. The flames were licking up its entire length. The two fires had now joined into one. And the decorative wooden scaffolding above the bar was currently being consumed. Time was not their friend.

"The new drone is headed towards the OG," said Ava, who'd gotten the best look at it.

"Better angle to shoot us," said Donna. She was putting the finishing touches of her tea towel bandage around her hand and forearm.

Colin nodded. "At least they'll be easier to defend if they're coming from a similar angle."

"We need to get Grace now," said Donna, searching for something to use as cover. The options were thin at best. "Shit!"

"You could use one of the bodies as a meat shield," said Ava.

Donna stared at her, horrified.

"What? *Gears of War* – retro gaming tactics," said Ava before scanning the space again. "Or there's some wooden cheese boards down there. You could tuck them inside your jacket."

Donna sighed, then nodded her approval. Ava passed them over.

Her daughter obliged, then looked at Colin. "Meanwhile, we can just go nuclear on them with the pint glasses."

Colin nodded. "I used to have a pretty good arm back in the day."

"Well, make it good today," said Donna as she padded her jacket with protection. "I'm going to need it."

The pair exchanged nods before Donna embraced Ava.

"Stay safe," said Ava.

"I will," said Donna. She gave the pair one last look. "Right, when I say—"

A loud fleshy thud came from the far end of the bar. Then another and another. It was followed by the raspy groans of several zambies.

"What the?" said Donna. "What's happening?"

"It doesn't sound good," said Ava.

"It's not," said Colin, using a broken segment of glass to look at goings on across the bar in safety. "The zambies have gotten in."

"What? How?" said Donna.

"Wait, is that Trevor?" said Colin, his eyes narrowing on the reflection.

"Really?" said Donna.

"Not a face I'm going to forget," said Colin before the piece of glass in his hand exploded under the weight of drone fire. He jumped. "Either way, time's up."

Donna breathed in heavily as she packed the last board into her jacket, then checked her range of movement. "OK," she said after a deep sigh. "I just want to say how proud I am of you."

"Thank you. I'm honestly just doing my bit."

"Colin, can I please just have a moment with my daughter?"

Colin nodded, and the mother and daughter embraced once more. Donna kissed Ava's forehead as she broke away.

She wiped a tear from her eye and turned towards Grace. She gave a hand signal to say she was about to head over. Behind her, she heard Ava and Colin pick up pint glasses. "Ready?"

"Ready."

"Watch my mark," she said before counting down finger signals behind her back. Three, two, one. She made a closed fist signal, then headed into a crouch-run towards Grace as the first of the pint glasses launched at the drones.

*

Suede ducked low and screamed as the sound of projectile fire filled the room. Tiny missiles rattled into the counter. There could be no doubt now the drone had his location. Whether it was through visuals, echolocation, heatmap, a Wi-Fi hack or some other method he wasn't aware of, it didn't really matter. All that mattered was there were two entities – one flesh, one machine – in the pro shop, and only one would be leaving.

That thought alone stopped him from cowering at the base of the counter, knuckles white on his grip on two potential weapons. He knew if he didn't fight back, he'd die.

He breathed deep, then reached out around the side of the counter where he still felt he had protection. He gritted his teeth and slung the net in the direction he believed the drone to be. He gave his wrist a little flick action like he was spinning a bowling ball in hopes it would fan the net out.

He watched the reflection of the drinks fridge to see the net sail through the air, billowing as he'd hoped. The drone detected the threat and backed away and up until he lost it in his reflective range of vision. He heard a sound he swore was the side of the net swipe past the drone's edge, but he couldn't be sure. What he could be sure of was a reprieve from drone fire.

He heard its motor roar and whirr until it seemed to resettle into a more consistent flight pattern. It fired a couple of pulses into the counter before he could hear it move position. He ducked low and moved his head back, hands ready on the putter in case it tried to hover into his airspace. As he did, he cursed himself for not taking advantage of the window for a return attack he'd created.

He started removing his jacket, knowing two more nets would give him two more shots to capture it or windows to attack if he missed. As he did, he raised the nail gun. After a quick scan of the tool, he found the on switch. He aimed it at the wall and fired a test shot. The device made a satisfying noise of engagement, and he felt a mild kickback. He spotted the damage the missile had created in the wall, smiled and turned his focus to his attacker.

He grabbed some golf balls, then searched the drinks fridge reflection for signs of the craft. Nothing. He trained his ear on the audible signals until he could make an educated guess as to its location, then he launched balls in that direction. He heard the drone take evasive action, then popped his head over the counter, aimed the nail gun and fired repeatedly. He felt the weapon slip slightly on his sweaty palms. He heard nails ricocheting but had no idea where the shots went, only that they didn't appear to strike the drone.

Meanwhile, the drone banked so that the barrel under its body faced him. He ducked to seek cover once more. As he did, a line of pellet impact points shattered the glove display shelf on the wall behind him. Several pairs fell around him.

"Sure, why not," he said, donning a pair to solve the slippery palm problem.

"Thanks, Colin. That was useless," he said as he retired the nail gun and grabbed a handful of golf balls instead. The ability to throw more than one at a time and actually see where his shots went made them a preferable weapon in the moment.

He grabbed one of the buckets of balls and moved it such that there was one at each end of the counter. He shuffled back down the counter a little and honed his ears on the rhythm of the drone's engines.

Once he was satisfied, he round-armed the next volley of golf balls. As he did, a line of pellet fire sprayed across the back of counter displays. Just as he released the balls, he felt a pounding against his hand, once, then twice.

He had been hit.

*

CHAPTER 44
THE END

Ava hurled a pint glass at the closest drone from behind the cover of a keg. The shot beamed directly at the target until it swerved to evade at the last second. She watched as she launched a shot from her non-preferred hand, then reloaded from behind cover with two more glasses. The second shot also missed, but it pushed the drone back until it hovered on the balcony.

To her right, Colin was firing at the other drone from the cover of the other keg. His first shots had a similar result to hers.

Behind them, they could hear footsteps as Donna crouch-ran to where Grace was pinned down. No shots were fired as she moved.

Donna dropped out of sight from the drone fire threat next to where Grace had huddled up. She leant against the side of the bar. Her skin brushed a stainless-steel water carafe, and it singed her arm. She swore as she leaned in close to Grace. “You OK?”

“Been better,” said Grace.

Donna saw the wounds in her side and nodded. “Me too. And cooler. Huddle in close, use your tray as a shield. Let’s get back to the others.”

Grace nodded her agreement and moved into position as instructed. She breathed out the pain through gritted teeth, then lowered the cutlery tray to cover both of their faces from attack.

Donna waddled into the potential line of fire. “And go!”

They kept their heads down and ran blindly under their cover. Grace grimaced with each step. She screamed. Donna screamed. A burst of drone fire sprayed across the tray. Then they hit something at pace and came to a crashing halt under the cover of bar safety.

That something was Colin.

He squealed as his feet were taken out from under him, then moaned as all the wind escaped from his lungs again. Both drones turned their fire onto Ava, who dropped back to safety.

"Everyone OK?" said Donna, as bodies untangled themselves near the bar.

"No!" said Colin. "No, I'm fucking not. Not only my shoulder and ribs, but now m—"

"Shut up, Colin." Donna looked at Grace. "You?"

Grace gritted her teeth through the pain as she nodded. Thoughts flooded to her of Suede – she needed to see him again. She steeled her expression and nodded. "Let's get these fucks."

*

Suede leaned back against the counter as he analysed his wounds. He could see a pellet caught in the ball of his hand through a broken segment of glove, while another had passed through the webbing between his fingers, leaving a red hole on either side of the white glove. There were also a couple of marks where it looked like pellets had hit bony sections and bounced straight off. With the adrenaline pulsing, he could barely feel any of the damage. He flexed his hand, sensing it would still function reasonably well when called upon.

He listened out for the drone. It was circling, probing, advancing – generally trying to press in on his quickly receding secure space. Time was on its side.

Suede laughed to himself. It had all come to this. A duel with a drone in a resort pro shop for his future. He positioned all the equipment he thought he would need into place for his last stand. As he did, he thought about Grace. How he wished he could be with her right now. There was something impossibly large about facing the end. How a familiar touch could've made all the difference.

"See you soon," he said, knowing that one way or the other, he'd be right.

He turned around, faced the cabinet, and dragged the nearest bucket of balls a little closer. After taking a deep breath, he hurled a handful of golf balls over the counter. Then, as he reloaded, he sent a second load around the side of the counter at the drone from a different angle. He heard the pulsing of fire but not the sensation of being hit. He unloaded another round, then another.

He could hear the drone's motors working overtime to evade the shots, which only added to his will to maintain the rage. Dip grab throw, dip grab throw – his arms moved almost in a freestyle swimming motion. They burned. The drone's engines roared.

But he couldn't stop, not until the moment he—

He heard a ball striking the craft. The tone and timbre seemed to indicate a flush hit. He stood up, grabbing the putter and the net resting on it in one hand and a final round of golf ball ammo in the other. He'd guesstimated the drone's location and had his eyes fixed on that spot as he broke free from cover.

The drone was already rotating around to aim its weapon at him when he took his final shot at it. This time, instead of launching lobs from behind cover, he was standing with a clear line of sight. He beamed three fastballs at the target.

The drone started shooting back before it had Suede in its sights. Small flashes of light popped from its underbelly. Until it was struck again. This time, the impact sent it flying and spinning until it found itself buried into a rack of this season's-coloured polo shirts.

Suede jumped around the counter and hurled the net at the stunned drone. It met the machine just as it was starting to fight its way free from apparel, ensnaring it. The drone continued to move and spin, trying to escape the new danger. It began firing blindly. It knew the tables were turned and it was now exposed.

Suede screamed as he ran towards it with the putter aimed and ready. A stream of pellets fired past his legs as he neared it, then, with one mighty blow, he sent the head of the putter deep into the heart of the drone. Sections of plastic flew out from the strike, and it tumbled from the sky, still trapped within the net.

It struck a display cabinet and more debris fell from it, including a rotor.

Its flight days were over before it hit the ground. It tried to manoeuvre itself into position to take another shot, but Suede had already closed the ground to it. Then, with a swift stomp of his boot, he ended the drone.

"Boom!" he yelled, then looked around for the support of a crowd of zero.

He cast his eyes back on the broken drone. He stomped on it again to make sure of the victory.

"Matchplay win for the human!"

And again.

"That's for my hand."

And again.

"That's for fucking up my whole week".

And again.

"And my species."

*

"And fire!" said Grace, launching pint glasses at the closest drone to her as she fought through the pain.

By her side, Donna did the same while Ava sprayed a stream of soda at them. Her s-shaped pattern managed to cover as much of the space as possible. Bursts of pellet fire shot back at them, but they were keeping the drones on the hop, and the shots were more general threats than targeted attacks.

Around the side of the bar behind them, the flames had completely taken over. The timber structure began to fall apart, and sections of ceiling became fuel for the flame's growing power.

Further down the bar, Colin used his spear to reduce the number of zambies gathering. There were already a dozen who had breached the door, and he began the task of prodding them out of non-existence. In the centre of his sights were the reanimated remains of Trevor. Hopefully, he was the holder of a valuable set of car keys. Trevor would be the last one downed.

It all seemed to happen at once. A section of bar fell outwards, dragging the wooden canopy from above into the new pit of fiery debris. The bar tore in two near where Grace was standing. While the fiery side fell safely away from her, it also totally exposed her flank to drone attack. She was working in tight proximity to Donna and there was limited space to find more cover.

The closest drone began to flank to further exploit the weakness, but it was clipped by a Donna-hurled pint glass. It spun, over-corrected, clipped the other drone, and then crashed into the wall. Ava focused her soda beam on it as it dropped to the ground. Donna chased up her strike with another pint glass direct impact, then reloaded.

Grace saw a chance to end the moment. She squeezed through the split in the bar with a wince and reached out for a burning beam of wood that had caught her eye. Picking it up by the untainted end, she wielded it like a weapon, striking it down on the fallen drone while the other two went to town on the remaining airborne drone.

Meanwhile, Suede had made his way back up the stairs with a bucket of balls, a putter and the drone nets. He saw the state of the fracas, dropped everything but the putter and sprinted in to help.

The final drone turned to shape its barrel at Donna while dodging multiple attacks. It emitted a clicking noise but no pellet fire. Its means of attack was now exhausted. It dodged its way under a twisting plume of sticky soda, rolled and yawed its way around a pint missile and then headed for the window.

Suede saw the moment unfold. Dodging burning wood, he reached the putter backwards and made a last-ditch swipe to strike it from the air before it headed for freedom. The drone evaded the shot, and he buried the putter in the window frame.

"Fuck!" he said as the shaft on the putter buckled, the head end flopping uselessly downwards

Ava jumped on the counter, did a half-turn on her backside and jumped down the other side, pulling her pistol from her waistband. She jumped through the open balcony door and leant out over the railing. She pressed what she assumed was the safety, prayed there was a bullet in the chamber, breathed out deeply and pulled the trigger.

She felt a satisfying click and recoil from the weapon. An instant later, the retreating drone popped in the sky. Pieces fell off as it spun downwards. It fought a brief battle to correct its situation, but the damage was terminal. It twisted and descended before crashing into the practice green in front of the balcony.

Donna, Grace and Suede stared at Ava briefly before turning their attention to the drone's demise. That's when Suede noticed the kangaroo with the unusual facial markings. It was standing on the edge of the green, grazing, but now it was fully aware of the nearby threat.

The drone tried to make it airborne once more. It reached far enough off the ground to briefly achieve flight capacity, but the short-lived attempt had it tumbling to the foot of the kangaroo. The roo leaned back on its tail and sent two enormous feet onto it, crushing it.

*

CHAPTER 45
GOOD FEELING

Grace and Suede turned to each other. In unison, his broken putter and her flaming slab of wood dropped to the ground, and they raced to be together. They collided in an embrace as deep and fulfilling as it was painful.

Grace wheezed as her eyes watered with pain and joy. Suede buried his nose into the side of her neck, and the tears flowed.

Ava made her way back to the bar and locked arms with Donna in their own embrace. They made up an impromptu dance as they hopped around in circles.

"We did it!" said Ava.

Donna moved her head up to her daughter's face, cupping it as they touched foreheads. "We really did. Where did the gun skills come from?"

Ava laughed and shrugged. "Gamer girl got lucky."

The right side of the bar made another seismic shift as the structural integrity of the burnt section lost its will to fight gravity's eternal pull. It seemed to roll in on itself, sending a wave of sparks out past where Grace and Suede were embracing. It was enough to bring the couple back into the here and now of their situation.

Grace pulled back and wiped her eyes as she beamed at Suede. "What happened?"

"Took up golf, killed a drone for humanity," he said. "You?"

She smiled, then grimaced at the pain in her side.

"Whoa," said Suede. "You OK?"

"I'll be fine," she said. "Less golf for me, more bot slaying."

They smiled like teenagers at each other.

She gestured towards the flames. "We should probably take the celebrations outside."

Suede nodded, and they headed to the remaining part of the bar, where they extended their embraces and winces of pain with Donna and Ava. For the first time since events began, they experienced a moment where their thoughts weren't prisoners of a scary and unknown future. And all it took to get there was overcoming a scary and unknown present.

Each knew the moment would be a fleeting one. No one wanted to let go of the embrace for fear they'd let all the other thoughts back in. They hugged and celebrated.

"Oi! Any chance you lot could help?" said Colin, striking away at the remaining zambies coming in from the far end of the bar.

The rest of the crew looked over at the stupidity of the scene – a demolished bar where a thin old man was holding back the last of a wave of zambies with a homemade spear in the aftermath of a mechanoid versus human bar brawl that had burnt the house down.

"Well?" he snapped as he prodded forward and downed another one.

The others laughed as they gathered their weapons and moved in to support him.

"That's the problem with you youngsters. You just can't finish a job properly, can you?" he said as he prodded his spear again. "If it's worth doing, it's worth doing properly – ever heard that?"

"Yes, Colin," they said in unenthused unison.

Colin gestured towards Trevor. "And nobody lays a finger on that one. He's all mine."

"Yes, Colin."

*

CHAPTER 46
BACK IN THE SADDLE

It was well past lunch as they loaded the last of the goods from Donna's crashed van to Trevor's rusty dual cab. Donna shut the door, and Suede whistled to Colin, then gestured for him to join them. Colin had been keeping watch over the skies from across the road with a pair of binoculars he'd swiped from the clubhouse. The clubhouse itself was now fighting a losing battle against the flames. Colin was soon in a golf cart and headed their way.

"Do you think, for once, that we could leave a location not in flames?" said Suede.

The others laughed at the brief respite from the aftermath of their lucky survival and the enormity of what lay ahead. The levity soon dissipated into awkward silence.

It was too much for Grace to deal with. "And you know where we're going?" she said to Donna and Ava.

Donna shrugged. "Not really, but fortunately for us, we have Colin in the van."

Grace smiled at the sarcasm. "And we've got the printed map-of-roads book. I'm sure we'll figure it out."

"It's called a street directory," said Colin as he pulled up alongside them.

Grace shrugged her indifference to the lesson. She was tired. They all were.

"Oh, and I found these in the maintenance shed," said Colin as he reached to his side, where a pair of two-way radios were clipped to his belt. He handed one to Grace. "It'll help communications between cars."

"Nice one, Colin," said Grace, as she accepted her radio. "And remember to keep an eye out for somewhere to stay the night."

Things went silent once more as if that collective silence was urging them to hit the road. Or was it holding them back for fear of what they might encounter? One way or another, it had its own heavy presence on the scene. Even though they'd only known each other a few days, it was the only familiarity they knew of that had survived the end of the world. Sure, it wasn't much, but they were still here.

"We could always sleep the night back at zambie-Judith's," said Donna. "We could head out before dawn with plenty of time to get to the meet-up point."

"This place will be teeming with drones and God knows what else by then," said Suede.

"We're, like, three-star *GTA* wanted right now," said Ava.

Colin scrunched up his face. "What are you talking about?"

"She means we've got to shake off any tail before it's too late," said Suede.

"Well, just say that next time," added Colin before giving him an uncomplimentary facial expression.

Suede scratched his nose with his middle finger in response. Ava laughed.

"C'mon, Halen II awaits," said Grace to Suede.

Another bout of silence set in. No one rushed to leave the moment, yet no one knew how to say goodbye or one of a hundred other things that could have been said.

"Wait, Halen. Van Halen!" snorted Colin. "I get it."

Suede stared at him. "Good lord, has a penny ever dropped slower?"

Colin glared at him. More silence.

"We're getting Plutoed, aren't we?" said Suede, eventually.

He looked up to see four confused faces looking back at him.

"Like, humanity. With everything that's happening right now, we're getting downgraded."

"What are you gabbing on about now?" said Colin.

"Pluto. It used to be a planet. You know, one of the big, important things in the solar system. Until they changed the definition of a planet. Now it's a dwarf planet."

"Is this going anywhere?" said Colin.

"C'mon, honey," added Grace. "It's been a long morning, and we've got quite the drive ahead."

"Hear him out," said Donna.

Suede nodded his appreciation. "Pluto still exists, it's still doing Pluto things, but it's just, you know, not the same. It's no longer top-tier. Like us, we're all just as smart as we were yesterday—"

"Is that true?" said Colin.

Suede stared at him. "We've just been reassigned to the second-best category, intelligence wise."

"So, we've got dwarf brains, is what you're saying?"

Donna clipped Colin over the head.

"Ow!"

Donna looked at Suede. "Go ahead."

"Yeah, I guess I'm just saying we're not in the smart club anymore, and maybe that changes everything in some ways, but maybe it changes nothing at the same time."

Colin scoffed.

"I get it," said Ava, in challenge. "Getting Plutoed," she added in thought.

Donna looked around the group. "Yeah, I see what you're saying, despite it all we're still just us."

"Hmm," said an unconvinced Grace, grabbing Suede's hand. "C'mon honey, why don't we workshop your idea further in the car."

"About time," said Colin. "I'm too old to be wasting two minutes of my life like that."

With that, they embraced each other one final time. They were hugs of shared survival. Of trust, need and camaraderie. It was a moment of hope and one to pretend fear was at bay, magically repelled by the collective power of the five of them. It was a hopeful wish that they'd see a tomorrow in a reality where their collective skills couldn't guarantee it.

But it was all they had.

In a world where they were getting Plutoed.

*

THE END. FOR NOW

###

GETTING
PLUTOED

RATINGS AND REVIEWS MATTER

Thanks so much for reading our story, we hope you enjoyed. If you do find the time to share your thoughts with others, you would be doing the aithors a big favour :)

Review on Amazon

Review on Goodreads

AUTHOR Q&A

(CONTAINS SPOILERS)

We're spent an entire novel reading about the zambies and we still don't know who's pulling the strings. Care to share?
Thanks for hanging in there, but if I was going to reveal that it would've happened before the words The End! I do have something in mind, though. You'll just have to wait for *Getting Plutoed* #sorrynotsorry

It's the first time you've written in your own new universe for a long time. How did you come up with the idea of Zambies?
It really is. Aside from *Hart & Sol* (Joint venture with Russell Emmerson – inappropriate sci-fi comedy), I haven't written in a new universe since 2015! It definitely gave me fresh energy to discover a new world and new characters.

As far as the Zambies concept goes, I've been working on it for several years. I've always wanted to write a zombie type series aimed at adult audiences, but I wanted to find a new angle on the concept and tying it in with AI seemed very on point. And, you know, a totally believable first wave attack in the circumstances.

And given how fast things were evolving in the AI world, I didn't think I could wait any longer before taking the idea from concept to manuscript.

You seemed to have a broad understanding of what's been going on in the world of artificial intelligence
Definitely. Once I had the story in the writing plan, I started watching videos about AI and robotics every day. I still do. Even then, it feels like I've barely got enough time to keep up with everything! And at the rate things are advancing that's only going to get worse.

Anyway, it's amazing what's happening right now. And the possibilities going forward, many of which will soon be realities, are mind blowing! One way or another, the world is about to change.

The all-generation cast bring their own kind of tension to the story. What made you choose that direction?

I really wanted to make this story accessible for everyone. The world of AI and the threats it poses can seem overwhelming, so I thought stripping them back into a comedy format would help people 'brave' the read.

The all-ages cast seemed like a natural extension of that. Not only did it give a variety of perspectives on the lens of technological change, but in real life there is a noticeable shift in attitudes between generations these days and I thought that was definite fodder for storytelling gold.

Do you have a favourite?

Oh, come on! Tough choice! They've each got characteristics to like/dislike and I enjoyed writing all of them. Having said all that, it seems Colin is the character that resonates most with readers in early feedback. Some really don't like him, while some think I've been mean to him, but everyone has an opinion on him, so I really like that.

Is there really any way out of the mess Grace and crew are in?

I genuinely don't even know the answer to this question. And readers of my work will know not all the main characters make it through all my books.

I can't promise the stakes will be raised in *Getting Plutoed.* We'll just have to see where all that goes.

*

BUY ONE OF SUEDE'S T-SHIRTS!

Yes, they're real! Want different way to support the author? You can order one of his (or Suede's) T-shirt designs at logofaux.com!

Check out
logofaux.com

About the author:

Like the legendary R M Williams, Matt was born in Jamestown in rural South Australia. But that's where the remarkable similarities between these two end. While Reginald went from bushman to world renowned millionaire outback clothing designer, Matt is a complete dag who was lured by the city lights of Adelaide. Kindergarten in the big smoke was a culture shock, but it is here he first discovered his love of storytelling.

In high school that love found an outlet in a series of completely unflattering cartoons about fellow students and teachers alike. He survived long enough to further his art into a successful career in multimedia design but, like a zombified leech, the lure of the written word gnawed at him, forcing him to pen his first novel, the award-winning sci-fi comedy epic, Kings of the World. It was followed the next year by Amazon Australia dystopian sci-fi best-seller Apocalypse: Diary of a Survivor. He has now published eleven books and won several international awards for his works.

Matt donates part-proceeds of each book sold to find a cure for Rett Syndrome, a neurological condition the youngest of his three children, Abby, has. As a gorgeous Rett angel, Abby cannot walk, talk or use her hands in a meaningful way. So, not only is each of your book purchases a ticket to fantastically rounded, character driven, hilarious and poignant sci-fi awesomeness, it wraps you in a warm feeling that you've made a difference to people who deserve your help the most. Like the zombified leech it's a no-brainer.

****

More ways to connect:

Facebook.com/
MattJPikeAuthor

Instagram.com/
matt_j_pike/

Subscribe to Matt's
mailing list

####

Printed in Dunstable, United Kingdom